PRAISE FOR CRAIG LANCASTER'S BOOKS

600 Hours of Edward

"Mr. Lancaster's journey . . . into the imaginative pages of fiction was one well taken, for himself, for readers and certainly for the lovingly created Edward Stanton."

—*Montana Quarterly*

"A masterful blend of character and action."

—Chicago Center for Literature and Photography

The Summer Son

"A classic western tale of rough lives and gruff, dangerous men, of innocence betrayed and long, stumbling journeys to love."

—*Booklist*

Quantum Physics and the Art of Departure

"Have you ever felt in your pocket and found a twenty you didn't know you had; how 'bout a hundred dollar bill, or a Montecristo cigar or a 24-karat diamond? That's what reading Craig Lancaster's

Quantum Physics and the Art of Departure is like—close and discovered treasures."

—Craig Johnson, author of the Walt Longmire novels

Edward Adrift

"Mr. Lancaster has triumphed again. With remarkable speed, he has made himself into one of Montana's most important writers."

—*The Billings Outpost*

The Fallow Season of Hugo Hunter

"This story ties it all together, from the boxer and the writer's eyes—the struggling middle, the bright beginning, and the path toward the end for Hugo Hunter and this Montana collection of characters. It's about the fraternity of the lost, and the tales they tell each other on their way back."

—Tim Kawakami, award-winning sports columnist,
San Jose Mercury News

"To describe *The Fallow Season of Hugo Hunter* as 'a story about a boxer and a sports reporter' would be too limiting. It's a story about the human condition, and about how, for better or worse, we all need each other."

—Elisa Lorello, author of *Faking It* and *She Has Your Eyes*

This Is What
I WANT

ALSO BY CRAIG LANCASTER

600 Hours of Edward
The Summer Son
Quantum Physics and the Art of Departure
Edward Adrift
The Fallow Season of Hugo Hunter

This Is What I WANT

CRAIG LANCASTER

LAKE UNION
PUBLISHING

Text copyright © 2015 Craig Lancaster

Published by Lake Union Publishing, Seattle
www.apub.com

Amazon, the Amazon logo, and Lake Union Publishing are trademarks of Amazon.com, Inc., or its affiliates.

ISBN-13: 9781503945111
ISBN-10: 1503945111

Cover design by David Drummond

For Angie, my friend. Still. And for the Buckley and Pederson clans. Thank you for letting me be part of your lives.

In Oil Country, a Struggle to Maintain Tradition Amid Change

GRANDVIEW, Mont.—*Fifteen years ago, this town of 600 people, in the northeast corner of the fourth-largest state and a stone's throw from the North Dakota border, put up signs on both ends of the highway that passes through it. The signs herald it as "Montana's Original Article—Where the Past Is Always Present."*

Town leaders say the signs were meant to entice passers-through to stop and visit the charming if a bit rough-hewn burg, which was founded 100 years ago on sugar beets and a can-do spirit.

But the year 2000 was a different time, and Grandview, sitting on the edge of the biggest domestic oil play since Alaska's Prudhoe Bay, is a different place.

Those differences, some say, threaten to transform Grandview, and the region, into something that can't be reconciled with what came before. Those fearful of such changes say it's already happening, pointing to a free flow of oil money and the associated social ills that have irreparably blighted the local economies of scale and the region's cultural heritage.

Others, some of them prominent leaders of not only Grandview but also the region at large, say progress cannot and should not be derailed, that the issue facing the area is one of managing the changes.

Whatever the case, it prompts the question: How does a plucky town such as Grandview, invested in its past as much as its present, find its way in this brave new, oil-soaked world?

THURSDAY

SAM

Even at eleven in the morning, the distant badlands shimmered from Sam Kelvig's vantage point on Telegraph Hill, the refracted heat waves licking at the horizon like a campfire. He tugged the bill of his ball cap low over his eyes, then reached for the binoculars and drew them up. Not even noon, ninety-two degrees, the hottest part of the day still to come, and the blast furnace of August lurking in the near future. *Damn*, Sam thought, *a guy could almost wish for October and an early snow. Almost.*

He started his scan from the northeast, as always, where the edge of town eroded into the bend of the highway. A half mile down the road, a flashing yellow light signaled Williston to the left, Watford City straight ahead, two boomtowns tucked into the folds of scoria far beyond Sam's searching eyes. North Dakota. The Bakken oil formation, and all that goes with it. In all his fifty-three years, Sam had been happy to keep his feet largely in Montana, thank you very much. He'd enjoyed the innate superiority of being a Montanan in a border town. He might well be a farm boy, but at least he wasn't some mud-hut dweller from across the line.

That kind of self-regard was a product of another time, however. Now, the rush was on, and it seemed that every eastern

Montana kid with a willingness to work—and more than a few shiftless layabouts—was being pulled across the border, drawn by oil that never ran dry and the promise of ninety grand a year. It made Sam sick sometimes to think of this: how easily the money flowed out there, and how hard he'd had to work throughout his own life to make that kind of dough. He remembered well the first year he and Patricia had seen more than fifty grand on their tax return, the way they'd looked at each other as if their fleet of ships had come in. Now the dropout kid next door made more than Sam did.

With that came another shift in thought, and he was back where he so often landed these days. It seemed sometimes that Grandview High pumped out the kids onto a conveyor belt to the oil fields, but his own son had run, hard and fast, in the other direction. Patricia, ever the optimist in the ways of family, kept saying Samuel Junior would be coming home this weekend. Sam wasn't inclined to believe it until he saw it.

Just beyond the state line lay the nest of simple white mobile housing units, the man camp for the rig that rose like a ship's mast on the flat land in the middle of Sam's view. He telescoped in. "Sonsabitches," he said. "Gonna have to keep an eye on them." He said it aloud, as if he weren't alone on Telegraph Hill, as if an absent conspirator might intuitively understand the rotten trade-offs inherent in an oil play. By night, the men shuffled westward into Montana—more particularly, and more galling to Sam, into Grandview—to drink whiskey and chase women, and while the Double Musky and Pete's Café might enjoy the fattening bottom line, others in town were paying the freight. Sam himself had found a nineteen-year-old kid up from Oklahoma curled into a ball in his garage one morning, sleeping off a drunk. While the young man was properly apologetic in his startled sobriety, that experience had changed things. Sam locked his doors at night now, and so did his neighbors. Parents told their children not to talk to strangers and to avoid certain parts of town after a certain hour—in a burg of six hundred souls, who would have imagined that a town could be so segmented? Not so long ago, there were no strangers, Sam often lamented to his pals down at the Country Basket.

He let the binoculars drop to his chest, then he pulled a bandanna from his back pocket and wiped his brow. At the Farm and Feed, before leaving on an early lunch break for this reconnaissance mission, Sam had looked up the ten-day forecast on the office computer and braced himself for the result. The third week in July was reliably a cooker, and this year looked to be no exception: high nineties across the board for the weekend, with brief scatterings of rain in the evenings. Good for the sugar beets, but not so for the humidity. It was a reminder that they'd need to double the number of water stations around the park. Last year, a few biddies were laid low with heatstroke during the homecoming parade. Sam didn't want that to happen again, not on his watch.

Binoculars up again, he fixated on Clancy Park. Some of the heavier set pieces had already taken root—the dunking tank, the kiddie Ferris wheel, and Alfonso's Funky Taco truck, on the corner adjacent to the Double Musky so Alfonso Medeiros wouldn't have far to crawl every night while Dea, bless her heart, ran things. Every year, it seemed, Alfonso engaged in some bit of inebriated foolery that put him in dutch with the town fathers, and every year poor, sweet Dea made a successful plea to keep the family's festival permit. They stayed afloat on a summer's receipts, hitting the various eastern Montana carnivals, and losing Grandview would be a crippling blow to Alfonso and Dea, and to their four kids.

Sam panned around the expanse of green. His mind's eye held the layout. In two days, the town would swell to about three times its normal population, and the park would be the center of it all, the venue for a weekend of community breakfasts, sack races, bingo, face painting, a quilt auction, food, drink, merriment.

The official name of the weekend party was the Greater Grandview Old-Timers' Jamboree, but nobody called it that anymore. It was, simply, Jamboree, no definite article needed. Sam had inherited the leadership mantle from his Uncle Rick, who took it from Sam's daddy, Herschel, when Big Hersch up and died in '86 of the throat cancer nobody saw coming. For the better part of that summer, Big Hersch had nursed a wicked cough that no one really noticed, and then—boom—he finally sees a doctor and gets a death sentence. In the aftermath, Sam guessed everyone just figured his daddy was invincible, until it was obvious he wasn't.

Next, Sam examined the knot of streets adjacent to the park. There, at the abandoned grain bins, was the parade staging area. He had commitments from twenty-four Grandview High classes to build floats or, more likely, to use flatbed trucks that would allow the returning grads to sit up straight in their folding chairs. Once Sam figured in the rest—the police car and the water tender and the American Legion and the classic-car club and Bobby Jensen's rusted-out '77 Bronco that had become a stale joke and everybody else—this year's parade stacked up as the biggest ever. They'd have to snake the lineup clear back to Dawson County, he'd joked to Patricia that morning.

Sam capped the binoculars and set them on the hood of his F-150, then he checked his watch. 11:21. Time enough to scoot down to Pete's for a patty melt before he had to be back at the store. He leaned against the grille of the pickup, content with his progress. A lot of work went into this thing, much more than anyone outside of Patricia could even imagine, but it satisfied him just the same. Big Herschel used to tell him that it took a certain kind of man to make things move in a town like Grandview, and Herschel Kelvig would have known, because Herschel Kelvig was that kind of man. That was the model, the expectation, for Sam. So he'd enjoy this, the realization of all his hard work, same as he basked in the opportunity to address the high school graduates at the baccalaureate service every May. He'd earned the good tidings coming his way. The uncertainty, too, for that matter.

A series of honks—like a car alarm but syncopated in a way that suggested a manual application—invaded his reverie. Sam cupped his hands around the bill of his cap and ran his eyes along Main Street, looking for the source. Alongside the Country Basket, he found something familiar, the green Dodge pickup belonging to Henrik. A window came down and an arm emerged, waving wildly as the honking resumed. From his viewpoint a good 250 yards away, Sam couldn't make sense of the gesticulating.

He reached back, shucked the binoculars out of their case, and brought them to his eyes again. Some minor adjustments zeroed Henrik's arm into sharp relief. At the end of it waved a middle finger. Sam couldn't see through the windshield for the glare, but he could make a pretty good guess what was going on inside the cab. Henrik would be scoping Sam out and shouting invective as if Sam could hear him, the dumb lug.

"He's glassing me," Sam said as he raised his own middle finger to the breeze. "Well, up yours, too, big brother."

NORBY

He'd slept through the alarm and would have kept on snoozing had the car-service driver not pounded on the door. Norby splashed cold water on his face, shocking himself into a halting readiness for what lay ahead. *Maybe that would have been better,* he thought. *Just miss the flight, phone in your regrets, stay here. No big surprise, right?*

The driver stood just inside the apartment door, ill at ease in a black sport coat and too-short slacks that showed a hint of white tube sock at his ankles. "Norby. That's your name?"

"Yeah." Norby spat a frothy mouthful of toothpaste into the kitchen sink, after having fetched his travel kit from his bag.

"Never heard that one."

"Family name."

"Huh." The driver removed his cap and used it to wipe his face. "You about ready?"

Norby wriggled into a button-front shirt. He could leave the rest of the grooming for the ride. "Yeah. Suitcase is over there."

Norby had to laugh about the driver's befuddlement at his name. After six years in Silicon Valley, punching in code at one start-up after another, he'd managed to slip quietly into a multi-cultural workplace churn of given names and surnames, where a

"Norby" wasn't more or less unusual than a "Queng." He liked that, how he could disappear into the melting pot as the westernmost member of a Scandinavian white-boy diaspora.

"Which terminal?" the driver tossed over his shoulder.

"A. United."

"Where you headed?"

"Denver."

Norby left it at that, knowing what would come next if he said "Billings."

"Where's that?"

"Montana."

"I've always wanted to go there."

"Uh-huh."

"You from there?"

"Yeah."

"I love the mountains."

The destination itself had been in some doubt until Monday, when Norby broke down and committed to buying the tickets. That he did so was the result of a full-court press by his mother, who first floated the possibility a month earlier in their usual weekly phone conversation and then ramped up the pressure in ever-more-frequent calls that weren't on the schedule. Norby hated talking on the phone. Why couldn't she just e-mail, like the old man did? She wouldn't have it. She said she needed to hear him. So that was that.

He'd resisted her overtures at first. "Aw, Mom, Jamboree's a pain in the ass. It's just too much."

"It would mean a lot to your father."

"Yeah." Debatable, that contention, but not worth the circular argument that would ensue if he pushed back.

"It would mean a lot to me, too."

"I'm awful busy."

"You can bring your friend."

"You mean my euphemism?"

"Hush now."

"I don't know."

"At least think about it. Denise and Randy could pick you up in Billings, and you could ride out here with them. Wouldn't that be nice? Denise says she hasn't heard from you in an age."

Now, Norby looked out the window at the steel-and-glass office towers sliding by. There was no way in hell he'd ride with Denise. Four hours in a car with his estranged sister and her amiable but dumb husband—or probably five or six hours after factoring in pee breaks for his two crumb-factory nephews. No, thanks. When he finally acceded to his mother's wishes, he lied and told her he'd fly into Bismarck and then make the drive into Grandview. Technically, it would be a shorter drive to do it that way, but he couldn't reach Bismarck with fewer than two layovers, so between flying time and waiting in airport terminals it would be a horribly longer day. No, he'd go to Billings, rent a car, and if he bumped into his sister and her brood at the Town Pump in Miles City, oh well— he'd be a found-out liar. Wouldn't be the first time.

His heart panged for Derek. He shouldn't have thought of what his mother said, shouldn't have let Derek back into his thoughts. He'd been doing a good job of playing defense against that lately— better by far than he had the first several days after the breakup, when he locked himself inside the house except to go to work—but Derek and the reason Norby was now shooting down the 880 in a town car were inseparable. If Derek hadn't said he wasn't happy and was leaving—over a plate of spaghetti at Original Joe's, as if it were just another dinnertime topic—Norby probably wouldn't be dragging himself back to Grandview, back to the past, back to the place where he'd taken Derek three years earlier so he could at last be honest with his family. What a fiasco that had been. The old man had looked at Derek kind of quizzically upon meeting him, as if trying to make sense of his twenty-five-year-old son bringing home a guy from the office and whiffing on the obvious, and

Norby had choked on what he'd intended to say. He'd put it off until dinner that first night, when he took Derek's hand at the table. The old man stared for an uncomfortable few seconds and then asked for the mashed potatoes. Norby's mother stood up and served everyone more salad. Denise, thick with child, snickered audibly. And no one said anything more about it, ever. Derek offered a handshake to Norby's dad at the end of the visit, and the old man accepted and then wiped his hand on his Wranglers.

From the gate, Norby called the house. Ten in the morning in California, eleven back home: the old man would be gone. All the better.

"Ten-hour flight," Norby told his mother, fudging the timeline. "I think I'll just spend the night in Bismarck and then drive up tomorrow. Unless you want me to—"

"No," she said. "That'll be fine. You don't need to be driving here that late. Besides, your father needs his sleep, and he doesn't like to leave the house unlocked anymore."

"It's that bad?"

"Oil-field trash," she said, the words expectorant. "Scum."

"That's pretty harsh, Mom."

"Well, it's accurate."

"OK."

"He's glad you're coming," she said, suddenly sounding chipper.

"Uh-huh."

"He is."

"OK."

"He's a particular man, Samuel. Like you, really. You ought to be able to see that."

He closed his eyes and winced. "No, no, I don't see that." *And don't put his name on me.*

"We'll see you tomorrow, then," she said. It was her way, the short-circuiting of something that threatened emotion or settling of old disputes. Stiffen the upper lip and move on. Straight out of the playbook.

"OK, Mom."

Norby settled into his aisle seat, on the wing as he preferred. The airline fascist at the gate had made him check his duffel bag plane-side, which cost him the new Raleigh Ridgeley novel he was slowly penetrating. He thumbed an in-flight magazine and waited for the pushback.

He glanced at his seatmate, readying a smile in return if one came his way. Nothing. Just as well. Smiles lead to talking and talking leads nowhere good. He remembered how Derek would fend off a talker on a plane by pulling a porn mag out of his backpack and reading it openly. *Oh, your kid goes to Santa Clara? That's fine. Really fine. Here are two guys fucking. You want to talk about that? No? I didn't think so.*

He shook his head, wiping away thoughts of Derek a second time, and tuned in to the last of the captain's preflight message. He buckled his seat belt. "We know you have your choice of airlines when you travel to hell," Norby said under his breath. "Thank you for choosing United."

His seatmate looked over. Norby fumbled a smile.

The plane pushed back from the gate.

PATRICIA

The phone had been ringing all morning, threatening to compromise the assembly line of strawberry-rhubarb pies Patricia Kelvig was running through her kitchen. She'd had to chase Samuel off the phone faster than she wanted, though it was probably for the better. The topic she'd tried to broach—the one she always poked at in some way—could blow up on her if she pressed too much. He was at the gate in California, and that was good enough for now. It meant he was coming. Of course, she had no guarantee that he wouldn't get to Phoenix or Minneapolis and buy a one-way ticket back. He'd done that before. She would wait, and worry, and hope for the best, and she wouldn't say anything to her husband until she was sure.

Her thoughts bounced again to that morning, Sam sitting at the edge of the bed, pulling on his boots. "I sent him an e-mail about it," he'd said. "Shouldn't have had to, though. It's his ten-year reunion. Wouldn't be right for the class president not to show up, but I haven't heard back. You?"

"No."

"I don't get it."

"It's a mystery, dear."

She'd watched in the mirror as his face scrunched up at that, as he tried to figure out if she was mocking him or agreeing with him. She had no intent either way. She'd just come to learn a few things in thirty-two years as Mrs. Sam Kelvig, and this was one of them. They came at problems from different directions, and their son was definitely a problem, or at least a mystery, as she'd said. She'd found that amid uncertainty it was better to offer up as little information as possible and do her best work behind the scenes.

The phone rang. Patricia whisked two pies out of the oven and onto the cooling racks, then slipped two more into the heat. Two more rings sounded before she could pick up. The barking from the other end of the line commenced, and Patricia fended off the charge.

"Yes, Maris."

"Yes, I'm on it."

"Yes, twelve pies."

"Yes, I'll have them there by five thirty."

"Yes, I'll remember."

"Good-bye, Maris."

She knew she could expect at least two more phone calls like that before tomorrow. Maris Westfall, the self-appointed doyenne of the Jamboree Friday-night supper at Clancy Park, had a management style that leaned toward hectoring. And yet every year, Patricia baked a dozen perfect pies, same as Marlene Wolters made five pounds of scalloped-potato casserole, Nancy Drucker turned out four huge bowls of garden salad, and Maris—or, rather, poor henpecked Jim Westfall—roasted a few pigs. The supper was the start of all the Jamboree festivities. Everybody in town came to eat, and then a goodly number of them bellied up downtown as the band began to play. The decent people, Patricia suspected, went home and waited for the drunken night to blow over. Sam liked to stomp around as if he were the grand marshal of this deal, but Patricia knew better. Without the Friday supper, the rest would fall apart. It gave her half a mind to turn off the oven and take a long drive to somewhere else. Let Maris deal with that.

Again, the phone.

"Maris—"

"Who's Maris?"

Patricia felt her cheeks flush.

"I'm sorry."

"Who's Maris?"

"Raleigh, you know darn well who Maris Westfall is."

A chuckle came back at her. "She's worried about the pies?"

Patricia leaned against the counter and smiled. "Earlier than ever. Will you be here in time?"

"Wouldn't miss your strawberry-rhubarb. Or you."

Her cheeks went red again at the easy flattery. "Where are you?" she asked.

"Billings. Just got in from Scottsdale last night."

There was more—lord, how Raleigh Ridgeley could go on about his travels and his houses in Arizona and Montana—but Patricia caught only snippets. She was lost now, stuck thirty-six years earlier, when the thirteen Grandview class of '79 graduates were spilling out into the waiting world. Could anyone have known then what Raleigh Ridgeley would become? Or what Sam Kelvig would become? Not Patricia. She might have chosen differently. Or, rather, she might have wished she had a choice. In her memories, Raleigh was the nice-enough kid who didn't fit in anywhere, and she'd taken pity on his obvious enchantment with her, unaware of his upside. Sam, on the other hand, was the popular boy and solid citizen and the owner of her heart when she cast it.

"I had to get a motel room in Glendive," Raleigh said. "Can you believe that?"

She caught a glimpse of her reflection in the kitchen window, goofy smile and all, and then hurtled back into the moment. "Glendive? That's fifty miles away," she said.

"Sixty-three," he corrected. "Everything's full up in Sidney. The oil fields, they say. I had no idea."

"It's terrible."

"Not if you own a motel."

She laughed. "OK, for everybody else. Did you know dogs are disappearing?"

"Dogs. Why?"

"They don't know. Sam thinks they're being stolen and used as bait."

"Dog fighting?"

"That's what Sam thinks. Mina Pollard lost her Chihuahua. Right out of her backyard, they snatched it."

"Shit."

"It's terrible," she reiterated.

"I'm looking forward to seeing you." He said it quickly, and she picked up on that. The nervous way he jammed it in there. She spun herself in a half circle at the sink, the phone cord draping her hips.

"It'll be good to see you, too."

"How is Sam?"

She'd been twirling her brown-gray hair but stopped. "You know. The same. He's making his rounds."

A pause moved into the conversation. She waited.

"I'd like to talk to him about what's going on up there," Raleigh said at last. "You, too. Maybe it's something I need to write about."

"Well, you know Sam. He'll talk to anybody."

"What about you?"

She smiled again. The tingle. The suggestion of a recovered youth.

"I'll talk."

"Good. See you soon."

"Bye, Raleigh."

After she hung up, she fairly flitted back to her duty. Twenty minutes more on the cooking pies. She started to fill two more shells as she waited them out.

Her thoughts now lay beyond the Friday-night feed, beyond the downtown bash, beyond the Saturday parade and the games and the blowout Saturday-night party. She wished it all away for Sunday morning, Clancy Park, the Raleigh Ridgeley book club under the bandstand. Every year he came home, and every year she and her friends took a swim in his vast intellect, like the grad-school kids in workshops in Brooklyn and San Francisco, only the Grandview ladies didn't have to pony up for it, because Raleigh Ridgeley was from here and never forgot it. She'd read and loved all five of his books, none more than the first, *The Biggest Space*. That one was like peeling back the lid on home and showing what was really inside, the posturing and the politics of a small community and the subtle ways in which people were anointed or undermined. Sam hated the book, but it's like Raleigh told her once: Sam was invested in the myth of the place, not the truth, and he was among the anointed. You couldn't blame him, really, Raleigh had said. Imagine all the things Big Herschel must have pounded into his head. All the false platitudes.

She couldn't wait for Sunday. This year, they'd be talking about Raleigh's new book, *Squalid Love*. She'd read it, she loved it, but she wasn't sure she understood it entirely. The inscripted copy she kept on her nightstand, which she'd driven all the way to Billings to receive from Raleigh personally, said: *For Patricia . . . May you find beauty in this romaunt. With affection, Raleigh.* She'd swooned over that.

She caught herself smiling again and reeled back into the moment. She flicked on the oven light and assessed her work. It wouldn't be long now.

THE MAYOR

John Swarthbeck led the petite woman and the trailing photographer a block north on Main Street, from his office to Kelvig's Farm and Feed. Every few steps, he tossed a glance over his shoulder to make sure they were still following. When she'd come in, he'd spotted the heels right away: dead giveaway that she was an out-of-towner. Grandview women were many things, wearers of sensible shoes most of all. And damn, these reporters were getting younger all the time, it seemed—this one from the *New York Times*, no less. *She must be a firecracker,* he thought.

He checked on them again. "Just up here," he said. "Sam Kelvig's the man you want to talk to."

"Mr. Mayor, we want to talk to you, too," the reporter said, moving in double time to catch Swarthbeck's long strides.

"Of course," he said. "Call me John."

Swarthbeck recognized the photographer, Larry Grubbs, from the *Billings Herald-Gleaner*, probably picking up some extra scratch by freelancing this assignment. He'd had a few laughs with Grubbs over the years, even one drunken night up in Plentywood when they fought their way out of a bar. But that was the '80s, a long time ago. Everybody who lived that time had a story like that.

The mayor reached the door and stopped.

"What did you say your name was, again?"

She smirked. At least, he thought it was a smirk. By his reckoning, she couldn't be north of twenty-four years old. Everybody that age seemed to be smirking.

"Wanda Perkins," she said. *"New York Times."*

He pulled open the door and bowed deeply. "Well, come on in, Wanda Perkins, *New York Times*." Grubbs cracked a grin at that as he passed, which made Swarthbeck feel better.

Swarthbeck cupped his hands around his mouth. "Where's Kelvig?"

"You don't have to shout." The interlopers turned and watched as Doreen Smothers came up the aisle toward them. "He's not here."

"Get him," Swarthbeck said.

"Actually, I'd just as soon—" the reporter began.

"*New York Times* here. Rude to keep this young lady waiting."

Doreen held up a walkie-talkie and pressed the button. "Where are you, boss?"

Kelvig's squelchy voice broke in. "Almost there."

"Mayor's here."

"OK."

Doreen threw a deadpan look at the mayor. "He's on his way, your majesty." She turned and headed back to her post at the cash register.

"OK, thanks, Doreen," Swarthbeck said. Then, to Wanda Perkins, he said, "She loves me."

The *Times* reporter filled the empty moments of waiting by slinging questions at Swarthbeck, who dropped his rump into a stack of bagged dry cement and feigned blitheness.

"Would you say Grandview is an odd place, Mr. Mayor?"

Swarthbeck chuckled. "Odd? No. It's a great place. Odd compared to what?"

"Compared to what it used to be."

"No. It's always been a great place. We're a progressive town. No time for sentimentality."

"Really? Isn't this whole weekend about sentimentality?" She kept her head down as she delivered the question. Swarthbeck frowned and remained silent.

Finally, the reporter looked up from her notebook and reframed the question. "What I mean is, how is it now versus before the oil boom?"

"Great then, great now, Miss Perkins. We've always had booms here, and busts. Booms are better. A lot more people coming through, and I guess you've seen that man camp just across the state line, else why would you be here. But jobs and money are coming through, too. Those are good things."

Grubbs moved around them as they spoke, snapping images. Swarthbeck had been in this game before, although never with the *New York Friggin' Times*. But the Minneapolis paper was no slouch, and it had been here, too, trying to draw a bead on What Oil Means. He could tell from the distances and angles Grubbs worked that this would be a feature piece, maybe even in the Sunday magazine. Wouldn't that be a kick?

"What about you?" the reporter asked. "Do you consider yourself an unusual mayor?"

Swarthbeck leaned back and laced his fingers behind his head. The sleeveless plaid shirt he was wearing would give her a good look at his pits and his tattoo-festooned arms. *Soak it up, lady.*

"I have my peculiarities. Care to be specific?"

"He sucks at poker!" Doreen shouted across the store.

Swarthbeck kept his eyes on the reporter's. "Sucking at poker ain't unusual. And I don't, by the way. At all."

"What about keeping a grizzly bear cub on your property?"

The mayor leaned forward, hands on his knees now, closing the distance. "That would be unusual. Not me, though."

"I've heard stories."

Swarthbeck smiled. "Lots of stories out there. I planted most of them."

Doreen had crept in close, peering at the mayor from around an end cap. He shot her a hard look, and she retreated.

Wanda Perkins, however, only moved forward. "What about selling moonshine?"

"Who, me?"

"Again, stories. Did you?"

"Moonshine's illegal. You know that."

"So is harboring a protected species."

"There you go."

"I see." She jotted some notes.

"What kind of a story is this, anyway?" he asked.

"Same as I told you before. I just want to talk about how the people in these small towns on the edge of the oil play are faring."

The mayor pulled his sunglasses from the top of his head and set them across his nose. He didn't want Wanda Perkins looking into his eyes anymore. "Sounds like it's about me. Or, you know, allegedly me."

Wanda Perkins glanced up. She smiled and closed her notebook, as if to say, *look, no more questions.*

"Well, that's the thing," she said. "You're one of them, aren't you?"

Swarthbeck broke into a wide grin. He liked this girl. He might have even told her so had Sam Kelvig not come through his own front door.

"Sammy!" Swarthbeck stood, clamping a meaty hand onto Kelvig's shoulder.

"What's up, John?"

Swarthbeck pulled him closer. "Sam, I'd like you to meet—"

Wanda Perkins stepped forward. "If you don't mind, Mr. Mayor, I'd just as soon handle my own introduction." She offered her right hand to Sam. "Wanda Perkins, *New York Times.*"

"—Wanda Perkins, *New York Times*," Swarthbeck repeated.

Sam looked to the reporter, then to the mayor, then back again. He shook her hand. "Pleasure."

"She's here—" Swarthbeck started.

"Really, Mr. Mayor," she said. "I'll be by to talk to you later, OK?"

"OK." The mayor's words came out half reply, half question. At once, Swarthbeck wondered where he'd lost control of this thing.

"Leave me to Mr. Kelvig now," she said.

"OK."

"OK," Sam said.

"OK," Swarthbeck said again. He looked at Grubbs, who looked at the floor.

"OK," the mayor said for the last time. He backed out the door, found the sidewalk, and tried to remember his bearings, and then he walked back the way he'd come.

MAMA

In recent years, Blanche Kelvig had given a lot of thought to the way she wanted to die, and the contemplations had achieved a critical mass in the past week or so. She'd come to the hard-won conclusion that timing (soon) and pain level (minimal) were more important than method. As to the latter: The safe money would have been on the pulmonary obstruction that had kept her tethered to an oxygen source for the past five years. That could be a long exit, though. Blanche had come to favor a stroke or a massive heart attack in her slumber. Whatever it took to do the job cleanly and without her active knowledge.

She sat in her threadbare recliner in the living room of the house Herschel had built them, and she thought about this, even as her eyes followed the pacing of Henrik, who blotted out her preferred view of that sassy-mouthed TV judge from New York. Such an unexpected visit, and yet such a predictable rant from her elder son.

"He's up there on Telegraph Hill, like he's the damn king of the county," Henrik said. He came to a stop in front of the TV. She looked up at him, stone-faced and silent. Nothing she could say. Nothing she wanted to say. Not about this. Not anymore. Advancing age hadn't been good for much—the wisdom overblown, the bodily breakdown undersold—but she figured she had at least earned some peace on this topic.

Henrik dropped to his knees and moved toward Blanche. It disgusted her, this hard veer between defiance and wallowing, but she let him take her hands, his thumbs rubbing across the paper-thin skin on her knuckles. She shuddered.

"I'm sorry I've been so long in seeing you, Mama."

Blanche licked her chapped lips. *Lord, come and get me.* "It's good to see you now," she said. She drew in breath, as much as she could in her compromised state. When Henrik seemed pleased with that declaration, she exhaled, light-headed until the regulator on her tank filled her nostrils again.

Henrik stood, and she gathered in her hands, intertwining the fingers.

Herschel, Lord rest him, had told her it would come to this, or something like it. Their first child, delivered on the coldest day of winter, 1959, had come into the world sour. They'd had such high hopes, had bestowed the name of Herschel's father on him, had imagined endless horizons for the boy and for the family they yet hoped to build. It wasn't to be, not with Henrik. Herschel had been the one to peg Henrik's erratic nature, saying it reminded him of Jhalmer, his father's brother, who'd unraveled publicly for years before dying, drunken and without clothes, in a snowbank.

It was Sam, arriving twenty-seven months after Henrik, who showed all the promise. He was eager to work the fields with his father, and earned good grades in school as well as praise from teachers, pastors, and neighbors in abundance. With Henrik, it was continual crisis management. He bit a girl in the first grade, and tore a chunk of flesh out of her arm. Skinned the neighbor's cat at thirteen. A night in the drunk tank at sixteen. The Marines and dishonorable discharge at twenty-one. After that embarrassment, Herschel welcomed him back to the farm. What else could he do?

That blew up as well, as they might have predicted had they been the kind of people who spoke their doubts aloud.

"It's not right, what Sam did to me." Henrik was calling to her from the kitchen now, as he fixed himself a bologna sandwich and chugged her last can of Coca-Cola. "He pushed me out and nobody said anything."

"I'm not going to yell across this house with you," Blanche said. The force of the words sapped her. She dropped her head back into the chair and waited for oxygenated relief.

"I'm sorry, Mama." Henrik came back into the living room and lowered himself into the chair opposite her. "Mind if I eat?"

Blanche brushed her hand at him, and he tore into the sandwich.

"The thing is—" he started, his words mushy.

"Eat," Blanche said softly. "Don't talk with your mouth full."

When Blanche's husband passed on, she let the boys split the two hundred acres on the farm. Herschel wanted it that way. He wasn't usually given over to sentimental pap, but in those last days, his voice gone and his body withering, he wrote a few notes to Blanche expressing hope that their boys would bond and keep carrying the family forward, together. Soon enough, though, the old patterns played out. Sam made a tidy haying venture of his acres, while Henrik went chasing some scheme—cattle, maybe? Real estate? Blanche couldn't remember. Anyway, he ended up flat busted and owing everybody and his dog, and Sam rode in with some cash to bail him out, demanding Henrik's land as security.

Henrik licked mustard from his fingers. "As I was saying, the thing is, I shouldn't be pushed out like this. Nobody says anything because Sam is so smart and so dedicated." Blanche closed her eyes. She hated this singsong mockery. She'd always hated it. "Well, this is my legacy, too, Mama."

Blanche opened her eyes and found her son staring at her. "It is," he said.

"Nobody's denying you anything that's yours. Sam says you have a debt." She closed her eyes again. Shut them tight. She knew as soon as the words slipped her lips that she'd chosen the wrong ones. It wasn't her fight, and she had no fire for it, anyway.

"Sam says, Sam says," Henrik mocked.

Henrik found his knees again in front of her.

Lord, I've been faithful.

He wrenched one of her hands free and held it between his own calloused fingers.

I've never asked for much.

"I'm sorry, Mama. I shouldn't have said that."

I've tried to do right.

"But Sam is pushing me aside. He is. You have to see that."

Blanche Kelvig let her hand go limp, and her son held it still. She closed her eyes tight, trying to hold back what was coming. A fresh blast of oxygen pushed into her nose, and she let go of her breath, and then she sucked it back in.

"This is my home, too, Mama."

Lord, hear my prayer.

SAM

For the second time in just a few hours, Sam stood in his particular spot atop Telegraph Hill and looked down on Grandview and the broad valley that cradled the town. He hadn't planned on another visit today. The reporter—"Just call me Wanda," she'd said—and the photographer had piled affably into the cab of his pickup for the ride up. Once there, and as Sam settled into his spiel, he grew more comfortable with the audience. Wanda didn't seem intent on busting his balls the way she had with the mayor.

"I've been coming up here before the third weekend in July since 1964," he said. "That's when my daddy started Jamboree, and that's what he did. He came up here, scoped things out, made his plan, and then spent a few days pushing it through."

The reporter stepped forward, even with him. "Back then, what did things look like down there?"

Sam chuckled. "I couldn't rightly say, ma'am. I was three years old. But the town's changed for sure. Maybe not fast enough for some, and maybe too fast for others, but it's changed."

He traced Main Street with his eyes as he spoke, and he conjured a mental image of pieces moving in and out. Where the Country Basket was now, the old Egyptian Theater used to stand, giving Grandview kids their last hometown picture show in

1977—*Star Wars*, not a bad way to go out. Three spots down, in the main downtown district, Barry Bristow's real estate office occupied the building that once housed the *Grandview Gabber*, quite possibly the most undistinguished newspaper in all of Montana. Across the street, the IGA wobbled on its last legs, headed for an August closure, a victim of the megagrocery stores moving into Sidney just twelve miles south.

"So you're the director of the Jamboree?" the reporter said.

"Just Jamboree." Sam smiled at her. "And yes."

"And on the town council?"

"Yes, ma'am."

"And president of the school board?"

"Yes, ma'am."

She raised her head and returned the smile. "I guess I have just one question: How?"

Sam laughed. "Lots of coffee."

"Seriously, though."

He doffed his ball cap and held it at his side as he raked the gathering perspiration on his head with his bandanna. Nobody had ever come out and asked him so bluntly, and he didn't like not having a pat answer.

"I guess," he said, "my daddy instilled in me a love of where I'm from. He used to say, 'Grandview ain't known for anything worth knowing, except for what we know about ourselves.'"

"That's a little cryptic," she said.

"Not to me. His point was that we're sitting out here on this edge of the state, pretty much all alone, and we get ourselves along just fine. Sidney is bigger, Billings is where nearly everybody goes to see a dentist or a specialty doctor, and Bozeman and Missoula seem to pull our kids away from us—those places, or the smell of oil—but we just keep on keeping on. So I figure it's my duty to do what my daddy did, to be there for my town the way he was."

Sam glanced to his left and for the first time realized that the photographer was snapping shots as he spoke. He turned the other way, his back to the camera. "I've probably said enough."

"You were great," Wanda said. She reached out and grasped his elbow, and Sam felt a silly fluttering through his chest and stomach.

"I have just one more question," she said.

"OK."

"What worries you most about the future of Grandview?"

She turned to face him after asking the question, and Sam suddenly felt a gravity that hadn't been in the conversation before. He took his hat off again and held it in front of him, caressing the bill between his thumbs and forefingers.

"We're getting old," he said. "The mayor, he's been in office thirty-three years. I'm fifty-three. We had thirty-one graduates in May, but just twenty-one the year before. Most of those kids are gone, and they aren't gonna be coming back, except maybe to visit for something like Jamboree. The lady who runs our museum, Myrtle Davis, she's eighty-three. Who's going to run this town? Some oil-stained rig jockey? I don't see any of them interested in that.

"Meanwhile, Sidney's growing. They'd love to have our tax base. We're probably going to need their water treatment capacity sooner or later. Are they just going to swallow us up? A lot of people think so. I can't help but think we'd be losing more than we know if that happens."

He turned back to the view. The photographer's camera fired off clicks.

"Do you have kids, Sam?"

"Two."

"What about them?"

"What do you mean?"

"Why aren't they following you the way you followed your father?"

It was a hell of an audacious question, yet delivered so dispassionately that Sam didn't take it in the hard way he might have had, say, Patricia dropped it at his feet. But then, he didn't have any history with this Wanda Perkins person, and he and the missus had history enough to fill a dozen coal trains. What struck him even more is that he hadn't considered it. The kids' hard break with the place—Denise living there in Billings like she was born to it, Samuel just a whisper in their lives—had made it clear that they wouldn't move the chains even before Sam had acknowledged his own limitations.

"They have their own things going on," he said.

The sun had turned now, making its downward rappel toward the western horizon. It backlit the scene, casting the yonder badlands in alternating shadows and fresh splashes of color.

"It's a lovely town," Wanda Perkins said. "Not what I expected."

Sam put his cap back on, mindful of the sun and of the tender skin under his fast-thinning hair.

"Best place in the world," he said.

NORBY

Norby hunkered down in his hotel room, with a meal from Denny's in a Styrofoam box, his phone, and the fifty-six channels on the TV set. He felt better, though, perhaps as good as he'd felt all day. When the jet banked over the Yellowstone River and made the final approach into Billings, he'd looked down at the city and felt a stirring he hadn't expected. Anticipation. Desire, even. He wouldn't have imagined that.

He couldn't get over how much the place had changed, how vibrant it seemed relative to his memories and his biases. A funny place, Billings. It fueled an entire region, with a banking center, first-class health care, and the might of more than a hundred thousand souls, but you'd be hard-pressed to find someone eager to love it. Billings was car lots and office towers and windblown buttes. If it's mountains and lakes and liberalism you wanted—Norby smiled to remember how much he had desired all of those things—you'd do better to point your nose toward Missoula. And that's what he'd done, the first westward unfurling of his ambition and discovery of self. It's where he shed his given name, Samuel, and took his first steps toward becoming Norby, because he was finally allowed to be who he believed himself to be. After four years there, summa cum laude tucked into his pocket, he also knew his desires lay farther still from where he'd come.

But today, as Norby piloted his rental car down the Rimrocks into town, he was forced to reconsider his long-held positions. In his absence, Billings had grown into itself, with high-end bars and restaurants crowding corners once blighted by neglect; a new city library, linear and beautiful and modern; a parking lot where the beaten husk of the old library used to stand. He spun through town in wonder, cutting his way through leafy neighborhoods and business districts to a new hotel on the city's southern edge, convenient to tomorrow's interstate escape.

Now, a few hours later, Norby finished the last of his pasta and dropped the to-go box into the trash can by the table. He stood, linked his hands above his head and stretched, a tingle moving through him from the small of his back and radiating toward his shoulder blades. He spread out perpendicular to the alignment of the queen bed, propping a pillow under his arm and taking in the industrial scent of the laundered linens. The display on his phone read 9:13. At home, his parents would be getting ready for bed, to take advantage of the last night of decent sleep before Sunday. He wanted to call and come clean to his mom, to tell her he was in Billings and that he wanted to come alone for his own reasons. Like most lies, the one about traveling by way of Bismarck had been spawned by expediency and expanded by necessity. He felt foolish, but his father would surely be there if he called now, and Norby didn't want to get into it with him, so he wallowed in the frustration he'd stoked.

He turned on the TV and rifled through the channels, settling on one of the ubiquitous police procedurals. He'd seen this one before; it was the brother, the seemingly normal one, who hid the bodies of those girls in the crawl space of the family home. The detectives always got at the truth of the matter, it seemed.

A message flashed on his phone.

Where u?

Derek.

Norby stared at the screen for the better part of a minute, caught between joy and revulsion. When would one name, five simple letters, stop holding sway over his emotions and self-regard?

Out of town, he typed back.

Shit.

What?

I came by.

Why?

The reply was long in coming, and too banal for the wait. *I wanted to get my shirt. The one from Seattle. U know the one?*

As if Norby could forget. Seattle, a year ago next month. A concert at the Neptune, the sweet scent of alcohol seeping from their pores as they moved in rhythm under the houselights. They'd spent the preceding day roaming the University of Washington campus, with Norby basking in sweet envy at his lover's fortune in having matriculated there. Before the show, Derek had found the shirt—disco purple with silver cross-threading and mother-of-pearl snaps down the middle—at a vintage shop on Brooklyn Avenue, and it hung perfectly on him. Such fun those buttons had been to pop open hours later, back at the hotel, in their drunken rambunctiousness. Derek's skin, hot to the touch. The scent of him on Norby as they slept, entwined. Yeah, Norby knew the shirt. If he closed his eyes and thought of Derek, something he tried to avoid, the shirt was part of the image. When he'd found it after Derek cleared out, he cast it to the back of the closet, not wanting to lay eyes upon it—and holding the furtive hope that he could keep it somehow.

Sorry. Not there.

Where u?

Montana.

The words lingered unanswered for a bit.

Oh.

Yeah.

When u back?

A few days. A tremor went through Norby's hands. Sudden anger at the imposition, and the inquisition. It came on sideways, at odd angles, with no percolation.

Can someone else let me in?

No.

Chill. Just asking.

The world doesn't turn on you and your fucking shirt.

Whoa. What's with u?

"You goddamn well know what's with me," Norby said aloud. He bolted into a sitting position, turned off the TV, and jabbed his finger at the phone's touch screen, tapping out a reply. The night of the breakup, he'd gone back to the house alone. Derek stayed in a room at the Hotel De Anza, having already packed a bag and cleared out before they met for dinner. That had been tough enough, but it was no match for the scattershot visits over the next week—sometimes when Norby was at work, sometimes when he was there—when Derek would swoop in and haul off some more belongings. Finally, Norby had set some boundaries: one more trip, get everything, leave the key, stay permanently gone. That had been eleven days earlier, and the agreement had held until tonight. The bile rose in Norby's throat faster than he could swallow it back down.

Nothing's with me. You can get it when I'm back.

K. Jeez.

You're so manipulative. Norby rapped it out before he had time to reconsider. If he could still wound Derek, that comment would get him. Their worst fights, and Derek's most extended bouts of pouting, had come in the wake of Norby calling him on his fouls. Norby braced for the reply. If he drew blood, as he expected, he could count on Derek to overplay the offense.

Whatever. U R mean. This is why I couldn't love u. Norby stared at the screen, absorbing it even as his mind screamed at him to just let it roll off him. He blinked, then blinked again. How wonderful it would be if he just couldn't feel anymore.

He pressed the power button and turned off the phone.

PATRICIA

She lay on her side in the darkened bedroom, feigning sleep after hearing Sam come in the front door. His unwinding brought forth the melody she knew well—the slap of his tossed keys on the kitchen counter, the concussive beat of his slipped-off boots hitting the floor beside the sliding-glass door, the insistent beep of the refrigerator as he pawed too long through the drawers looking for something to ease his sweet tooth, the padded footfalls through the living room as he headed toward her.

She opened an eye and found the glowing display of the alarm clock: 9:21 p.m. A late arrival for Sam, even by eve-of-Jamboree standards. She knew better than to have expected him for dinner. Once the pies were out of the oven and cooled, she'd wrapped them in aluminum foil and set them high on her grandmother's buffet in the dining room, well out of the reach of the grabby grandchildren she expected to see in about twenty hours. After that, she drove the twelve miles to Sidney and ate a double cheeseburger from Dairy Queen in the privacy of her car, euphoric at every bite. She knew what such a luxury demanded. She would be back in Sidney the next morning, in league with her CrossFit group, ready to keep that greasy delight off her thighs.

A crack of light fell on her from the opening of the bathroom door as Sam brushed his teeth before bed. *Praise be for that,* she thought. He often didn't take such care, and on those occasions when he went in for a good-night kiss, she would quietly endure the detritus of whatever he'd consumed for lunch at Pete's.

Lights out, she waited for his touch as he slid into his side of the bed. A serpentine arm slithered over her hips and across her belly, drawing her into him.

"You awake?" he said.

"Barely."

"I'm sorry."

She patted his arm. "It's OK. How'd it go?"

She closed her eyes and let him speak his piece. Conceit moved to the forefront on this particular occasion, where Grandview and Jamboree became the revolving planets and Sam became the sun. Patricia supplied all the proper cues—the "uh-huhs" and the gentle, reassuring rub of his arm—that kept Sam's story rolling forth. She deviated into true interest only when he mentioned the visitor from back East.

"The *New York Times*? Here?"

Sam sat up a bit and pressed his whiskered face against her bare shoulder. She liked that. "Yeah. You should have seen Swarthbeck. He was sweating like a hog after the fair. I guess she kind of got under his skin with her questions."

Swarthbeck. Patricia's face twisted into a sour-milk frown. It wasn't that she didn't care for him; indeed, it went much deeper than garden-variety disregard. But the mayor was a useful idiot, she often reminded herself, a hedge against even greater ambition from her well-meaning husband. This Jamboree thing essentially came with the marriage, a duty passed down the family line that she knew was going to fall on Sam eventually. And she couldn't very well begrudge the position on the school board, because what kind of troll opposes the education of kids? But as long as Swarthbeck was mayor—and indications were that he'd sooner die than give it up—Sam couldn't be. As for the other aspirations, the county commission or maybe a seat in the statehouse, she'd exercised her nuclear option long ago: Sam could do that or be married to her, but he couldn't do both. She wanted a husband, not a public figure.

"What's her interest?" Patricia asked.

He kissed her ear. She rolled her shoulder to cover it up.

"Oil," he said. "Same old story, just a different way of going at it. She wants to know what the future looks like for a place like this."

"What did you tell her?"

"I told her we're in a lot of trouble."

She rolled toward him, face-to-face. "John isn't going to like that."

"It's true, though," Sam said. "I get it. Everything's hunky-dory to Swarthbeck. Money's rolling in, times are good, we can replace the town pool, whatever. I'm looking at the bigger picture."

She touched his face. Good old earnest Samuel Einar Kelvig. Thirty-two years had a way of putting distance into their marriage, and in some significant ways even discontent. Other times, though, she remembered why she'd loved him in the first place, and why she'd stood by him, even when he was flat wrong or just entrenched and pigheaded. Because his heart was right.

And about pigheaded . . . Her thoughts turned to their son and his impending arrival.

"Kids'll be here tomorrow," she said.

Sam propped himself on an elbow. "Samuel, too?"

"He called me from the airport this morning."

"Where is he?"

"Bismarck. I told him to drive the rest of the way tomorrow."

"And you know he's there?"

Patricia clucked her tongue, trying to chase her husband off the territory he was claiming. This had been Sam's go-to on matters of their son ever since that disaster of a first visit with Samuel's friend, and Samuel and Derek's subsequent turnaround in the Minneapolis airport after she and Sam had bought them tickets and asked them, pretty please, to come back at Christmastime for another try. To Sam, that had been an unforgivable snub and a demonstration of the immaturity that still hung heavy from their son. Patricia had found a softer spot in her heart. The boys had gotten spooked, and she and her husband had done the spooking.

"He said he'll be here," she said.

"OK. Good. Glad to hear it. He bringing anybody?"

"He didn't say."

"Well, we'll roll with it, I guess."

Patricia exhaled. She couldn't say this was promising, but among all the reactions Sam might have conjured, it was on the safe side. "Denise and Randy and the kids will be here in time for supper in the park," she said. "Randy's got a dentist appointment in the morning."

"OK."

Sam rolled away from her, prepping his pillow for the coming slumber. She reached for his shoulder.

"Sam."

"Yeah?"

She caressed him, dribbling her fingers down the length of his arm.

"What, Pat?"

"It's important to me."

"What?"

"Samuel's visit."

"I know."

She paused, the words caught in her throat. She swallowed, straightening them out.

"No, listen."

Sam rolled back to face her. "What?"

41

She swallowed again. Lord, how many times had she rehearsed this in her own head? How many ways had she looked at this breach with the child she loved and yet didn't understand? All she really knew is that she felt incomplete. It had happened as Samuel pulled away from them by degrees out there in Missoula and then extended the distance when he moved to California. Three years ago, the rupture came, and she'd spent the intervening months and years trying to mend the broken ground. She needed help, and only Sam could give it to her.

"Make time for him this visit," she said. "He'll be here by noon, he said. Come home for lunch. Will you do that?"

Sam thrashed in the bed to sit up and to face her again. "Good lord, Patricia, I've got a to-do list longer than the Missouri River. Send him to me. I'll put him to work, and we'll talk then. I could use the help. It's gonna be hell for me and Omar to get it done alone."

"Sam, I need you to be gentle with him."

"Gentle!" The word leapt from him, ready to thrash away at her. She leaned back, aghast, and listened to him strangle on the others trying to get out.

Finally he spoke, softly, as if to compensate for the things he had nearly said.

"He's not a delicate flower, Patricia, he's our son. I love him, but I am not going to pretend that I understand him, and I'm not going to let him disrespect us just because he's . . ." He fumbled about for the closing, and Patricia silently filled in the blank he'd left in a dozen uncharitable ways.

"I'm done," he said. "I'm wiped out. Let's talk in the morning."

He flopped over again, for good, and found the groove into sleep faster than he had any right to. Patricia lay on her back, listening to the rise and fall and blinking into the darkness, her mind scattered to the wind. *This funny life,* she thought. *Sometimes it shows you everything you love and everything you'd leave all in the same moment.*

THE MAYOR

Nowhere else did John Swarthbeck feel at home the way he did in the inner room of his Main Street office, a shame because only a few of the six hundred or so people in town had ever visited the temperature-controlled sanctum. Coltrane's *A Love Supreme*—on vinyl, the very copy Swarthbeck's own father had given him back in '65—made the rounds as he tallied the cases. One hundred four prime bottles of River City Select, his one-of-a-kind, homemade hooch, sat waiting for delivery this weekend into waiting hands. And Swarthbeck would, of course, hold back five bottles for his own use, to bestow upon those friends, old and new, who tickled his fancy over the next couple of days.

Tonight, though, he fondled his usual glass of port as he wound down his business. He lifted it in a toast to the framed-and-mounted centerfold of Jenny McCarthy from the June 1994 *Playboy*, which hung over the desk. He'd paid 125 clams for that at a brothel in Nevada, and so on price alone it was deserving of a place of honor. It stood, too, as a symbol of class, as Swarthbeck was inclined to define it. These kids today can see any number of vulgarities with a quickie Internet search. Miss McCarthy represented a better era and a more respectful time. It pained him to say that honor and respect were mighty hard to come by these days, and getting harder all the time.

Take that mouthy dame from the newspaper. She'd come sniffing back around, seeking him out after the trip up Telegraph Hill with Sam Kelvig. She said she wanted to let the mayor know that she'd just been messing with him, asking those questions about the bear cub and the moonshine.

"Like I didn't know that," he told Jenny. He bit the end of his pen, then got back to his figures. He'd been bottling the stuff all year to meet the demand of Jamboree, with its private parties and inevitable drunken trysts. Even now, the still pushed forth his product. Thanksgiving and December were never too far away, bringing another spike in demand and more cash to feather Swarthbeck's bed.

"God bless Sammy Kelvig," he said as he toasted Miss McCarthy again. The punctilious peckerwood could grate on a guy, but he'd made this Jamboree business a boon by turning it into a foot-tapping, body-swaying, beer-guzzling, rock-band-intensive tribute to town history. Sam Kelvig had a vision and he implemented it, and John Swarthbeck would by God make his annual nut on this event alone. Not bad for a guy with little more than some sugar-beet byproduct, yeast, water straight from city services, and a length of copper tubing.

That girl had some nerve, Swarthbeck thought, ping-ponging back to Wanda Perkins. Somebody in town had done some gum-flapping, or the reporter was sourced up better than he was inclined to give her credit for. The thing was, he knew that no paperwork could come running back to his door. The forest service guys had been content to take the cub back—impressed, even, that the mayor had done such a good job of fattening him up, and for Swarthbeck it had been a relief, as he wasn't quite sure what he'd do when the cub became a full-on bear, with appetites beyond his ability to sate. The cub had ended up in the sanctuary in Rapid City, disingenuously if accurately billed as an orphan, and Swarthbeck had even made a couple of pilgrimages out to see him. *Now where was the harm in that?* he wondered. As for the hooch, the feds had made the boundaries—and the considerable running room between them—perfectly clear: don't embarrass us by selling the stuff out in the open, and we won't come back to town and bust your still, embarrass you in front of your people, and throw your ass in the pen. Swarthbeck had found those terms agreeable indeed.

The reporter had said Watford City was her next stop; she was going to dig into the way oil money had changed downtown and transformed a town built on agriculture. A "renaissance," she called it. Five-dollar words aside, Swarthbeck had to think it didn't amount to more than slapping fancy siding on a rattrap of a house. *Watford,* he sniffed. *You couldn't pay me enough.* "Well," he'd told her, "be sure to come on back for Jamboree. We'll show you a good time." And she'd said she wouldn't miss it, that she'd be back Saturday with Larry Grubbs. Swarthbeck figured he could get on her good side yet.

The mayor checked his figures one last time. Finding them satisfactory, he capped his pen, gave Jenny McCarthy a little squeeze where it counted, silenced John Coltrane for the night, and wheeled the dolly holding cases of spirits toward the door and into his office proper, where they would wait for placement with their rightful owners.

Swarthbeck drove into the sullen blue of night, up Telegraph Hill and toward his place. The old farm lay three miles due southwest of town, set off the road a piece and given shelter by a cotton-wood windbreak. He ciphered out some quick math in his head to put recent events in perspective. Martha had run off thirty-one months ago now, chugging hard toward three years, and the mayor found himself caught between amazement that he'd survived the breach and consternation that he still didn't understand exactly what had happened. She'd never been afraid of him, which made her something of an anomaly in town. She said she was going, and she promptly did so, leaving precious little time for Swarthbeck to say anything of value. Her point had been that she didn't want this anymore, and didn't want him for sure. That she was now living in Grand Forks and going to college, at her well-curated age, was proof enough of both contentions. His point had been that he could fix anything. He was wrong about that, he often reminded himself now. You can't fix that which insists it isn't broken.

Since she'd been gone, he'd taken to sleeping in the office more than he did at home, catching his showers and his breakfast at the truck stop. He didn't see much reason to do it any other way. He'd let the fields go fallow, and he didn't have any livestock unless you counted the barn cats, which seemed to be doing just fine, multiplying and replenishing without his involvement in their greater well-being.

Tonight, though, he yearned for a proper bed and a proper sleep. Come Friday evening, from the supper on through the weekend, he had hands to shake and babies to kiss and deals to close.

At the turnoff, he crossed the small bridge over the creek and made his way toward the darkened house.

The New York Times, *Saturday, August 1, 2015*

The physical manifestations of oil's influence in the region are clear. On the 12-mile stretch of highway between Sidney, the seat of Richland County in Montana, and Grandview one can see upward of a dozen clusters of single-wide mobile homes and fifth-wheel trailers, the shelter for oil-field workers who can't find more traditional housing in town. And while there is a surfeit of work available in the region, it is work that requires some initial qualification, a message that doesn't necessarily get passed on before desperate people make their way to the area.

"They find out that they won't get hired because they have a criminal record, or they can't pass a drug test," Sidney mayor Brad Shulman says. "Meanwhile, they've used their last dollar to get here, and now they're our problem."

And a problem they can be. Sidney has doubled its police personnel on the second and third shifts, when workaday citizens tuck into bed but the rig workers—overwhelmingly male and young and single—are most active. In Grandview, the town council recently hired a new police chief, Adair Underwood, who came to the small town from the sheriff's office in Cass County, North Dakota. In a bit of irony, Underwood, 34, said she was drawn to Grandview for the challenge of getting its criminal problems under control after 12 years in the much more sedate—and much more populous—Fargo area.

FRIDAY

THE CHIEF

Adair Underwood figured nobody had it better than she did. Here, in her police cruiser on a tree-shrouded corner of Clancy Park, she could watch, unseen, as most of Grandview breathed in peaceful slumber. The trucks moving through town at all hours provided steady fodder when she got bored, and she found a perverse delight in pulling the drivers over for riding their compression brakes or failing to heed the thirty-mile-per-hour limit through the heart of town. Chief Underwood always fancied herself a sociable sort, and depending on how much guff she got from the detained drivers, she'd let a fair number of those old boys go on with just a warning. Give her a little lip, and she could fill the city coffers right quick with a violation or two. Good cop, bad cop. Whatever she needed to be, whenever she needed to be.

Her well-guarded view on this night came with another advantage, one particularly germane to her present attentions. If anybody was up to no good—say, stealing a dog for pit fights out in the fields, as the current rumor held—they'd be hard-pressed to get out of town without her seeing the attempt. The challenges of law enforcement here on the state line, with a mishmash of federal, county, and tribal land nearby, were legion, and frankly she had enough to do with only one deputy and one officer, and a town that lived bigger than its size would suggest. Still, she longed to tear into a piece of the big action. If somebody was sneaking into Grandview and stealing dogs, especially with such a nefarious purpose as pit fights, she would find out and bring the weight of her office raining down. Any vehicle that crossed her vision with out-of-county or out-of-state license plates tonight was subject to suspicion.

She'd given her two underlings, Joe LaMer and Phil Sakota, the night off. They were family men, for one, and in a few hours they would be pressed to the limits of their service, along with a cadre of officers from Billings and Glendive whom the city had hired as security for Jamboree. LaMer, her deputy, would still be awake, she knew. They'd taken to trading the late shift and the responsibility for keeping each other engaged in the work.

Quiet, she wrote in a text message. She was careful to use her personal phone. Back home in Fargo, she'd seen a colleague's life turned inside out by her work emails slipping into the public realm. Adair had no stomach for that.

The reply came back quick, as if Joe had been waiting for her to open the conduit. *Enjoy.*

What do you think of this dog business? she wrote back. *Real thing or no?*

Dunno.

She liked LaMer. Maybe too much. He was rough around the edges and two college degrees behind her, but he had an earthy wisdom about him and about this place that Adair didn't yet know as well as she would like. She smiled at the simple reply. He made her laugh.

It's just the one report, she rapped back. *And that Chihuahua is older than Yoda. Maybe it just wandered off somewhere and died.*

Mebbe.

Adair grimaced. She didn't care for texting shorthand.

Now came another message. *WTF is Yoda?*

She opened her mouth, a squawked "What?" escaping it.

Are you a real person? she typed.

Seriously.

OK, she wrote, *that's it. You're ORDERED to report for a viewing of the first three* Star Wars *movies. Popcorn is mandatory.*

LOL. I was a farm kid. I didn't go to movies.

And you're not allowed to talk to me again until you've absorbed them.

K. It's a date.

She came to a hard stop, looking at the words and the particular way they had been arranged. Once, twice, a third time. It was, of course, a pie-in-the-sky proposition. They never had the same hours off, for one. She hadn't even unpacked the DVD player yet, for two. Julie LaMer, for three. And yet on a still night in Grandview, the last one Adair could count on seeing for a while, she felt as though she could indulge the fantasy for just a bit before practicality had to be given deference.

She closed her eyes, and she imagined things she would never have to admit to, and she smiled deliciously.

The sound came first, an awful, thunderous noise that jerked Adair out of her reverie. The discombobulating nature of it, and the thump in her chest from the sheer power of the concussion, seemed to slow everything down. Adair felt as though she were underwater and moving at half speed, as she looked first to the street to see if there had been a crash, then to the main stretch downtown, and finally skyward, where she saw the fireball snap off the propulsive stem pushing it into the sky. Once free from its tether, the massive orb made one last upward surge and then dissipated into flickering embers heading back the way they had come.

"Jesus Pete," Adair said as she gunned the car to life and tore out onto the highway, laying down a rubber scratch on the asphalt. She mashed the accelerator to the floor, and the car responded as designed, shooting like a bullet across the straightaway. She stormed past the Sloane Hotel downtown before she realized she hadn't hit her lights, but that was of little import now. She slid her cruiser into an angled stop at the mayor's office—or what remained of it, anyway—and got out, urging back those who had already emerged from their homes across the street.

"What in *the* hell?" LaMer came running up to her, in a white T-shirt, sweatpants, and rubber flip-flops, his holster and gun strapped to his hip. From the lurching of his chest, she figured he'd covered the three blocks from his house in sprinter's time.

"We gotta keep people away from it," she said, retreating to her cruiser to dig out the bullhorn.

"That's the fucking mayor's office," LaMer said. "He in there?"

Adair took three steps toward him, eyes locked on his. "How should I know? Damnit, Joe, get them back."

Folks were streaming from their homes now. Gawkers, yes, but also people who tugged at Adair, asking what they could do to help. She didn't know. Amid all the jostling, she took a moment to trace what remained of the building. The flattop roof was gone, blown clean off, and she now saw the trails of shattered masonry that spread out from the site like tendrils, and the collateral damage to nearby cars and windows. The back wall was blown out, too, and inside the remaining structure a blaze gobbled up the remnants.

Adair did a quick inventory of the adjacent buildings and found them intact, if a little beaten up cosmetically. The pregnant question, of course, was the one she couldn't answer just yet: What the hell had caused this? If it was a gas leak, she feared the chaos might just be starting.

She scanned the crowd, now in the dozens, she reckoned, and saw that LaMer and a few helpers had managed to push everybody back.

"Joe!" she called to him.

He moved off the line of humanity and trotted back to her. "Yeah?"

"You got your cell handy?"

"Sure."

"Better call the Sidney Fire Department," she said. "I don't think the volunteers are going to be able to handle this."

LaMer placed the call, and Adair went back to alternating her attention between the growing throng and the devastation in front of her, until she found the eyes of someone she'd come to trust in her short tenure. Sam Kelvig, standing on the periphery, gestured to her, asking if he could approach. She waved him in.

"He's not in there, I don't think," Kelvig told her. "I don't see his truck."

"What happened?" She didn't expect him to answer, but it was the only question that seemed worth asking.

Kelvig shrugged. "Welcome to Grandview, Adair."

"Listen," she said, deflecting things back to business. "Do you mind running out to his place and checking? I'd sure hate to be wrong about this, you know what I mean?" Swarthbeck was prone to dumping his truck wherever he found purchase for an evening, be it in the back of the Double Musky or in some lonely widow's driveway. It didn't mean he hadn't made his way back here. If a body extraction was in the offing . . . Adair shook her head. *One thing at a time, girl.*

Sam nodded at her and offered a little half smile that she decided was an apology of sorts for his cheekiness. *Good enough.*

LaMer tugged at her shirtsleeve, and Adair turned to him. "On their way," he said.

"OK, thanks."

LaMer went back to crowd control, and Adair leaned against the hood of her cruiser to wait and worry. She took a long toke off the night air, a flavor reminiscent of campfire filling her senses. She was no expert, but she didn't think she could detect a hint of gas. The pros would be on the scene soon, and they'd know.

She reached back and pulled the scrunchie from her dirty-blonde hair, taking care to hold tight to the base of her ponytail. She pulled the hair taut and slipped the rubber band back into place.

Off to her right, standing on the sidewalk outside the Country Basket, a group of teenagers, maybe five or six of them, broke into song: "Disco Inferno."

Adair looked at them, a bunch of skinny kids, linking pinkies and swaying to the chorus, and then she turned back to the fire, which seemed to be dying out on its own. The cinder block walls of the mayor's office were splashed with black where the flames had licked at them.

Now the kids moved on to "Burning Down the House," and Adair couldn't help but smile. Smart kids, queuing up songs that predated them, even predated her. She envied them for their carefree ways. Adair had a feeling she wasn't going to get off so easy where this was concerned.

"Quiet night," she said, under her breath. "My ass."

THE MAYOR

By four a.m., it was a done deal. The remnants of the mayor's office stood there, a steaming heap of rubble doused by thousands of gallons of Yellowstone River water, a smaller crowd than before still milling around it, murmuring, wondering, engaging in conjecture. Swarthbeck stood there, too, close to the burned-out husk, shoulder to shoulder with Chief Underwood. He was most assuredly alive, no small comfort to the folks who'd been first on the scene.

His eyes watered from the smoke, but he stared straight ahead through his blinking and wrestled with the implications of this awful thing. Nobody had been hurt, and nothing beyond the office had been harmed in a way that some new glass and a coat of paint wouldn't fix. The real losses he couldn't talk about, now or ever. The hooch, the still, the money that was not yet in his hands. *Coltrane.* Jesus, the record. Maybe that stung most of all, the last connection he had to a daddy he barely knew. Some things exist beyond monetary value.

"Any idea what happened?" the chief asked him.

He shook his head, silent.

"We'll figure it out," she said.

Now he nodded, even as he wondered what she meant by "we." He could get to the bottom of that, he figured. There would be time enough for conversations.

"Mayor!" a voice called out from the crowd. Swarthbeck turned and squinted. A man with a walrus mustache and the frame to match took a step forward. "I was just wondering, you know, about tomorrow, er, today. You know?"

Swarthbeck broke into a half smile. He always did like the spirit of this place.

"Nothing's broke that can't be fixed," the mayor called out. "Hell, yes, the party's still on." He punctuated the final few words, and a whoop went up.

"You folks get on back to sleep," he said, ushering them to their homes by pushing his hands forward, palms up. "We got a lot of boogying to do in a few hours." He caught a glimpse of Sam Kelvig and gave him a thumbs-up. Sam shook his head, laughing, and turned to walk up the street toward home. The mayor watched him move away and gain distance from the diffusing crowd. The burden of the next couple of days would fall disproportionately on Kelvig's shoulders, the mayor knew. A good man, that guy. The only guy for the job.

When Swarthbeck pivoted back to the devastation, the wrenched-up face of his new police chief met him.

"What's your issue, Adair?"

"The party," she said. "Jamboree. You sure that's a good idea? We have a . . . well, I'm not sure what we have here. Maybe we should wait till we find out."

Swarthbeck squeezed his eyes shut, drawing his thumb and forefinger across them until they met at the bridge of his nose. "There's nothing here that won't keep till Monday," he said.

"I don't know."

"Adair," he said. "Trust me. You gonna have somebody from the state fire marshal's office come up?"

"I hadn't thought about it yet."

"Well, look," he said, "it's Friday morning, and Helena's seven damn hours away. I'm telling you, it'll keep for a few days. Meanwhile, we have a couple thousand people set to come into town. Let's keep our eye on the ball."

"It's the couple thousand I'm—"

"Adair," he said, "it's been a hell of a night. You got any coffee at the station? My pot's suddenly on the fritz."

Swarthbeck sat in a molded plastic chair, gripped his thighs, and ran his hands down to his knees. In the harsh white light of the police station, away from the din outside, he realized how silly he must look. He wore a white T-shirt, holes chewed in the neck of it as the manifestation of a nervous tic. His pajama bottoms were multicolored and striped, reminiscent of the pants his mother used to put on him when he was a boy. And his feet were snuggled into faux-fur-lined slippers. He hadn't had time to consider wardrobe when Sam, panicked, had come rattling his door.

Chief Underwood handed him coffee in a Styrofoam cup.

"Thanks, Adair." He took a tentative slurp as she slipped to the other side of the desk and found her seat. At once, he felt ill at ease at the juxtaposition.

"How's it going, Chief?" He cocked a smile at her as he said it, both to calm her a bit and to remind himself of her underlying position. Otherwise, it would be too easy to think of her as just a girl, two years younger than his own daughter.

"Tonight aside, just fine."

"You're settling in, then?"

Her return smile, showing up at last, was unyielding. "Yep."

"That's good. Real good." He took a full-on swig of the coffee now, letting it play on his tongue before swallowing. A little weak, but it'd do in a pinch.

Swarthbeck liked her. Liked the job she was doing. If anybody ever said the mayor wasn't capable of changing his mind—not that anyone would, to him—he could present Adair Underwood as his counterpoint. When her application crossed his desk several months back, she had two big strikes against her. One, she was a woman, and Swarthbeck figured the liberals of the world could cry him a fucking river if he didn't think some jobs were best handled by a man. Two, she was young as hell. But this being America and all, other people had a say in the thing, and sure enough, the town council drew a bead on Adair as one of the finalists. On three consecutive nights, the candidates met with the council and anybody in town who cared to drop in and ask questions, and Adair Underwood made the assistant chief from Glendive and the twenty-year officer from Colstrip look like right fools. The vote was unanimous, the job was hers, and Swarthbeck figured he was entitled to wave his feminist flag around a bit if he damn well wanted to.

"OK," he said, "let's talk about it."

Chief Underwood ground into the seat and fixed him with a hard gaze. He liked it, respected it, the way she'd always look him in the eye when they spoke. A lot of people wouldn't.

"It wasn't a gas leak," she said.

"No."

"Does somebody want to hurt you?"

Swarthbeck smiled. "That question coming from any particular place?"

"Just routine," she said.

"You think there's a bomber in town?"

The chief rocked forward in the office chair. Swarthbeck, in turn, pushed back and cupped his hands behind his head. Call and response.

"I don't think anything," the chief said. "Wouldn't do any good to have a theory at this point. It gets in the way of the questions."

"I don't know of anyone who would try to hurt me," he said.

"So what's your theory?"

He stared at her for ten solid seconds. He counted them off silently. He wanted this to stick. "I don't have one. Maybe it wasn't a leak at all but an exploding gas main. Maybe it was a hot-water heater. You know Jordy Jameson?"

"Yeah, I think so."

"His water heater blew clean through his roof a few years back. That thing was like Sputnik."

"OK."

"My point being, it's done, and nobody got hurt, thank God, and"—he looked at his watch—"it's 5:37 in the a.m. and I've got bigger fish to fry."

"I hear you."

Swarthbeck let his shoulders fall. Indignation took a lot out of him. He offered a rueful smile and shrugged, and Chief Underwood at last gave him more than a puckered mouth in return.

"Can you drive me home?" he said. "I wouldn't ask, but my regular flophouse has come in for some renovations."

That did it. Earnest Chief Underwood, so very astute and devoted to her job, cackled at the joke, a mouth-wide-open, mirthful reaction that made the mayor want to get at her funny bone again sometime.

Swarthbeck marveled at how different the ride up the hill to the farmhouse looked just a few hours later. Where once the coming of night had been painted in hues of deep blue, he now found the emerging day soaked in a spotty gray, like a newspaper page that had been thoroughly creased into ink smudges.

He asked the chief to pull over at the lookout so he could get out and take a quick glance at town. He was cutting into the scant time he had available, but he wanted a distant view on things.

The blemish was obvious. From above, they could look right down into the crater bordered by three walls, a big black puncture wound to the town.

"It's gonna be an eyesore," he said.

The chief nodded. Swarthbeck set to equivocating. "But most of the action will be downtown." He traced a line along Main Street with his index finger. "You ready for this, Adair?"

She nodded again. "All set."

"Let's get to it, then, I guess."

They piled into the cruiser and made short, silent work of the remaining distance. As the chief pulled off the road onto Swarthbeck's property, he flashed on a conversation he'd had with Joe LaMer during her first week on the job. LaMer, the kind of macho-but-pliable type the mayor preferred for social interaction, hadn't been much impressed with the council's choice of new chief, and Swarthbeck had inferred that the deputy's objections matched those the mayor himself had voiced initially. Swarthbeck had made an informal approach, a how's-it-going gesture over beers at the Double Musky.

"She's good, John," LaMer had said. "Resolute."

The mayor hadn't forgotten the word; it wasn't the kind a guy like Joe LaMer would ordinarily deploy. Swarthbeck had seen hints of that quality in her in subsequent weeks, none so remarkable as the foregoing few hours.

The chief pulled the cruiser in behind Swarthbeck's truck. "Here you go."

He offered a handshake, and she met it with a worthy grip. "Thanks for the help, Adair. And damn good work tonight."

"Sleep well," she said.

He saluted and then clambered out, closing the door behind him. The chief backed the cruiser up and wheeled it left, almost to the barn, and then was on her way back to the county road.

Swarthbeck pushed out his arms and gave them a quarter turn, stretching the muscles. He took in a prodigious breath, the freshness of a new day sweeping into his system. Sleep, nothing. He had calls to make. *Bad timing for a still explosion,* he thought. That had to have been what happened. He couldn't remember the last time he'd checked the pressure, lulled as he was by the steady production. Now he had a mess on his hands.

Dead center in his view, the rising sun sprayed the eastern horizon in pink and orange. Maybe he was getting soft in his advancing age, but he tended to see something bigger in each fresh spin of the planet, and he needed his thoughts aligned there now. If he were to pile up his yesterdays and tomorrows, the future would be the shorter stack. God, yes, he had memories of sunrise. He recalled a similar morning—he couldn't have been more than four or five years old, if that—when he'd taken hold of his mother's gingham skirt as she brought him out of that tenement in Billings to watch the sun come up, the light brushing her alabaster face.

Swarthbeck went inside. Much awaited his attention, and he couldn't dawdle in days he'd already spent. It's like Sam Kelvig told him after Martha left, when Swarthbeck was damn near inconsolable: the only way to bury the past is to build tomorrow on top of it.

PATRICIA

It couldn't be anyone else crossing the street, arms spread wide as if to welcome her back from a long trip. She'd have known Raleigh's round Charlie Brown face, his bulbous nose, and John Lennon glasses anywhere. The black, frenzied hair gave him away, too, spinning outward from his head like that of a whipsawed pencil troll. He was an unmistakable guy, and Patricia's only wish was that he didn't have to see her this way after her workout—wet hair, no makeup, sweat pooling in places she didn't want to contemplate. She nearly choked on a laugh as Denise's word sprang into her head. *Swussy*, her daughter had called it. Sweaty pussy. God, why did she think of that now? She teetered on the edge of hysteria. Would Raleigh like to talk about that word?

"As I live and breathe," he said, taking her hand. "I thought I wouldn't see you until the supper."

She gave a curtsy. "Here I am."

"Here you are." He released her hand and stepped back, as if to take her in. "What have you been doing?"

She nodded at the building behind them. "Gym. Staving off old-ladyhood."

"And doing a mighty fine job of it." Raleigh punctuated it with a wolf whistle, and she gave it the laugh it deserved. Some things never changed. The banter, easy and mildly suggestive, had never been a problem for them. There had even been times when they had walked it to the brink of having to make some hard choices. Patricia knew she cared a bit too much about how she looked when Raleigh was around, and she could think of a dozen hugs that lingered a bit too long, or a hundred times when she'd constructed an alternative reality in her head where they belonged to each other. She hadn't worked out to her satisfaction whether that was out of bounds or just what any woman married thirty-some years might conjure to keep her romantic synapses firing.

"I thought you were staying in Glendive," she said.

Raleigh pivoted from foot to foot. "Funny thing," he said. "You remember Tommy Barron?"

"Vaguely."

"He lived next door to us when I was a kid. I remembered he owns the Lazy Z, so I called him up and snagged a room."

"Disinfect the sheets," she said.

Raleigh laughed and took her elbow between his thumb and forefinger, and Patricia felt herself go a bit weak.

"Have you had breakfast?" he asked.

"No, not before working out. Are you kidding me?" She puffed out her cheeks and lifted her arms to demonstrate bloat.

"Your workout's done, so you must. With me."

Yes, please, she wished. "No, I can't. There's so much to do."

"A cup of coffee, then."

"No, I shouldn't."

"One cup." He took off his glasses and made his eyes sufficiently pathetic, and that did what little doing was required.

"OK. One cup."

Patricia gripped her coffee cup with both hands. The willingness to talk with Raleigh was always in her; it was just that finding the right place to start could prove so nettlesome. His mind, the way he brought such crafted, powerful language to yearnings she thought were hers alone, was an endless source of fascination, so much that she had to tamp down the compulsion to do nothing but ask questions about the books she had read into a tattered state.

Today, though, she had a more topical subject in mind.

"The mayor's office blew up last night," she said before she took her first sip.

"What? Like . . ." Raleigh threw both hands into the air and flared his fingers.

"Yep."

"Was anybody hurt?"

"No, thank God."

"What happened?"

"Sam thinks the still got plugged."

Raleigh removed his glasses and rubbed his eyes. "So the theory is that our rum-running mayor had a distillery in his office and caused an explosion?"

"I guess so."

Raleigh's mouth, hanging open after the incredulity of his question, flapped a couple of times before he found more words. "How in the hell did we come from this place?"

Patricia shrugged and then downed more coffee.

"And why are you still here?" he added, making it sound like a lament.

Patricia grimaced, something she hoped he didn't see or that she sufficiently covered with the cup at her mouth. Raleigh, of course, would have no idea how that query could wound her by feeding into questions she'd been asking herself for a while now. He had it easy. He'd gotten out, been to places she had seen only on TV, made a name for himself. He couldn't really hold regrets about Grandview, not the way she could. When she allowed herself to think of them, in those moments when she wasn't preoccupied by the day-to-day of being a wife and a mother and an auxiliary member, she had her own lamentations. Why was life stacked in such a way that she'd had to make binding decisions—where to live, whom to marry, whether to subjugate her own aspirations to those of Sam—before she had any way of knowing what she wanted? It seemed a cruel stroke that a willingness to wrestle with those questions came only after youth had been expended.

She would not answer his question. She could not.

"I think *Squalid Love* is your best book yet," she said.

The server swung by and went to top off Raleigh's cup. He pressed a finger against the mug, about a half inch from the top. "Leave me some doctoring room, OK?"

The woman—girl, really; she couldn't be much more than eighteen, nineteen, Patricia figured—giggled and then complied with the request, leaving them to their conversation.

Raleigh dropped in the cream and sugar and twirled the spoon through the muddied coffee as he looked back at Patricia. "The place has changed," he said. "All these new stores and hotels swamping the fields I used to wander into with my BB gun."

Patricia met his smile with her own. "It doesn't seem so sudden if you're here every day," she said, and then she wondered if he'd hear a slight in that, so she made haste with an addition. "You got the better deal."

A fresh approach by the server jerked Patricia's head up, but the young woman had another target.

"You're Raleigh Ridgeley. I wasn't sure—I mean, you look bigger, I mean taller, than in your photo, but that's dumb because the photo is small," she said. "What I mean is, you're Raleigh Ridgeley."

"Guilty," he said, and Patricia noted that as if on cue the server flushed a hearty pink.

The young woman kept going now, zeroed in on Raleigh and oblivious to Patricia. "I had to read *West of My Heart* in college," she said. "Listen to me—had to. It sounds like I didn't want to. I did. I knew you were from around here. Anyway, I loved it. Do you mind if I sit down?" The sentences tumbled out a half beat too fast, collapsing into each other.

Raleigh gestured to the chair opposite him. "Please." Patricia scooted her own chair over to make room.

The server folded herself into the seat and put the coffeepot on the table in front of her. Patricia watched as Raleigh smiled at the girl, and she wondered how often he had to deal with impositions such as this.

"What's your name?" he asked.

"Skyler Fitch."

"Pleased to meet you." He extended a hand over the table, and she giggled again as she met his grip. "So you had to read it in college. Where was this?"

"Minot State."

"When did you graduate?"

She placed her hands on her legs below the table and shrugged her shoulders. Nervous, Patricia noted. Nervous and pleased.

"I haven't graduated yet. I mean, I've dropped out. Not permanently, I have plans. I mean, I'm not going to work here forever. I don't want you to think I'm dumb or something."

"Of course not," he said.

"It's just that my husband is making bank in the oil fields, and we've been saving up for a house and, I don't know. I just thought I'd help us out, you know?"

"Sure."

"I wish I had my book here! I'd get you to sign it." She made a pouty face, and now Patricia wanted to throttle her. "I mean, wow, Raleigh Ridgeley."

Raleigh leaned forward, giving himself room to retrieve his wallet from his back pocket. He extracted two business cards and passed them across the table.

"How about I send you signed copies of all of the books?" he said.

"Would you do that?"

"Absolutely. Just write your mailing address and your email address on one of those cards, and I'll get the books out to you. I have some things to do for the next few days, but I'll send you a note when they go out." She made to hand the second card back to him, but he waved her off. "It's for you. Write to me anytime. I love hearing from people who love books."

She grabbed the ballpoint pen from her blouse and scratched out the information, then handed the card back to him. Raleigh made a show out of tucking it back into his wallet, and Patricia almost choked on a chortle. The server cast her a look.

"Skyler! Pick up!" came a call from the kitchen.

"Oh, crap," she said, standing and straightening her skirt. "My boss. I gotta go."

"Thanks for saying hello," Raleigh said.

"Bye, Skyler," Patricia tossed in. And then, when the young woman was gone, she gave him a devilish look and said, "Such a tough life you have," and they both cracked up.

Patricia stayed as long as she could, until there was no margin left between where she sat and the obligations that awaited, and then she offered her regrets and her reasons: Samuel, Denise and the grandkids, Maris Westfall and her damned old pies. And Sam. Always, Sam.

Raleigh walked her to the car. She demurred, but he insisted, and she was glad of that.

He hung off the door as she started the engine.

"I'm serious," he said.

"About what?"

"Why are you still here?"

She smiled. Damn him for pressing it. She rummaged through her purse, giving herself cover while a reason she could use swam for the surface. "It's just—"

Raleigh ducked into the cab, and he kissed her. The move was quick, but the kiss lingered. She closed her eyes and she let him do it, and then she pulled back, as if stung. He retracted.

"I'm sorry," he said, a contention that didn't match the look on his face. She knew that look, long though it had been since she'd seen it.

She was breathing heavily, as though her air were being consumed by the fire burning her up.

"I have to go," she said.

"I know."

"See you later, Raleigh."

She closed the door and gunned the car to life, and he stood there, ambition in his eyes, and she wondered why he had to look at her like that.

OMAR

The boy fixated on the strip of white skin between Sam Kelvig's slipping belt line and the tail of his shirt. The upper crease of Sam's ass peeked above the leather belt, and Lord help him, Omar Smothers couldn't help but stare. Old men and their plumbers' cracks. Is that what he had to look forward to in some distant tomorrow?

Sam continued rummaging through the small storage shed adjacent to the town hall, which itself was just a Quonset hut painted in simple white and well insulated for the angry seasons of the northern plains. Omar rubbed the sleep from his eyes, then idly picked at the line of acne standing sentry on his right jaw while he waited for instructions.

"The damn things are in here somewhere," came Sam's muffled declaration.

"What are you looking for, Mr. Kelvig?"

"Sam. The damn pylons."

It was always this way between them: Mr. Kelvig asking him to ditch the formality, and Omar being mindful of what his mother was forever telling him, that he needed to respect how wonderful the Kelvigs had been to them, with the job and the friendship and the support of Omar's aspirations. It had been Sam who paid for Omar to go to that basketball camp in Las Vegas two years ago, and Omar now received a bucketful of mail nearly every day from college coaches who wanted him to come play for them. That doesn't just happen for everybody, his mother was always saying, and while Omar had his own talent to credit, he shouldn't discount Mr. Kelvig's role in things.

Omar got it. He did. There weren't many men in town who'd do what Sam Kelvig had done, who'd embrace a single mother and her bastard son and treat them like his own. He appreciated it. He just wondered sometimes why he wasn't allowed to feel embarrassed when Mr. Kelvig's voice would sail out from the stands, louder than everyone else's, scolding him ("Damnit, Omar, you've got to grab that ball with both hands!"), or when Mr. Kelvig singled him out for a chat after church on Sundays or insisted on buying him a malted at Pete's when Omar just wanted to be with his friends. Or why he had to be up at this ungodly eight a.m. to help Mr. Kelvig. Omar yawned. Why? Because his mom had said so. End of discussion.

"Isn't that them right there?" he asked.

Sam looked back at him, annoyed. "Where?"

"Just let me . . ." Omar slipped his slender frame between Sam and the shed's door frame. The pent-up mustiness hit him at once, flavored with hints of stale gasoline and parched soil. He reached for the top shelf in the far back, a simple task at his height of six foot eight, and he plucked the stacked pylons with his oversized hands.

"Hot damn, Omar," Sam said. "I'd have never seen them up there in the dark. You got X-ray eyes?"

"No, sir."

"All right, come out of there. Let me get the rest of the stuff and we'll get busy."

Omar stepped out the way he'd gone in and went back to waiting, making patterns in the dirt with his feet.

Sam whistled a tune while he gathered the signs that would direct traffic around downtown, some spray paint, and some boundary ribbon.

"You're going to be a big star at the U, Omar," he said between whistle blasts.

That was another thing, Omar thought. Mr. Kelvig was always talking up the University of Montana, like it was a done deal that Omar would be going there, the way Sam's own son had done back when Omar was just a little boy. He had to be nice about it, because like his mother said, Mr. Kelvig meant well, but privately Omar figured the old guy could kiss his half-Indian ass. Coach Boeheim wanted him at Syracuse. Coach K wanted him down at Duke. They wanted him at UCLA. The University of California at Mother-Fucking Los Angeles, as Coach had said. Mr. Kelvig might think the world stopped at Montana's borders, but Omar had a few ideas of his own. He'd always need his mother, but he wasn't going to need this town much longer, and he wouldn't need Montana, either. All he needed was beaches, basketball, and girls. Stuff that in your ass crack, old man.

NORBY

For a long while, Norby had harbored a theory that places acted like dry-cell batteries, storing remnants of the lives of everyone who had ever passed through them. Even as he had put steady distance between himself and where he'd come from, he'd held to that notion. But now, as he cleared the last bend in the road before Grandview loomed into view, he wasn't so sure anymore.

Apart from the physical layout, nothing here looked like he remembered. Fields that had once lain open, alternating between fertilized and fallow, now held mishmashes of RVs and travel trailers. Holding tanks and oil pumps sprouted in front yards and back forties. An infusion of oil tax money had allowed the town fathers to slap a new coat of paint on everything—Norby knew this from the email exchanges with his dad, who could talk up a storm about everything that didn't much matter. The whole effect was a mash-up. Old farms, new alignments, cheap housing alternatives fronted by all the trappings of quick oil wealth—dirt bikes and watercraft and gleaming new pickup trucks.

The butterflies flapped around his stomach again, same as with his struggle with creeping doubt that morning in the Billings hotel room, as he endured the tug-of-war between expedient desire—find a flight, now, and just go back—and practical consideration for his folks' point of view. *You get to do that once,* he reminded himself before he set out on the four-hour drive home, *and you've already burned your chance.*

And then, before he could give himself time to consider bailing out one last time, he was upon it. On the left, the cluster of three schools—elementary, middle, and high—where he'd spent thirteen years. On the right, a constant amid the change, the Rifleshot Pizza Company, where three generations of Grandview kids ate and worked and settled their differences in parking-lot fisticuffs. Then he made his left turn, and the new, foreign Grandview fell away and familiarity flooded the scene. It was like cueing a movie in Norby's head. Childhood, at first idyllic and then chaotic as he learned more about himself, sped through his mind's eye, and when Norby came to a stop in the driveway of the house he grew up in, just a short walk across the street from his old schools, disorientation set in, as if he had no idea how he'd gotten here.

"You've changed your hair," Patricia told him after she'd held him tight and then ushered him into the living room. ("Sit down, and let's talk while we have the time," she'd said, and Norby had fought with himself not to read something more into that. He'd spent the better part of the morning reminding himself of the thin margin between innocuous chitchat and a deliberate message, with his final pronouncement being that he should just give his folks the benefit of the doubt.)

He dragged a hand across his brow, pushing the intransigent shock of hair back. "Yeah."

"I liked it better short. You shouldn't hide your face."

"Mom."

"I know," she said. "I'm nervous. Is it OK if I say I'm nervous?"

They sat across from each other. Norby wished she were closer, so he could take her hand and give some indication of how alike they really were in this. Instead, he smiled through pursed lips. "Yes, it's OK. I am, too."

"I'm just so glad you came. That's the main thing."

"Yes."

"That's a nice car you got."

"I guess so."

"Montana plates. That's strange, isn't it?"

The heat flushed through Norby. The stupid, pointless ruse about where he was flying. *What is wrong with me that I thought that was a good idea?* he wondered.

He aimed to move her off the topic.

"Where's Dad?"

"Down at the park by now, I should think. You should go see him."

"I don't know."

"He wants you to, Norby." He looked at her. Though he'd made his wishes clear about the name he wanted to use, neither of his parents had acceded, until now. "I'm trying," she said.

"OK. I'll go."

Patricia stood. To Norby, it was as if she wished to hustle him off before he changed his mind.

"Good," she said. "Be sure to drop by the mayor's office and see what kind of foolishness he's been up to."

Norby decided to cover the distance on foot, the better to poke around in his memories at a gentler pace. He pressed due north on Mission Avenue, past the most memorable settings of his younger days, connecting the threads of time and place as he went. There, in the backyard of the house on the corner of Fifth Street, was the clothesline he and Marc Ray had raided in the summer of 1997, intending to hold Marcy Yaw's underwear for a ransom. No, wait, he thought, that would have been '96, because Marcy's older sister, Kate, was class of '97 and was killed by a drunken driver out on Cutoff Road the following spring, two days before graduation. That had been a solar-plexus punch for everybody in town.

At Sixth Street, he turned right, and the reason for his mother's urging him to go this way shoved into view. Three skid steers were being loaded and locked down onto a flatbed trailer, and another truck carried a container stacked high with singed lumber and blackened cinder block. Where Norby expected to see the mayor's office building, he saw nothing but a view to the alley behind it. Standing well back but front and center and assuredly in charge of the bustling work site was Mayor Swarthbeck.

Norby jogged the final few yards.

"Mayor," he said.

Swarthbeck did a literal double take before recognition finally triggered.

"Well, I'll be," he said, gripping Norby's hand and shoulder and giving both a considerable shake. "How the heck are you?"

"Pretty good. So what happened here?"

Swarthbeck, still holding on to his shoulder, commandeered Norby and moved him a few feet farther away from the cleanup. "Oh, you know, little mishap. Jeez, kid, I've gotta tell you, didn't expect to see you around, so I'm sorry it took me a minute. It was like opening the door to the fridge and seeing an aquarium. A little hard to ponder."

"No biggie."

Swarthbeck looked him up and down a couple of times. "So this is the California look, huh? Long hair. No socks in your shoes."

"I guess."

"That what they call metrosexual or something?"

Norby clenched his fists instinctively, without any real plan for what to do next. He searched the mayor's face for some indication of intent behind the remark but couldn't suss any out.

"I'm just joshing you," Swarthbeck said at last, nudging Norby with an elbow. "Naw, you look good, kid. The coastal life's been good to you, I guess."

"I guess." Norby switched gears. "You seen my dad?"

The mayor cast a dismissive wave toward downtown. "Down at the park, putting up the bunting or some shit. It's his show, you know."

"Thanks, Mayor."

"He's there with that kid, Omar. You know about him?"

"I've heard some stories."

"He's the real deal. Better basketball player than you, that kid."

There was no mistaking that one. The words had been sharpened and aimed at the heart. Norby turned and walked away, ears burning. At least half of the sting, he told himself, lay in the fact that he allowed the stupid comment to pierce his skin. It wasn't that he hadn't heard it all before from people much more significant in his life than the mayor. He'd been called a coward, though he had no idea how anyone could support that contention. There's nothing cowardly about telling your coach you won't play again, no matter how much he's counting on you. Nobody with fear ruling his heart stands in front of his father and says the same, while offering no explanation, because who would have believed it? He'd had ten years to make his peace with what he'd done, and he knew, in the deepest part of him, that given another hundred chances to make the decision, he'd do it the same way. Every time.

THE CHIEF

At the north-side downtown blockade, Adair nosed the squad car off to the right, up a street, and into the alley. She didn't care for not being able to drive the full length of Main, and she'd told the mayor as much several weeks earlier, when the nuts-and-bolts planning kicked in. Still, she couldn't argue with the general principle of keeping a rowdy, alcohol-fueled crowd penned in once the night-time festivities began.

She emerged from the alley onto Sixth Street, and what she saw brought her to a stop. She couldn't believe it. Here, hours earlier, had stood the charcoal ruins of the mayor's office. Now it was a hole in the street, just a bare foundation, like the gap left by a missing tooth.

"What the hell?" she said.

She checked the mirrors behind her, and craned her neck out of the window. Nobody on the street. Just an empty space and dust stirred by a gentle wind.

Adair's cell phone buzzed. She checked the text messages. LaMer.

You coming? These guys are ready to eat.

Yeah.

You got everything?

Yeah. Where's Sakota?

On patrol. You want him?

Loaded question, Adair thought. Yeah, she wanted him. She wanted his head on a spike. A building doesn't just up and disappear, and if it does, the police chief damn well better get a call.

No. Be a sec.

With little trouble, Adair got food ordered for the hungry men in her charge, and while they waited for Pete to knock out the orders, she made a show of handing out yellow T-shirts with the town insignia on them, as well as zip ties for each man to use as handcuffs should the occasion warrant it.

The mayor had been direct about his wishes when Adair decided to hire the extra security. "We don't need a show of damn force, Adair," he'd said. "Tell everybody to dress casual and blend in." The T-shirts had been her compromise. They weren't exactly unobtrusive; these guys weren't going to be mistaken for a boys' choir in the matching duds. But Adair knew she needed a quick way of identifying who was who once the sun went down and the rowdiness kicked up a few notches.

She sat with LaMer at lunch, working on her bottom lip and grinding her hands.

"What's wrong?" he said.

She plucked a french fry off her plate and jabbed it in the air at him. "You see what was going on at the mayor's office this morning?"

"Yeah. He had a crew come clean up the mess. So?"

"A little unusual, don't you think? I mean, I just dropped him off at his place, what, six hours ago?"

"Yeah."

"How come nobody called me?"

LaMer took a bite of his burger and talked through it. "I don't know. Why are you so sore?"

"It's just weird. He even asked me about calling the state fire marshal. Not much point in that now, is there?"

"Guess not."

Adair threw the fry back onto her plate. Sometimes, she got a nasty mouthful of just how dumb Joe LaMer could be, which wasn't his most attractive quality. When she'd finally gotten home after the explosion, keyed up and exhausted all at once, she'd used him—or, rather, her imagination about him—to get off, to cut the tension down to something manageable and bring sleep on. She thought now that he wasn't deserving of her fantasies or her touch.

"What I'm saying, Joe, is that it shouldn't have gone like that. There's a protocol."

LaMer wore a look of boredom, and that goosed Adair's discontent.

"It's his building," he said. "I figure he can do what he wants."

"Oh, come on—"

"Listen, Chief," he said. He never called her chief, and the invocation startled her. Maybe she should have insisted on it. In an effort to get along, and with such a small staff, she'd encouraged first names. A little deference, a little thought to keeping her in the loop, might be nice right now.

"Yeah?"

LaMer looked down, as if he didn't want to get into it, and then he brought his face back up. He set a hard gaze on Adair. She found it unnerving.

"This isn't any big deal," he said. "Maybe you ought to let it go."

Quick as it came on, the stolid look from LaMer slipped away, and he went back to his plate. Adair pushed hers to the middle of the table and stood up.

"Have half of these guys at the park at four thirty," she said. "Other half need to be posted around the downtown area. We'll swap places at five thirty so everyone can eat. OK?"

LaMer nodded. "You got it, Chief."

Adair walked away, fighting to conceal the wobble in her legs. She'd never seen such straight-up insolence from LaMer before. No, not just insolence. Creepiness. It had jerked her antenna up, this subtle yet strong indication from him that she should shut up and let it go, and that left her caught between rattled and pissed off. A few guys in her hired crew acknowledged her as she headed for the door, and she responded with a pursed smile.

Outside, in the cruiser, she gave herself a minute to gather her composure. One minute, just sixty seconds, and then she had to get on with it. She set a timer on her phone, and she watched the seconds tick off. One minute, and then Adair would be a rock.

No fear.

32 . . . 33 . . . 34 . . . 35 . . .

She slammed a fist on the empty seat beside her. "What the hell just happened?"

SAM

When Sam saw his boy striding across Clancy Park toward him, he felt a wave of thankfulness that he hadn't had time, before now, to ponder his reaction to the moment. He realized that he couldn't have anticipated it all—the gladness to see him and the instant, eternally renewable regret for things said in frustration or not said at all, and the trepidation over what more might come out or be held back this weekend.

Samuel gave a wave as he approached, enthusiastic enough and friendly enough by Sam's reckoning. He responded in kind, and then they shook hands. This, Sam had projected through his thoughts maybe a hundred times. Could he hug his son? Would Samuel hug him? When the moment came, it didn't feel like the thing to do, and that hurt.

"Mom said you need some help."

Sam doffed his cap and polished his forehead with a bandanna. "Sure do. Omar's left me high and dry here." He caught Samuel's eye and offered a rueful chuckle to let him know he'd expected as much. The kids would be swimming up at the river. Couldn't blame a kid for being a kid.

They went to stretching a canvas banner—"GREATER GRANDVIEW OLD-TIMERS' JAMBOREE"—across the west face of the bandstand. They alternated turns tying it down, Sam at the top right edge, Samuel the bottom left, then top left and bottom right. They worked wordlessly, in rhythm, and Sam liked that. It reminded him of his first year running the show, when Samuel was about to be a senior in high school. They'd been inseparable that summer. Fishing trips, camping in the Missouri Breaks, a golf getaway in Billings. Then, just a few months later . . .

Sam pulled his head up, on alert. He moved around the perimeter of the bandstand to the other side, watching.

"Dad?"

Across the way, in the back parking lot by the swing sets, Henrik climbed out of his truck. Sam spat out a "damnit" and took off toward him.

"Dad!" Behind him, Sam heard footfalls as his son ran to catch up. At a more leisurely pace, Henrik closed the distance, too.

"Can't park there," Sam said. "You see the sign?"

"Relax, little brother. I won't be long." That smug grin. Sam wanted to punch him in the face, a compulsion tempered by the inconvenient fact that Sam had never gotten the better of Henrik in a physical way. His older brother came by big the way Big Herschel had, a genetic blessing that had bypassed Sam.

"Uncle Henrik?"

Henrik moved his gaze from his brother to his nephew. "Samuel. Been a long time."

"Norby," Sam said.

"Huh?"

"He's Norby now," Sam clarified. *Goddamnit*. "Get that truck out of here."

Henrik reached out to grab his brother's shoulder, and Sam shucked him off.

"I just come to tell you something, and then I'll be on my way," Henrik said.

Sam closed his eyes, a search for some vestige of serenity to latch onto, and then opened them again. "What?"

"I come for what's mine. I've already talked to Mama—"

"You stay away from Mama."

"—and now she knows it, too. People are finding out you're not such a straight arrow, Sam."

That self-satisfied grin again. Sam balled up his fists. "You stay away from her. She's sick and she's old, and she doesn't need you dragging her into your horseshit."

Henrik reached for Sam again, and this time Sam drew back as if to strike. Norby grabbed hold of his father and pulled him a few steps away. Henrik backed off, too, still smiling.

"You know, little brother," he said. "She's my mama, too. You don't get to hog everything and everybody."

Sam stood his ground. The tension lingered in him until Henrik was in the truck and on his way, and then it released all at once, expending him.

"Dad," Norby said. "What the hell was that?"

"Just your uncle, being a dumbass."

"Yeah, but—" Norby said, and Sam cut him off.

"Look, there's too much to do," he said, which was true enough but also a convenient dodge. Sam had no stomach for swimming the depths of Henrik right now. "Let's just get on it, huh?"

PATRICIA

Randy, Denise, and the kids had been in the house less than an hour, and it was wrecked. Bags and baby paraphernalia were strewn from the entryway to the living room; the smashed scatterings of soda crackers dotted Patricia's hardwood floors; and to compound matters, Maris Westfall had called twice with reminders of what Patricia should bring to the park, as if she had not done this for thirty years.

When it all threatened to be too much, Patricia stepped out onto the enclosed veranda, shutting the glass door behind her and choking off the sounds of Randall Junior and Chase screaming baby invectives at each other as they fought over the plastic horses Sam had given them last Christmas.

She had to wonder when she'd developed such intolerance for the sensory overload of children. Lord knows she'd been down those trails with her own kids. Denise, in particular, could bring an abrupt end to a trip to the grocery store or a restaurant once she got it in her head to explore the octave heights of her voice. Patricia smiled now to remember one lunch in Williston, just the three of them, and Denise's warbling discontent that sent Patricia out into the snow while Sam grimly paid the bill for food that sat untouched on their table.

Samuel's arrival, three years behind Denise, didn't compound the noise and aggravation to any great degree, praise be. On the contrary, he was a happy, contented baby from the get-go. Patricia chuckled to herself. Denise probably wouldn't appreciate hearing that now. In any case, Samuel's—Norby's—discontent came on with a vengeance later and raged to this day. All the more reason to keep her mouth shut, Patricia thought. Denise would point that out, too.

The difference, she decided as she breathed in and out a few more times, steeling herself for going back inside, was that she and Sam had put some years between their two children. Randy and Denise had theirs fourteen months apart, prompting Sam to tell Randy to stop hanging his pants on the bedpost. Patricia chuckled again to remember that directive, delivered over a celebratory dinner in Billings. It was difficult to harness Randy Sternslaw into silence—there'd be a lot of people interested in knowing that trick—but Sam's words did it. For a while, anyway.

Patricia peeked through the kitchen window at the microwave clock. 2:09. She'd be due at Clancy Park in less than two hours, and that was an appointment she aimed to make on time so as not to invoke further Westfallian ire. Between Denise's family and Norby, she hadn't had much time to think about anything other than the rote duty of Jamboree. Not such a bad thing, considering the events of the morning, she thought. And still that unresolved matter lay in wait. Raleigh would be at dinner tonight, and she felt sure he'd have something to say. He'd left a lot on the table. So had she, for that matter.

She reached for the handle of the sliding glass door. *Smile,* she told herself.

Maris called again. Minnie Lane had fallen ill, and could Patricia run over there—"It's only three doors from you, don't you know, so that's why I called," Maris had said—and get the pickles and grape tomatoes and the rest and cut them up for the relish trays? Please and thank you and all of that. Patricia galloped down there, cooed appropriately over poor Minnie, and came back and pressed Denise into a supporting role.

"So he hasn't said anything about his . . . whatever you call it?" Denise said.

"Boyfriend, honey. I think the term is boyfriend." Patricia followed this with a smile, to send the message that she didn't mean anything cutting by it, but Denise still wrinkled her nose. Patricia appreciated, at least, that Denise had waited until Randy had taken the boys down to the basement for a nap before broaching the subject of her brother. She didn't want to have this conversation on two fronts. Randy had about as much acquaintance with considered debate as a rabid dog has with decorum. She didn't think she could face that.

"No," Patricia said. "I've barely talked to him. I thought he and your father would be back by now, but maybe they're just going to meet us at the park."

"You know what I think," Denise said, as if the vastness of her thoughts were common knowledge.

"No, I don't."

Denise made two perfect slices, turning one dill pickle into four spears, which she stacked on the tray. "I think he's got too much of that California in him, that's what I think."

"Oh, Denise."

"I'm serious. He wasn't like this before he moved out there."

Patricia dropped the cutlery, pressed her hands against the cutting board and turned to her daughter. "How do you know?"

"What?"

"What he was like. How do you know? How do you know this isn't who he's always been?"

"Because I have memories, Mom. Because I lived here with him. Something changed when he moved to California. They're freaks out there, you know."

"Oh, good grief. They're not freaks." Patricia flashed on the one trip she and Sam made to the Bay Area, six years ago, before any of the mess started—or, at least, before any of the mess was known to them. She loved California the first time she set eyes on it. She remembered City Lights, where she lost herself in the stacks of books. The worst meal they had in a weekend in San Francisco was better than the best meal she'd ever had in Montana. The ocean, so wild and vast and beautiful. The weather. When she and Sam came home, she no longer had any questions about what Samuel saw in the place. How she wished to return. How she hoped that they might square away the pain on this trip and open up such possibilities again.

"You want to know what I think he ought to do?" Denise said.

Not really, but you're going to tell me, anyway. "What's that, dear?"

"He needs to go to Peace Lutheran with you and Daddy on Sunday and get right with his God."

"Oh, Denise!"

Patricia's daughter scrunched her face into the little-girl scowl she'd developed long ago and never refined in her subsequent years, and Patricia had been down this route with her enough times to just let her pout. Denise crossed to the dishwasher and began loudly arranging the soiled stoneware and silverware, her displeasure registered in every metallic clank.

Patricia waited it out, and in doing so gave her thoughts over to a worry she'd harbored on and off ever since Samuel lit out for California. He and his sister had never been close, dissimilar as they were beyond the blood coursing through them, and now they had distance working against them, too. Time was still an ally, in that there might be enough of it for them to find their way to each other, but Patricia also knew well how the years tended to stack up. If the next thirty went by as quickly as the previous thirty . . . She shuddered. She wasn't ready to contemplate mortality today, on top of everything else.

"Denise," she said.

Her daughter slammed the dishwasher shut and set it on its task. There'd be no opening now. Patricia clamped down on the rest of what she wanted to say.

A reliable alignment had taken root in the family long ago. On matters of principle or emotion, Denise would flock to her father's side, looking at the issue through the same lens Sam used. That perspective, for lack of a better assessment, tended toward the authoritarian. Suggesting that Samuel hew to what religion had to say fell in line with that. That's the position Sam had staked out, too.

Samuel, on the other hand, would find communion with his mother on family divisions. If Denise's feelings were a hammer that she wielded without discrimination, Samuel's were fodder for introspection. Patricia remembered talking to Mina Pollard about that one time, and Mina had told her, "Your boy, he's more girl than boy when it comes to feelings." She hadn't meant it in a disparaging way, but Patricia was happy all the same that Sam hadn't been there to hear it. It would have left him chafed and angry.

Patricia's own reading had backed up her friend's diagnosis. Where Sam had turned to the Bible to fortify his stance against their son's sexuality, Patricia had thrown herself into books that she hid from her husband, dense distillations of anima and animus and the archetypes of masculinity and femininity. She thought she'd learned a lot. She wished she could impart some of it.

"Denise," she said again, and at this her daughter turned to her at last, silent and fuming still, but at least open to Patricia's thoughts.

"I don't think it's a matter of God," Patricia said. "This is who he is."

Denise turned and walked away.

OMAR

The Grandview railroad bridge—just "the Bridge" to anyone in the know—had, in its nearly eighty years, come to be viewed as a bitter metaphor for the town that shared its name. It took root but never really matured into fullness. In the time of the WPA, great notions held that the bridge would span the width of the Yellowstone River and establish a rail route for the goods produced on the fertile farms of the river valley. Had that come to pass, Grandview might well have sprung into something larger, economically and socially, for it was generally agreed at the time that neither Sidney nor Williston nor anywhere else in that tucked-in corner of the map had more potential than Grandview did.

History, of course, had the final say, as history is wont to do. One section of bridge and one river piling were built before the plan was scrapped and the funding was diverted. The railroad didn't come, and Grandview never got its bridge. What it had, for a short, tragic while, was the world's most expensive diving platform, until one or two kids came home in body bags after ill-fated leaps into the water and the open end of the bridge was sealed with fencing and barbed wire. Now it was a mild curiosity in a no-man's-land. The town that gave the truncated bridge its name actually had no responsibility for it, as its spot on the river sat east of the state line, on McKenzie County land in North Dakota. This between-two-worlds quality—out of the reach of Grandview's authority and miles from any active police presence in North Dakota—had made the place a draw for restless teens for four generations.

Omar Smothers stood now on the half-baked bridge and leaned against the railing as he watched a cross section of Grandview denizens—classmates and mothers and fathers and small children—play in the water, lie on blankets in the sun, and tend to portable barbecue grills on the river's shore. Beside him, Clarissa Axtell stood sobbing.

She'd called the night before and asked him to come, and Omar had been noncommittal. There was this thing he had to do for Mr. Kelvig, he'd said, and he had some other chores, too. It was mostly a lie, the bit about Mr. Kelvig notwithstanding. The bigger truth was that although Omar badly wanted to see her, to talk with her, to be in her space again, he didn't think he should. The vagaries of a small town and a school where everyone knows everyone else already clawed at the distance he was trying to keep from the first girl to smash his heart.

"Please, just come," she had said, and that had more sticking power than his resolve did. It dug at him and agitated him all morning, and it must have shown, because Mr. Kelvig had finally told him, "Omar, I don't think you're gonna be much help to me today. Go enjoy your friends."

So now he was here and Clarissa was sobbing, and he didn't know what to do except reach out and stroke her hair.

"No," she said, pulling back. Omar tucked his hands in his pockets.

"I'm sorry." His cheeks burned.

"No, I'm sorry," she said, and then the crying came on again. Clarissa dropped her head into her hands as her shoulders heaved.

Omar watched the throng below, and he wondered if anyone was looking up at them, seeing this, wondering what was going on, building their own assumptions. There'd been plenty of that already, in other venues, and though Clarissa had never come out and said as much, Omar figured it had spelled the end of them. In high school shorthand, Clarissa was slumming by being with him, and he was trying to climb out of his social caste by being with her. Soon enough, she was in the passenger seat of John Rexford's Mustang and in the booth opposite him at the Rifleshot, a restoration of social order in which the Axtells and Rexfords remained part of the town fabric and Omar remained the half-Indian son of a single-mom store clerk.

"Tell me what to do," he said, low and sideways.

"I can't." Her words crumbled as they met his.

"I'm going home, then."

He said it with intent, to force the issue, and if she hadn't reached for him, he knew he'd have been unable to find the gumption to actually walk down the hill to his bicycle and ride away.

"I'm scared, Omar." She raked her face with the palms of her hands, trying to clear her eyes. "I need help."

"Tell me."

Clarissa knelt before him and asked him to sit with her. He folded himself onto the steel platform, long arms and legs akimbo, the transferred heat of the day scorching his skin. When Clarissa first touched her stomach through the purple tank top she wore, Omar knew, and the words that poured forth from her thereafter simply provided confirmation of the mess she was in. *And what a mess it is,* Omar thought as he swallowed down the waves of nausea. The boundaries that he had dared not cross—not out of deference so much as fear and his mother's reminders to know his place—had been breached with impunity by his romantic rival. By August and the start of school, Clarissa would be showing, and that, she said, would bring the whole works down upon her if she didn't do something first. She had a plan, she said. First thing Monday, they could drive her Honda to Billings, where things like this were done. They would be back that evening. She could tell her parents she was spending the day in Minot with a girlfriend. Omar could conjure a fib for his mom. No one would have to know.

"You're sure?" Omar said.

"I made a mistake," she said. "A mistake."

"Why me? This isn't my problem."

Omar said it to make it hurt, and he could see that it did. She dropped her head again, and regret spread across him at once. He took her hand, and she let him, and the sensation he missed so much came back to him. He held her hand, his brown fingers contrasted against the pale white of her knuckles.

"I can't," she said. "I have to do this."

"OK."

"Will you help me?" she asked.

"OK."

"Thank you."

"Can I tell you something?" he asked her.

"Yes."

He let go of her hand.

"I feel like I'm going to throw up," he said.

THE CHIEF

Adair sat in her cruiser behind a cottonwood windbreak on the southern edge of town, positioned as if running point on a speed trap—a reasonable place to be, given the impending event and the steady rush of cars heading into Grandview. The radar, however, was not engaged. She had instead descended deep into a phone call.

The whole series of things stuck in her craw, and Swarthbeck's unconscionable actions stood at the top of the roster. That was a crime scene, or at least needed to be treated like one until some answers came through, and the mayor should have known it. It frosted Adair's ass now that she hadn't run some police tape around it. The hell with the mayor and his desire to get some sleep. That was plainly a lie. And then Joe LaMer with his I-wouldn't-cross-the-mayor posturing. What the hell was that about?

She'd made her rounds after lunch, hit the checkpoints, offered to help with setup, chased some kids away from potential mischief around the food trucks that lay silent in Clancy Park. She'd done her damn job, but more than that, she'd stewed on this thing until her anger went on full boil. That's when she drove out to the town line and looked for a release valve.

On the other end of the call, back in Cass County, her mentor and former commanding officer, Jim Fuquay, took it all in and dispensed questions and advice in equal measures.

"What do you think caused the explosion, Underwood?" It made her smile, even now, to hear him call her that. Not just because it was reminiscent of another time, but because from the start Fuquay had inspired memories of her father, and hearing her last name bantered about injected just enough dissonance into that association to keep her grief at bay. In her own head, though, a raspy, barked "Underwood" followed the same path as Linus Underwood's "darling girl." It went straight to the most sentimental part of her.

"I don't know, Cap. Not my area. I've heard some stuff about him, though. Selling moonshine and things like that."

"So that's why they call it Montucky, I guess." Fuquay chortled at his own joke. "You check it out?"

"Of course. Nothing to it, that I can find out."

"Doesn't surprise me. And nobody talked, I'm guessing."

"Cap, I'm not exactly rolling in informants here. I'm an outsider. I'm a curiosity, the chick cop." Just that afternoon, in fact, some smart-ass kid who couldn't have been north of fourteen looked at her and slipped a tongue between his two fingers, as if that were something original. Little fucker.

"I don't know, then," Fuquay said. "You might have some obstruction of justice there—or you might just have a mayor who wanted a clean town to show off when the big party started. Do you like this guy?"

"Does it matter?"

He cleared his throat, then dealt with a full-on coughing attack. "Sorry about that. No, I don't suppose it does. But if you like him and you're worried, that tells me you're keeping an even keel. That's good. I don't have to tell you to be careful."

"No."

Another coughing fit busted in.

"You all right, Cap?"

"As the one-eyed man said, I am what I am." At once, Adair wished she were there. "I know this much for sure," he said. "You've got a deputy who's talking out of turn. You need to stomp a mudhole in his ass for that, and make it stick, or you're going to have bigger problems."

"I know."

"Then what'd you call me for?" That rasp again, a laugh, and then another coughing fit. She knew not to press her luck by asking about his health again. She'd just have to worry silently.

"I guess to get backup on being right," she said. "It's lonely sometimes."

"Well, Underwood, you said a mouthful there, didn't you?"

About twenty minutes later, Sakota's voice came bounding across the radio as Adair made her downward run off Telegraph Hill.

"Adair, you better get down here."

"Where?"

"Grandview bridge."

Jesus on a palomino. "You're out of jurisdiction, Officer."

"McKenzie County sheriff called, asked for us to go out there until they could spring somebody loose. Joe took the call, and he called me."

Adair's cauldron tilted again and spilled a few more gallons. "We're going to have to do a refresher on chain of command, you know that?"

At that, LaMer broke in. "Just come, Adair."

Adair threw on the lights and challenged the cruiser by pushing her foot to the floor. The bile, the nausea, rose up in her. Her officers hadn't been willing to talk freely on open air. That meant that whatever it was would be bad. She tightened her grip on the wheel and began putting her concentration on dispassion. She'd seen some depravity. In North Dakota, that first year on the job, she'd worked the scene of a dismemberment, a young woman's arms and legs and fingers and toes seemingly plucked from her body like ripened fruit. You can't get used to something like that. You just tighten up and you get on with it. Dispassion. That was the key. You could cry in solitude later if you needed to.

Two miles past the state line, she whipped the cruiser off the highway, down the rutted dirt road that led to the shoreline. Maybe three dozen people lingered there in a tight clump, a couple of them talking to Officer Sakota, the rest watching LaMer, who was down the shore a piece, standing next to a black garbage bag.

She got out and approached Sakota, all six feet of him looking vomitus green. "What is it?"

"Our missing dog, I think. This one"—here, he indicated the young woman, maybe seventeen, who stood next to him—"stepped on it."

"Jesus," Adair said.

The girl's chin quivered, and a friend wrapped her in an embrace. Adair kept moving toward the spot where LaMer worked. Once there, she reached down and pulled back a flap that LaMer had cut into the plastic bag. A putrid blast of air belched up, immeasurably worse than any rotten meat Adair had ever smelled. The dead eye of a Chihuahua stared back at her.

"My god," she said. "That our dog?"

"I think so." LaMer stood a few steps away. He had his T-shirt hiked over his nose and mouth.

Adair covered up with one hand and took another look. Bloated entrails spilled from puncture wounds in the Chihuahua. "He's been tore up," she said. "Figure he was used as bait? We looking at dog fights?"

"That's what I'm figuring."

"How many dogs are we missing in town?" she asked.

"Just Mina Pollard's, I think," LaMer said. "This one."

She looked back at the congregation along the shore, then checked her watch. Coming up hard on four p.m.

"OK, here's the deal," Adair said. "I want you to stay here until the McKenzie sheriff arrives. I'm going to go get those people out of here and head back to town with Phil. Now listen to me: This isn't our case. It's North Dakota's, but I want you here to hand it off, and then come straight back because we've got a lot of our own problems."

"Sure thing."

She looked at the bag and felt the stirrings of revolt by her lunch.

"Has anybody had a good look at that?"

LaMer pointed at the crowd gathered on the shore. "You mean them?"

"Yeah."

"Just the girl and her boyfriend. I guess she came out of the water like a shot. He pulled out the bag. That's when we got called."

"But the others would have seen at least that, right?"

"Yeah, I guess."

Adair lifted her face to the clouds and closed her eyes. She thought she'd do just about anything to keep Mina Pollard from having to know too much about this.

"OK," she finally said. "Those people are going to talk. Nothing we can do about that. We can keep from making it worse by not saying anything that we don't get officially from McKenzie County. You understand?"

"Yeah."

"OK," she said. "I'm going back to town. I'll find Mina and talk to her. You get back as soon as you can, understand?"

MAMA

Blanche sat in her chair, the window AC unit blowing cold air on her neck, and she held tight to the hand of the boy who'd come back to see her at last. Little Samuel—not so little anymore, of course, in fact a full-grown man on his own in the great yawping world—was her favorite of the grandchildren, not that she had a whole passel of choices. There was Samuel or Denise, a rude girl that one, always sneering and back talking. Of course, Blanche reminded herself, you love all the little children, for they are God's creations, but it was a sin to lie, and she'd be lying if she said she didn't like Samuel best.

She patted his hand, and he looked at her again, and she smiled. He leaned over and kissed her cheek. Blanche had given a lot of thought to dying—she thought of it every day, and she was ready, oh, Lord, yes, she was—but she'd also hoped that Samuel would come to see her again before she departed. She was all the time asking Sam when his boy would be back, and Sam would mumble something about the cost of airfare, and she knew her son wasn't telling her the full truth about his own boy. *What can I do about that?* she often wondered. The answer: Nothing. Nothing at all.

Sam, her son, came back into the living room with the ice water Blanche had asked him to fetch. She took it in both hands and held it like a scepter, feeling the coolness from the sweaty glass on her hands.

"You sure you don't want to come tonight, Mama?" Sam asked.

Blanche put the glass to her lips, which were cracked like a dry lake bed. She drank gingerly, careful not to spill but also treasuring the ripple that rode to the back of her mouth, down her gullet to her insides, spreading out and cooling her down as it traveled. When she was done, she found only shallow breath, and Sam reached for the cup so she could lie back and let the oxygen do its job.

"No," she said, closing her eyes. "Not tonight." Not tomorrow, either, for that matter, but Blanche knew that one wasn't up for a vote. Tomorrow, she'd have to be there. Ten years for Sam running Jamboree, ten years since Samuel graduated and left, and she was this year's Queen of the Grandview Parade. A banner day for the Kelvig family. She would have to wear a dress—a light one in this heat. Blanche remembered that Patricia said she'd come over and help with the makeup and the tiara. A tiara, perfectly silly.

"We can have Norby bring you a plate, if you want."

Blanche opened her eyes. "Norby? Who's Norby?"

"That's me, Grandma."

Sam broke in. "It's what he wants to be called now."

Blanche waited for a couple of toots from her oxygenator. "But you have a perfectly good name. Samuel Einar Kelvig Junior. Do you know how you got that name?"

"Yes."

"Well, apparently you don't. Samuel was my father, a great man. He worked his whole life and didn't have much, but he put up the money for your Grandpa Herschel and me to buy this farm, because that's the kind of man he was. Einar was your great-grandpa's favorite uncle back in Norway. These are fine names."

"Yes, Grandma, I know. But Norby's a family name, too. That's why I picked it. Shouldn't I get to call myself what I want?"

This is a confused boy, Blanche decided. She figured it fell to her to set him straight on his mother's father, a man of such prickliness that even his own kinfolk would cross the street to avoid him.

"Dennis Norby was the biggest no-account, lowdown dirty scoundrel this county's seen in many a year," she said. She had more harsh words on deck but couldn't find the air for it. Wheezing set in.

"Take it easy, Mama," Sam said.

Blanche's eyes grew wider the more belabored her breathing became, until at last the oxygenator caught up with her and filled her lungs again. She curled a finger at her grandson and beckoned him to move closer. Norby leaned over the arm of the couch, almost to where he was half in her lap.

"Honor your name," she whispered. "You come from good people." She reached out and gripped his hand. "Do you understand?"

"Yes, Grandma."

"A name tells you something about yourself, where you come from. It's something you can rely on when you don't have anything else." Her eyes drew wide again, and she waited for replenishment. Norby hung his head and waited.

"Mama, it's OK," Sam said. He moved in on her and brushed her hair back with his thumb. Norby held on, and a fresh shot of oxygen got her going again.

"Remember who you are," she said.

"I will," Norby told her.

NORBY

They rode back to town in Sam's pickup. The sun, with hours to go before it slipped below the western horizon, had begun spackling the sky in pinks and oranges. Norby leaned toward his father, looking for the temperature reading outside. Eighty-seven degrees. The night ahead would call for short sleeves and plenty of mosquito spray. During Jamboree, it was ever thus.

"Tell me about Grandpa Norby," he said to his father.

Sam wiggled his fingers on the steering wheel and took a quick glance at Norby in the passenger seat. Norby caught, and appreciated, a tight smile that played across his lips. "Didn't know the man, really. We were just in grade school when he passed."

"How'd he die?"

"Liver gave out, I guess."

"Alcohol?"

"Yeah."

This was the game Norby remembered. It wasn't that his folks didn't have feelings, exactly. Everybody does, and Norby knew enough about how to get at them that he'd stung the old man and his mother more than a few times. It's just that when anyone dared venture into territory where difficult feelings would have to be discussed—regret or shame, in particular—a not-so-subtle shift to shutdown mode kicked in. They'd keep answering questions, sure, but there'd be no substance to the answers. Eventually, you just give up. It's easier to leave it to the wind.

Norby tried another way in. "Grandma sure didn't like him, I guess."

"I guess."

"Was he as bad as all that?"

"I don't really know. You'd have to ask your mother."

Norby clammed up. This was getting nowhere. He felt foolish about his appropriation of the name and the way it had just made everything worse with his father. It had been such a snap decision, anyway. When Norby felt like he'd run as far from home as he could and still needed some distance, he'd fixated on his mother's maiden name: Norby. *That'd work,* he remembered thinking. It came out easily enough in his first wave of classes in Missoula. "Call me Norby." They called him that, and he became that, in a practical sense. No legalities, no stationery to change, no fuss, no muss. It hadn't been until Derek called him by the name, in front of his parents, that there had been any reason to explain, and then all of his explanations plummeted to the earth, impotent. No matter how he presented it, the facts still came out against his interests. He'd forsaken the name he'd been given, turned his back on his father, brought shame into the house. No one had said any of that, of course, other than Denise. That's the thing about a place where feelings aren't given room to breathe. The vacuum pulls in everything else. He'd talked about who he was, what he wanted, how he viewed himself in this world. He'd tried to explain it. They'd sat grim-faced and silent.

Sam made the last turn toward the house.

"Almost time for supper," Norby said.

"Yep. You can use the shower downstairs if you want."

• • •

Norby sat at the kitchen table, watching Denise dandle baby Chase on her knee after the little nipper had raised holy hell when placed into Norby's arms. Next to her sat Randy, wiping Randall Junior's snot from the shoulder of his shirt. Food for the town supper, ready for transport, formed a mound between them. As soon as their parents were ready, they could head for the door.

"Uncle Henrik, huh?" Denise said.

"Yeah, down at the park," Norby said. "It was creepy, the way he talked to Dad."

"Well, he *is* a creep."

"He came and saw me, what was it—a year ago? Two?" Randy looked at Denise, who shrugged. "Maybe two. Anyway, he asked for a job in the rail yard. I told him, 'Well, you know, Henrik, you'll have to pass a piss test.'" Randy let loose with a braying laugh. "He said he'd get back to me."

"Dad seemed pretty rattled."

"What do you mean, rattled?" Denise said.

"Shook up. You know. Bothered."

"Dad's got enough to worry about without his idiot brother showing up," she said.

"I guess."

"Yeah," she said. "You guess. I know."

"Honey," Randy broke in.

"No, listen, I'm just going to say this and be done with it, OK?" That shut her husband right down. Norby waited for it. It wasn't like he could stop what was coming. Might as well lean into the inevitable pitch.

Denise craned forward, her voice low.

"They won't tell you this, because they're nice people," she said, "but you're breaking their hearts."

"I am?"

"Yes, you are," she fairly hissed. "Don't smart off to me."

Randy tried again. "Couldn't we do this another—"

"They're trying hard," she said. "Maybe you'd notice that if you came around more often. We're here all the time and all we hear is *Samuel this, Samuel that, I wish Samuel could be with us.* It's getting old. And you don't care."

"I'm here now."

"Well, congratulations. You only made Mom beg and plead. How courteous of you."

Norby tried to find valor in silence. Ten or fifteen years earlier, he might have batted her volleys back at her for the balance of the evening, quietly drawing a thrill from his uncanny knack for making her angrier even as his own tone remained level. It was almost Pavlovian, the way he could bring Denise to a boil just by repeating what she said back to her without inflection. But now he watched as her anger grew, his nephew's head bobbed with advancing speed as her knee fired like a piston, and Randy looked increasingly worried that the situation would spin out of control. It was the rare talent who could make Randy Sternslaw appear to be the reasonable one in a social interaction, so bully for Denise on that count.

"Come here, buddy," Norby said, reaching a hand across to three-year-old Randall Junior. He liked the towheaded little boy. Randall Junior took Norby's hand and toddled over from his father's side.

Norby tugged at the bill of the little boy's cap. "Minnesota Twins, huh? Do you like baseball?"

The boy balanced himself with his left hand on Norby's knee. His right hand balled up into a fist and drove into Norby's crotch. Direct hit. As Norby's knees slammed together, the ache moved into the pit of his stomach.

"He's a dick hitter," Randy said, a bit too cheerfully.

Denise made no effort at concealing her glee. "I think that puts it in perspective, don't you?"

THE CHIEF

Adair didn't like anything about this.

To start with, the rumor grinders beat her to Mina Pollard's place. The women from her knitting group formed a ring around her to offer succor, with Mina alternating between crying jags and offering assurances that she'd leave the whats and the whys of Fredo's horrific killing "to the Lord." Somebody had even rousted her boy Carl from his job at the service station, because he was there, too, jabbing a meaty finger entirely too close to Adair's nose and telling her that he wanted someone's head on a damn stick. And by someone, he said, he meant the oil-field trash out by the highway. She'd had to warn him off twice before finally saying, "Carl, you poke at me once more and I'm running you in," and that had shut him down right quick. Here he was, forty-two years old and already six DUIs on his record. He didn't need more trouble.

With that, Adair had said, "Now, we don't know anything for sure yet, and we don't even know it's your dog, Mina, but when we do . . ." and it had pretty much gone south from there, with Mina launching into a new round of crying and gnashing. "What do you mean it's not my dog? Of course it's my dog! Would these people be here if it wasn't my dog?" Adair was left to crease her hat while Mina and the others accused her of not taking seriously her missing-dog report. "Look what's happened now because you couldn't be bothered," one of them said, as the rest of the knitting ninnies had clucked their disapproval. When Adair left, Carl had shouted at the closed door, "Get a goddamned man on the case."

Now, Adair stood behind the serving line at Clancy Park and watched the way folks moved around. Her weekend deputies had been the first to eat, and four of them had taken up positions at the corners of the park, munching on burgers and trying not to be too conspicuous. They weren't the problem. It was the civilians—the ones who congregated in small packs and talked in low rumbles—and Adair didn't have to wonder if she'd grown paranoid about the topic of conversation. Every now and again, someone would point across a borderline beet field, and she'd follow the trace of the finger to the rig encampment. What was being said and bandied about was clear enough, and she figured it for a problem sooner rather than later.

She scanned the growing crowd till she found the mayor, jimmied up next to the author, who'd caused a bit of a stir himself when he went through the food line. Raleigh Ridgeley. She'd read *The Biggest Space* in college. Liked it, too, though she thought the main character, Perry, suffered a bit too eagerly for his art. Roman à clef, perhaps? Ridgeley, though a bit taller and more athletic looking than she had imagined him from his book-jacket picture, looked like he could tilt toward the delicate-flower end of things.

She made a straight line to them, getting there just as Sam Kelvig approached.

"Mayor," she said, "need a word with you."

"Sure thing, Adair. Have you met Raleigh?"

She shook hands with the author. *Yep,* she thought. *Delicate flower.* "Pleasure."

"Likewise," Ridgeley said. He and Sam nodded at each other.

"Raleigh here is our celebrity," the mayor said, and Ridgeley closed his eyes and shook his head. "Only person in Grandview, past or present, with a Wikipedia page."

"That's great," Adair said. "Listen, sir, can we talk real quick?" At this, Sam inched in.

"Of course," Swarthbeck said. "Is it . . ." He held a finger to his lips.

"No," she said, "here's fine. I assume you're going to get on the microphone and say something."

"Planned to."

"Well, we've got a situation—"

"Mina's dog."

"Shocking," Ridgeley said.

"Look," Adair said, "we don't know anything, so let's not go there just yet. I just think it's a good idea, considering what everybody thinks they know, that you tell folks to keep their cool. After you welcome them, of course."

"This is what I was going to suggest, too," Sam said.

"Yeah, OK," the mayor said. "You want to do this now?"

"I think we should," Adair said.

The three of them left Raleigh behind and walked to the bandstand, maybe thirty yards away, where the microphone and speakers had been stashed. On the way, Adair radioed Joe LaMer and got a status report from the roped-off downtown stretch.

"All clear here," he said.

"OK, send your four down here for dinner. As soon as they get here, I'll send the others back to you."

"Roger."

The mayor took up the microphone and gave it a couple of taps with his finger. A squeal of feedback diverted attention to him.

"Good evening, everybody." His voice boomed across the park.

"Listen," he continued. "I say the same thing every year, so you know it by now. We're pleased to see everybody for Jamboree on this, the centennial of our town, so thanks for coming out to the annual town supper."

He waited for the applause and the hoots to die down.

"Just one other thing," he said. "There's a lot of talk about something, and a lot of people assuming they know what's happened, but let's keep our cool, folks. We don't know what exactly happened, so let's let law enforcement do their job"—here, he gestured to Adair—"and let's concentrate on having a good weekend. We've got all kinds of good stuff over there at the tables if you haven't had something to eat yet. Thanks, everybody!"

Adair watched as the downtown crew arrived on foot and got into the chow line. She radioed Phil Sakota and told him to get the park crew moving out to replace them.

"Well, Adair, that's that," the mayor said. "Looks like you're going to be busy tonight." He wore the kind of smile that made her wonder now if he'd just been playing games with her all along. Was every kind word calculated? Was every inquiry loaded with an agenda? She didn't know, and she didn't like not knowing, and she especially didn't like having to be so suspicious. Not about the mayor, anyway. She had plenty of suspicion for those who demanded it. She hated to see it spent in his direction.

"Looks like some people have been busy all day," she said, and she walked away, the radio at her mouth.

"I'm headed that direction," she told LaMer.

PATRICIA

She wore her favorite yellow dress, the backless one she got from Herberger's the last time they'd gone to Billings, and to that she added the white pumps she found at that wonderful store in Denver. She'd made up her face and dabbed on just a bit of Cashmere Mist, and sure enough, Denise had looked at her and said, "Mom, it's just the stupid town supper," and she'd been ready for that, too. "Hush up, Denise," she'd said. "This is a big weekend for your father."

Now she stood at the serving line and dished up slices of pie, and when she could, she stole glances at Raleigh, who was making the scene. She liked how he glided in, lightly dropping a hand onto the small of the ladies' backs to say hello. She giggled at the reactions, how rigidly they seemed to hew to gender. With the women, she could see the light behind their eyes flare up when Raleigh was near. The men would take a step back, faces tight, while Raleigh moved in with the easy banter. He intimidated them, and she liked that he could do that.

She'd had only a brief exchange with him when he came through the line, but it had made her heart flutter just the same. "You are a vision," he'd said, and she responded by dropping an extra-large dollop of potato salad on his plate.

"Thank you, sir," she'd said, just a smidge of coyness threaded into her voice. He'd promised to come back for pie, and she had a big slice pulled back from the rest, waiting just for him. Elmer McFadden had reached for it a few minutes earlier, but she'd managed to slide a smaller one his way.

Now she watched as Raleigh stopped Sam and initiated a conversation, and the trilling of her fanciful notions gave way to a spreading dread. There, in a single frame, lay fantasy and reality. She and Sam had traded sharp words while they got dressed for supper. His contention was that she needed to make some extra time for his mother, that he didn't like her cooped up by herself like that, especially with Henrik lurking about. She had countered with the pies she'd baked and the emergency fill-in on salad duty and the hundred thousand tiny things she was always doing that he couldn't possibly fathom, and besides, why did he always choose these moments before they went somewhere to upset her so? The angry words had come out incongruously soft, from both of them, because the kids were just a couple of rooms away, and they didn't need this stress on top of everything else. Patricia had a hard time with staying circumspect amid disagreement. She wanted to shout it as loud as she could, to flail against what the marriage had become—a series of debates over protocols and procedures.

That morning, in Sidney, she'd silently acknowledged the truth of the matter, and a hard one it was: reality and fantasy couldn't exist without each other. The kiss had been a mistake. No, the kiss had been delicious, but letting it happen had been a mistake. On the drive home, she had searched her memories for the last time Sam had made her feel that vibrantly alive, and she couldn't fixate on it. They'd come home last Fourth of July and screwed into sweaty exhaustion, but that was as much the mayor's hooch as it was rampant desire. She was thinking of something more considered and delicate, some moment where she felt again as though she were treasured beyond anything else in Sam's life, and she couldn't find it. And it was in that gaping space of discontent where imaginations of Raleigh Ridgeley could take root and flourish. *He doesn't really want me, does he? No, he couldn't.* She shook her head. She knew whom he'd been with, whom he could have. Refined women, famous women, tempestuous women. She thought of Marisol in *Squalid Love.* The critics all said the real-life model was that French actress with whom he'd been connected for years. Pretty, petty Marisol, who left Jefferson Voorhees and took up with an extra on her latest movie, banishing Jefferson to an artistic stubble field, where he drew only her for a year before regaining himself. Women like Marisol, or their real-life equivalents—that's who Raleigh Ridgeley could have. He'd been nice that morning and made her feel wanted, and she appreciated that, but she knew it couldn't be real. And knowing that, of course, made life with Sam seem all the more unstable.

Their chat over, Sam and Raleigh shook hands. As Sam headed for the street side of the park, he threw a grim glance at Patricia, his work never finished, while Raleigh a few moments later caught her looking and smiled, bringing her nearly to a blush. He walked over.

"You haven't forgotten my pie, have you?"

She slid the paper plate across to him.

"Sam says we're good to go for Sunday. Jamboree book club, right here in the park."

"I wouldn't miss it," she said.

He shoved a bite into his mouth, then closed his eyes, savoring it. "Nobody does strawberry-rhubarb like you."

Patricia took up the sides of her dress and curtsied. When she spotted Maris giving her a look, she wrinkled her nose. *Eat your heart out, Westfall. He's talking to me.*

"Are you coming downtown?" he asked.

She'd have liked to say she hadn't considered it, that she and Sam usually retired early on the Friday night of Jamboree and left the drunken revelry to the younger folks, but her dress said something else. She knew where she'd be going when she put it on.

"I'll probably be there for a little bit," she said.

"Let me buy you a drink."

"Promise?" she said.

"Promise, pretty lady."

She laughed at that, and batted her lashes. Oh, this was fun. She reached for Raleigh's hand and she rubbed a thumb across the top of it, and she laughed some more. *Oh, Raleigh. You do make a girl's heart do flip-flops.*

OMAR

Every year, it was the same thing. The other kids tended to stay away from the town supper, populated as it was by adults and self-styled dignitaries and old-timers with their incessant hobnobbing. But every year, Omar had to go, dragged there by his mother. So he ate the overcooked hamburger and the mustard-heavy potato salad and the pie—now, the pie was actually pretty good—and he tried to keep his distance from the smattering of his peers who'd been forced to be there, too.

He got it. He understood. When he added up his time in school and her work and his sports, the two of them had only a few hours together each week, and those tended to be spent on rushed-through meals and church, another place Omar would just as soon not be. He knew his mother was grabbing moments while she still could, while he was still her little boy. While he was still here. There'd been some battles over that topic, for certain, but the momentum had swung his way. He was dead set on UCLA, and his mother was making her peace with that.

They sat on the grass on the east end of the park and cleaned their plates, and Omar at last scratched the itch he'd been digging at all afternoon.

"Gabe wants me to go fishing with him at Fort Peck," he said.

"When?"

"Monday."

"Don't you have—"

"Postponed till Tuesday."

Omar set his paper plate on the grass and wrapped his arms around his scrawny, hairless legs. Coach had told him he'd need to add ten, fifteen pounds of muscle before he got to college and then even more after, because those big boys would toss him around like he was nothing. They'd been working out together every week-day morning during the summer. Technically, Omar supposed that was a violation of the high school association rules against organized workouts, but nobody in Grandview was going to go tattling. People in town were invested in him, urging him forward. He was going to first bring them a state title and later a mention on network TV every time he touched the ball out there in California. The workouts were just part of the plan.

That's why Omar hated to have to lie about Monday to his mother, and hated to lie about Gabe, too. He hated that he'd have to ask Gabe to cover that lie. As for Coach, another lie would be required to get Omar out of the Monday workout. He didn't like the way this was adding up.

"I guess that would be all right," Doreen said. "When will you be home?"

"Late."

"I want the garage swept out before you go."

"I will."

She set her plate on top of his.

"Nice evening," she said.

"Yeah. Are you going downtown?"

His mother slapped her knee, squashing a mosquito. "Goodness, no. I'm too old for that scene." She smiled at him, and he smiled back. She *was* old. Omar certainly couldn't see himself at thirty-eight. He wondered sometimes if she'd squandered her youth on him, unplanned as he was. It wasn't a question he dared ask, but he thought he could see some wistfulness in her some-times, as though the life they had together wasn't everything she had wanted for herself. He had a plan, though. A couple of years at UCLA, grow into his body—the coaches there said he could get up to six eleven or so—and get a pro contract. He and his mom could leave Grandview forever. Whatever she'd given up could be hers again. He could do that for her.

"What are you and Gabe doing tonight?" she asked.

"You know, hang out. The usual."

She reached around him and pulled him in, and he took it. Her public displays were something else he'd just have to live with this last year at home.

"Be careful," she said. "I'm proud of you."

It was the worst thing she could have said, given the heap of dis-honesty he'd just dropped on her. After Omar kissed his mother good-bye, he trudged up the street to the Country Basket conve-nience store, where Gabe was set to come off his shift. They hadn't really made any plans for the evening—it seemed that every sum-mer night ended up with them back at Gabe's house, playing Xbox into the wee hours, Omar sometimes sleeping over—but Omar fig-ured they'd do what every other kid would be up to tonight. They'd lurk on the edges of the downtown party and try to scam their way into some booze.

It wasn't a difficult trick if you knew the right people. The cops kept the street pretty well locked down. You could get in, but if you weren't of age and wearing the designated wristband, you'd be found out pretty quick. The kids who'd been successful at filching drinks in years past either had somebody on the inside—a cousin or a brother who'd hand cups of beer over in the alley—or they got lucky and slipped into an unlocked storeroom at the Sloane Hotel or the Double Musky and made off with the goods. It reminded

Omar of what he'd read about computer systems, how hackers were always probing them, looking for a way in, while the security experts tried to keep the invaders at bay. Cat and mouse. He could think of worse ways to spend an evening.

Omar nodded at the police chief as he made his way along Main Street. That afternoon, he and Clarissa had still been on the bridge when the commotion started down below, and they'd clambered down when they heard Ashley Teaford screaming. Once he'd heard the words "dead dog," he didn't bother looking. He didn't need to see that to know it was awful. He just wanted to go home. He'd made sure Clarissa was all right, assured her again that he'd help her get to Billings, and got on his bike. The chief had passed him on the highway. She must have been doing ninety, ninety-five.

The streetlamps flickered on, the official ushering in of night. Omar looked up at the Country Basket sign, cast against the purple-pink dusk. Gabe emerged from the glass doors, his work smock folded under his arm. He gave a wave, and Omar jogged over to join him.

"How'd it go?" Omar said. The friends bumped fists.

"It's a job, you know," Gabe said. "Same old."

"No, I don't know."

"That's because big-time basketball stars don't have time for jobs." Gabe chuckled, and Omar playfully punched him in the arm. It was the first time all day Omar had felt halfway decent. Gabe was a good friend—probably the only real friend Omar felt like he had, certainly the only one he knew he'd be in contact with a year from now, when Grandview would be just part of his story. Gabe, the only black kid in town, was going to be valedictorian. Omar, the only half-Indian kid in town, was going to be a sports star. A couple of high-achieving misfits, they'd been tight since the eighth grade, when the Bowmans moved to town after his dad took a job as a pipeline supervisor. They'd sized each other up quick and realized their commonalities in skin tone and background. No matter how long Gabe stayed, he was the black kid from Oklahoma. No matter how long Omar lived, he was the kid with half-Indian blood and no known father.

"So what do you want to do?" Gabe asked.

At that very moment, as if an answer straight from the gods, the first electric notes took wing downtown, and a mighty cheer went up from the gathered crowd. Stone Cold Cherry set down the opening bars of "Hold On Loosely," the electric riffs and the boom- ing bass drum rattling the street, and the two boys looked at each other, smiled, and took off running in the direction of the action.

MAMA

Blanche wished for a lot of things. Too many, she suspected, which was why she was always mindful about ending her prayers with thanks for the bounty she'd already been given, so the merciful Lord didn't think she was pressing her good fortune. What she wished for now, at this moment as her prodigal son circled her favorite grandson, was breath enough to say, "Sit down, the both of you," and make it stick. *Lord, if you could just make this stop, I'd never ask for another thing from you.*

Henrik, as usual, was overplaying his hand. He'd set upon the boy when Samuel had arrived with a plate of food, asking him questions in that rapid-fire, sneering way that made people so blasted uncomfortable around him. She'd tried, oh how she'd tried, to explain this to Henrik clear back to when he was a little boy, that too much offense creates an equal overabundance of defense. More flies with honey. Any cliché will do. The point is, she and Herschel had tried to break him of it long ago, and nothing much came of their efforts except for Henrik's wounded pride.

Blanche laid back her head, drew in a raspy breath, and watched it unfold in her living room; how she wished Sam had come with his boy.

Uncle and nephew had moved off the topic of Samuel's appearance back in town after so long—and Samuel's backboned reply that Henrik had a hell of a lot of gall casting that particular stone, given his own ebb-and-flow absences and reappearances—and were now on the larger topic of family, and who had a right to speak and who should just remain silent.

"Just lay off my dad," Samuel said.

"It's between me and him, Junior." That sneer again. "So you just keep your fag nose out of it."

Samuel shrank from that. He balled up a fist, a follow-through Henrik would have relished, but then he faltered and moved back a couple of steps as the force of the words rushed over him.

Blanche had seen enough. She leaned over and retrieved her cane lying against the wall and rapped it hard on the wood floor three times, enough to leave her spent.

The squabbling men looked at her, and she thrust a finger at them in turn, silently telling Henrik to take the chair on her left and Samuel to set himself into the one on the right. Each did as she instructed, and Blanche gulped in breath and waited for reinforcement from the oxygenator.

When she felt as though she could speak again, she turned to Henrik. He hid behind that scolded-puppy-dog face, a hard enough sell when he was eight, and one she couldn't countenance now.

"I won't have it," she said.

"Mama—"

"I won't."

She gulped air and put her attention on her grandson.

"Thank you for the food, Samuel. You go on home now."

"I don't think I should, Grandma. Not while he's here." At that, Henrik kicked at the floor but said nothing.

"You go."

"You're sure?"

"Yes, child."

Samuel rose slowly, then leaned over to her. She watched Henrik as Samuel's lips found her cheek. He never took his eyes off the boy, his face darkened by menace. *Such ugliness in that man. Where did we go wrong, Lord?*

When at last Samuel was out the door and they heard his car start, back out the gravel driveway, and disappear into the night, Blanche turned a cold gaze on her son and said, "Whatever you want, whatever it is that will give this family peace, you must take it up with me. Do you understand?"

Henrik fell forward from the chair, onto his knees, and he crawled to his mother and lay his head in her lap. His shoulders heaved and quivered, and she set her hands on his head and whispered to him. With each word that passed her lips, the violent outpouring of his body increased in fervor, until he'd expended everything he had. His mother stroked his hair, the way she had when he was but a boy and she could still see a world that would open itself to him.

She couldn't say she saw such things now, but that hardly mattered. No mother worth the title throws in the towel on her own child. There wasn't much she could do for Henrik, and she didn't hold out much hope that he would do for himself. But the love never stops. That's the way Blanche had it figured, and she slid her fingers through his hair again.

RALEIGH

Raleigh Ridgeley had been a public figure for twenty years, and he'd come to learn a few things about the privilege. His audiences were mostly female, and in the wake of his first book and all its renown, it had been quite the surprise to him to learn that these women were predominantly interested in more than whatever book he was shilling. He'd noticed it first with *The Biggest Space*. There he was, thirty-three years old and unhappily married, a Billings PR man by day and a slave to his manuscripts by night, and it all happened seemingly at once: publication, glowing *New York Times* review, National Book Award finalist, being flown around the world to writers' conferences. And at every single one of them, threaded among the tweed jackets and the academics and the fawning and ambitious MFA candidates, he'd find women who knew his book and assumed, by extension, that they knew him just as intimately. He learned the signals. The unyielding smile. The light brush of a hand upon his. The eyes that lingered a beat too long. He knew, and he allowed himself the fruits of such knowledge.

Now, he looked across the table at Patricia Kelvig, once the object of his secret teenage lust, and he picked up on the same pulses. She laughed at his jokes, no matter how slight. She twirled her hair. She leaned forward when he spoke. The difference between Patricia and every fan to whom he'd given the vapors was that she actually did know him, from a time long before he'd been touched by fame. And that, he thought, was perilous and seductive in equal quantities.

"I'm glad we came inside," she said. "It's too loud out there."

By Raleigh's reckoning, inside the Sloane Hotel was only marginally better than outside. Stone Cold Cherry was two doors down, ripping through the holy canon of southern-fried rock, and the muffled reverb sent ripples through Raleigh's old-fashioned and Patricia's coffee.

"That's not what I had in mind when I said I'd buy you a drink," he said, pointing at her cup.

Patricia wrapped her hands around it. "That's as daring as it gets for me, mister. One cocktail would do me in."

"I'm not seeing the problem with that."

"You wouldn't!"

He laughed, because that's what would be expected in such repartee, but there it was again: the peril of their familiarity. She could reduce him to his barest components, if she wished.

He hunkered down, physically and in voice. "Should we talk about this morning?"

Patricia, bless her, didn't straighten her back or withdraw or give any facial suggestion that his inquiry was unwelcome.

"I don't know. Should we?" she said.

"I'd like to. If it's not too uncomfortable."

"OK."

Now it was Raleigh's own spine that went stiff and his own chair that slid back, if only a smidge.

"It was an impulse," he said.

"Yes."

"But it came from somewhere real. It was something I felt—I feel—deeply."

He watched her as she considered that, her half smile sympathetic and her eyes glistening and soft. She bore him no anger; that much had been obvious back at the park, but he searched for some indication of where her heart lay with regard to this matter, and he could not find it.

"It felt like you felt it," she said.

"I did."

"I'm glad."

"You left so quickly," he said. "I wondered all day what you thought of it."

She looked now at her coffee, and it seemed to Raleigh as if she were seeking the answers she couldn't conjure. "I'm sorry I made you wonder," she said. "I liked it, and that's why I had to go."

"I don't under—"

"No, Raleigh, I think you do."

He slumped in his chair. Nothing here matched his expectations.

"I'm sorry," he said.

She reached for his hand, and she forced his reluctant fingers to lace with hers.

"Don't ever be," she said. "Now, will you walk me home?"

They brushed past the Farm and Feed on Main before turning up Ellison and pushing west, toward the Kelvig house. Raleigh wondered, not for the first time, if he'd played it wrong all those years ago, beating a furious exit to the East Coast and college and as far away from Grandview as a train ticket and his own wherewithal would take him. By his midtwenties, both of his parents were gone, and that cut his final ties with the place until fame finally brought him home again. *Had I stayed,* he thought, *I could have been the one with a thriving little supply store, two kids, and Patricia Norby on my arm.* Would he have traded all of the running away, and everything good it brought him, for the one person who might have made him stay? That was the unanswerable question.

He kept his hands jammed in his back pockets as they walked on. The kid, Samuel, had come to see him at a signing in Mill Valley last year, and they'd had a cup of coffee afterward. Nice kid, and a marker for how much time Raleigh had let slip by in his own self-aggrandizement. Samuel had grown up, earned a degree, made a life for himself in California. They spent the better part of an hour talking, and Raleigh gleaned enough from the conversation to know that not everything was as it seemed back on the home front. The kid bore an animus for his father. It wasn't anything he said explicitly. It lay in the arrangement of the words, the way they were deployed, and particularly in the ones he didn't use at all. Raleigh had wondered then and wondered now whether a finer examination of the family's masonry would reveal other fault lines. Did that make him a scavenger, picking through the bones of other lives for his own sustenance? By definition, he supposed it did. But Patricia. *Oh, Patricia.* Maybe she would be worth that.

He caught her eye, and they smiled at each other again, and Raleigh let go of some of the earlier embarrassment. He'd dreamed of this so many times in his callow youth, that he could find the gumption to squire her through these streets. Back then, he knew the houses and the people in them—some of them, anyway—and he couldn't wait to get away, but if he'd had Patricia Norby, well, he'd have had some gravitas that was denied him then. The people in this town mostly deserved their lot, always groveling for the next boom, but he'd long believed that Patricia settled for too little.

In the alley behind the Kelvig house, out of the powder spray cast by the streetlamp, Patricia took his hand. Together, they walked behind the garage. Raleigh nervously scanned the adjoining houses for lights in windows, finding only darkness, his heartbeat rising over the ongoing thump from downtown. She pressed him against the wooden doors, and he let her. She moved into him and brought her lips to his, and he tasted her. And when he reached for her hips, she let go and stepped back, out of his grasp.

"Never be sorry," she said, and then she left him, running past the garage and through the backyard grass to the front of the house, the soles of her shoes clapping against the concrete driveway.

He stood in the darkness, and he waved at the nothingness in her wake.

PATRICIA

She shut the front door behind her and leaned against it, eyes closed and her heart doing the rumba in her chest.

"Hi, Mom."

Eyes fluttered open. Samuel sat at the dining room table in the dark.

"You frightened me," Patricia said.

"Sorry."

She gathered herself as best she could, feeling foolish just the same. That moment with Raleigh, bad as she wanted it, had been reckless. She wouldn't have done it had she known Samuel was here and awake. Once she had her breath back, she stepped through the kitchen to join him. She flipped on a light, then sat down in the opposite chair. "I thought you'd be downtown seeing some of your friends."

"Didn't feel like it."

"Everybody else asleep?"

"Yeah."

She reached for him, covering his hand with hers. He didn't retract. A small breakthrough, that, after the hesitation and uncertainty of the afternoon.

"What's wrong?" she asked. She knew that something was, of course. A mother always knows. More than that, Samuel had never been able to keep distance between his feelings and her, and for that she had given thanks untold times. And wasn't it funny how that worked? She and Sam had two children, created in the same way, her egg and his seed, brought up in the same house, fed the same food and given the same water, raised up in the same church, and they couldn't be more different if they tried. Denise seemingly had come out of the womb with a point of view and using self-ishness as a blunt weapon. Samuel was the quiet, eager-to-please child, the one who was disarmingly comfortable talking about his feelings. Until he wasn't, of course. That had come later, and she and Sam were still reeling from it.

"I ran into Uncle Henrik at Grandma's," he said.

"Oh?"

"He really hates Dad."

"No, he doesn't."

"Mom, yeah, he does. You should have heard the things he said."

Patricia gave up on the bluff. She could only imagine what Samuel had heard, and when it came to her husband's brother, her imagination could be vivid indeed. Her own experiences with Henrik ran a short gamut from uncomfortable to offensive, and she'd been happy enough to see his repeated failed ventures carry him away from Grandview for much of the past twenty or so years. It was a view she kept to herself, though, because Sam didn't share it. To him, the breach with his big brother was a wound that couldn't be sutured, and one he took personally. Being a Norby, Patricia had learned early on that survival meant cutting and run-ning from those who would do you harm, even—no, *especially*—if they were family. But Sam was a Kelvig, and the Kelvigs put more stock in the merits of blood.

"Are you OK?" she asked.

"Yeah. A little rattled. Grandma told me to go home. I've been sitting here for an hour, wondering if I should go back. I didn't want to leave her with him."

Patricia squeezed her son's hand. "You don't need to worry about her. Your grandmother's a tough old bird. Henrik wouldn't cross her."

"But Dad."

Yes, Patricia thought, *there is that*. The brotherly relationship was more difficult to plumb. Sam was the one who'd done well, who'd been true, who'd stuck to his responsibilities. That made him a good man, but none of it would ever make him the big brother. Henrik had a mighty big trump card, and he knew well how and when to play it.

"Your father will handle it," she said.

He looked up at her. "Can I ask you something?"

"Yes, of course."

"Is Dad telling people about me? You know . . ."

Patricia felt the bottom drop out of her. "What happened?"

"Uncle Henrik called me a fag."

"And you think your father—"

"No. Maybe. I don't know."

Damn the trepidation that has seized hold of us, Patricia thought. She wanted nothing more than to go to Samuel now, take him in, hold him, comfort him, and still she stayed rooted to her side of the table, unsure of the reception that move would receive in these frosted-over times. As to the question of Sam's loose tongue, she'd made it clear to him that family business was not for public consumption, though she knew well that her actual control in that area was limited. In any case, she couldn't imagine any conversation with Henrik that would lead to such a revelation.

"Son, no, your father wouldn't do that," she said.

"OK."

He didn't sound convinced. Patricia figured she'd have to go deeper.

"When you were here last, we were—"

"Shocked?" he said.

"Taken aback. We hadn't expected—that is, we didn't know—we don't have any experience with this. It surprised us."

"Yeah. I didn't want to surprise you. It was unavoidable."

Patricia exhaled. She'd wanted this for so long, a way into this tangled briar.

"Your dad has struggled." She put it out there. What she needed now was a way to set a road between them. This struck Patricia as the route forward. "You know, he was raised a certain way, he believes certain things, and this wasn't part of that. It's not that he doesn't love you. He does. I do. We do. It's just—"

"I'm a heathen." When the words came out, Patricia's thoughts flew at once to alarm, and she wanted to smother that notion so he couldn't resuscitate it. When she saw that he was smiling, the tension left her. Still, he had no idea just how close his assessment hewed to reality. They had gone to see the Reverend Franklin in the aftermath of Samuel and Derek's visit and the subsequent botched attempt at a redo. Their hearts were burdened, and their attempts to ease the load for each other had only threatened to drive a wedge into their marriage. Patricia had come to view that visit as a mistake. The pastor had counseled them in the ways of love and intolerance—love the sinner, hate the sin. She had found it completely inapplicable to their son, their flesh and blood, the greatest thing either of them would ever do. That was her take. Sam, on the other hand, found reinforcement for his lifelong grounding in scripture, and now he and Patricia were poles apart, anyway, the very situation they'd hoped to avoid.

"You're not a heathen," she said, soft as Sunday. And then: "I'm glad we're talking about this."

"I am, too. I wish Dad were here, instead of in there asleep."

"You can talk to him, too." *You need to*, she might have added. This was a message she couldn't carry to Sam. Samuel would have to find a way across the gap between them.

"Derek and I broke up," he said.

"I'm sorry." It occurred to her then that she actually was, and that was a revelation. She had consigned Derek to being a problem in their lives rather than a living, breathing object of love in their son's. She flushed with shame. "When?"

"A couple of weeks ago."

"Are you OK?"

He sighed and rocked back in his chair, and she had to swallow the urge to scold him the way she used to about keeping all four legs on the ground. "I guess."

"Really?"

"No."

"You cared for him, didn't you?"

"Mom, I love him."

In the cracking of his voice, in the plaintive way he said it, the curiosities fell away and the commonalities moved forward, and Patricia thought that maybe she understood her son in a way she hadn't before. She'd seen heartbreak. She knew it. She'd endured a slow-motion unfurling of it these past several years with Sam, as active, pulsing love took a secondary position to expedient need and the narcoleptic inertia of the day-to-day. Viewed in abstractions, love is the same thing for everybody. It thrills the same way, and devastates with bloodless efficiency.

"I'm so sorry," she said. "I am."

"I know."

"Is there anything I can do?"

He sniffed. "No. I just need time and distance. That's the only cure."

"I'm glad you're here."

"Me too."

She made her move. She stood and she went around the table, coming up behind him. She dropped her chin onto his shoulder and draped him with her arms, and then he was all hers again, a full-grown, whiskered man who was still her little boy. She nuzzled him, the way she would do when he was a toddler, and she would gather him up and say, in that teasing singsong voice, "Be my baby."

He covered her hands with his, and they swayed together, and the house swaddled them in silence.

CRAIG LANCASTER

The New York Times, *Saturday, August 1, 2015*

To be sure, maintaining control in Grandview is a more daunting task than it is in most towns of its size. While most of the active drilling in the area known as the Bakken occurs on the North Dakota side of the line, the border town sees the spillover effect. While much of the money goes home with the rig workers—wherever home happens to be—the latent need for a good time often plays out in Grandview's streets.

"They spend their money here," said Sam Kelvig, who owns the Farm and Feed store in town and is a member of the school board and the town council. He's lived in Grandview his entire life, except for four years spent at the University of Montana. "That's good, as far as it goes. But things are out of balance, too. If you're offering a basic sort of salary, like I do, you can just about forget it when there's oil money just across the border. It puts an enormous amount of pressure on the businesses that have been here a long time. They can't keep help.

"But it's more than that. If you've got a family living in a fifth wheel on some rented piece of land, we get those kids in our schools, but we don't get the tax base that goes along with it. The state will give us a certain amount of money per pupil, but it still puts pressure on the system. Something's going to have to change."

Mr. Kelvig is also the director of the town's annual cele-bration known simply as Jamboree. During the third week-end in July, as the town's inhabitants swelled in number to more than 1,800, tensions between some of the townsfolk and the roughnecks living across the border reportedly spilled over into a downtown brawl. Though there were no official arrests—indeed, the Grandview Police Department still uses a paper ticketing system and has no database of crime information—several residents said the issue was that the oil workers had been committing criminal acts for sport, including the killing of a woman's dog. Police Chief Underwood referred all questions about the so-called man camp to the McKenzie County (N.D.) Sheriff's Office, which declined to comment.

Chief Underwood also declined to go into specifics about the incident downtown.

"There was some scuffling," she said. "It was a misunderstanding that flared up, and we got the situation under control. Alcohol, a big crowd, and loud music can be an explosive combination if you're not prepared for the possibilities, but we were. If I had to write a ticket every time somebody took umbrage with someone else in a bar, I wouldn't have time for anything else."

SATURDAY

THE CHIEF

Adair knew what she saw first: Roger Simons came out of the Sloane Hotel itching for a fight, and he got one from the first roughneck he met on the sidewalk. Simons got in a shot—at seventy-three, the old fool should have known better, but he was a hard piece of iron—and the roughneck, Joel Branford, got in the next three before Adair made it across the street and wrestled Simons to the ground while one of the officers up from Billings took down Branford.

But she heard later from Officer Sakota that it had started a few minutes earlier down at the Double Musky, with Carl Pollard squaring off against a nineteen-year-old rig hand who shouldn't have even been inside the ropes. Once Adair dealt with more pressing matters, she figured she'd try to deconstruct where the kid got in and who should have stopped him. But that could wait.

Simons, bloody-mouthed, and Branford sat now before her in her cramped office, with Pollard and another eight men in zip-cuffs out in the hallway waiting to be interrogated, and Adair could feel a doozy of a headache coming on.

She was getting nowhere with this crew. Simons, who ran about a hundred head of cattle west of town, kept yammering on about "atrocities" and "no-accounts," and Adair figured he meant Mina's dog specifically and the oil culture in general, but damned if she could get Simons to say that directly, as he was already neck-deep in a bottle and fading fast. And Branford still had spittle around his mouth from his own outburst there in the office, having turned in the molded plastic chair and kicked at the rancher, swearing so violently and colorfully that Adair had simply tipped his chair over, spilling him to the floor and setting Simons into a round of old-man cackles.

"You going to shut the hell up for a minute?" Adair said to Branford as she pulled him and the chair up. His hands were behind the back of the chair, cuffed tight.

"Fuck you," Branford said, and she dumped him again.

"You fucking bitch!"

"Keep talking, kid. You're just ringing up a bigger bill."

That launched Simons into a fresh round of laughter, but Adair short-circuited it by asking him if he wanted to join his friend on the floor.

"You wouldn't," he slurred.

"Try me."

That shut the old fool up.

Adair dragged a hand through her nest of hair. She figured she could bid farewell to sleep tonight. She and her hired officers had cinched things up tight when the guys from the man camp started showing up just after nine p.m., and the grumbling discontent at the interlopers was more or less quelled for the next few hours. A couple of townies got mouthy and were shown the exit. LaMer and his crew chased down the little irritations that they'd all expected going in—mostly kids trying to get behind the ropes, including one group that made off with a case of beer, a few once-a-year drinkers who couldn't hold their liquor, and the vomitorium created by the millennials. Adair herself had escorted Alfonso Medeiros out of the Double Musky because he was panhandling patrons in the casino. She walked him over to the taco truck and tried to give him back to Dea, who asked her to put him in the cab and let him sleep it off. Poor Dea. She really loved him, and when he could manage sobriety, Adair had to admit, Alfonso was pretty easy to like.

"All right," she said, "if you guys don't want to cooperate, you can cool your heels in the cell." She yelled for Officer Sakota, who peeked his head inside the doorway.

"These two in the cage," she said. "Make sure they can't get at each other. And bring me Pollard and the guy he was tangling with."

She fell in behind Officer Sakota and the two men as he escorted them down the hall. When they turned right toward the cell, she bore left, into the restroom, and closed the door. She flipped the switch, and the translucent lights flickered on.

"You look like hell," she said, gazing at herself in the mirror. Her eyes were bagged out again, her skin ashen. Adair never wore makeup on the job—too distracting, too much a reminder that she was somehow different from the men with whom she worked and, more directly, supervised—but she couldn't help but think a little color would be helpful. *When Jamboree is over,* she told herself, *you're going to take two days and just sleep. Let Joe and Phil handle it. Two days, nothing but sleep, and then you're back and better than ever.*

She splashed water on her face, toweled off, then looked again. *Better? Marginally.*

When things had gotten hairy, just past midnight and about a half hour before the band was to shut it down and last call would go out, everything happened fast. Adair counted herself lucky that she happened to be watching the door of the Sloane when Simons came stumbling out. She was on the opposite sidewalk, by the Oasis, and she didn't like the looks of the old rancher. That set her feet to moving, and sure enough, the old fart threw a spastic right hand that caught Branford square. That's when she heard the Billings officer—Gilluly—yell out her name. She made eye contact with him and pointed at herself, then Simons, and Gilluly nodded and made tracks for Branford. Good teamwork. She'd have to remember to send a commendation to Gilluly's commanding officer.

In patching it all together there at the sink, the next thing she remembered was the yelling, up and down the main drag. Once she got Simons under control, she looked up the sidewalk toward the Double Musky. Six deputies had six men on the ground, in various states of submission. She rotated her weight atop Simons— "Jesus Christ," he'd said, "are you a brick shithouse?"—and saw that LaMer and Sakota had two guys down in front of Pete's Café. *Holy hell*, she remembered thinking. *The whole joint lost its mind at once.*

Once they'd collected the guys, they'd marched them up the street like a regiment, into the station. Adair had told LaMer to take active charge of the street along with the rent-a-cops. In another half hour, he could send everybody home for the night and shut down the works, at least until tomorrow rolled around.

"We OK?" she'd said, in a moment when it was just her and Joe.

"Yeah, sure."

"Just checking."

"*Star Wars*," he'd said, and then he grinned, and damned if she hadn't felt all of a sudden like she was ablaze from the crotch up.

Adair splashed more water on her face. "Don't go losing focus now," she told the reflection.

She shut off the light and stepped back into the hall. Officer Sakota was waiting for her.

"Carl and that other guy are in there," he said.

"Thanks, Phil."

"You OK, Adair?" He looked at her funny.

"Yeah. Why?"

Sakota averted his eyes from her gaze. "Nothing. Just making sure. You look a little flush."

She clapped him on the arm. "I'm good. I promise. Long night, getting longer."

"That's for sure."

Adair moved along, reminding herself to breathe, and chasing herself off the kind of thoughts that would get her in trouble. A big chore, that.

"Carl Pollard," she said as she approached the door to her office, "didn't we talk just a few hours ago about keeping your nose clean?"

THE MAYOR

Upstairs at the hotel, Eldrick Sloane's infernal voice pulled Swarthbeck's attention out of the card game. And that was too bad, because Swarthbeck had Tut Everly right where he wanted him, stuck in that hard space between a winning hand and Tut's own grandiose sense of self.

"Mayor, Adair and one of them deputies got two guys on the ground," Eldrick said, his voice coming out in a scratchy cough developed in those years before Montana went all pussy and banned smoking in its bars.

"Unless she's fucking them, Eldrick, I don't give a rat's ass."

"It's Roger Simons. Don't know the other one."

"In that case, I take it back," Swarthbeck said. "I don't want to see anybody fuck that old canker sore."

The other players, Lael Rostrom and Gale Grinich, guffawed. They could afford to—they'd dumped their cards. Not Tut Everly. He kept going, and now he was going to pay, and he wasn't laughing.

Tut was a degenerate gambler. That was bad enough. He was also as predictable as a John Wayne flick. The mayor had already whittled a grand out of him on earlier hands. Now, before the flop on this one, Tut had come hard with a thousand-dollar bet, and Swarthbeck figured he had double queens. Poor Tut. He always got a boner for those broads, and they gave him blue balls more often than not.

"Mayor!"

"Jesus, Eldrick, what is it?" Swarthbeck appreciated the discretion the Sloane's owner provided for the weekly poker game, not to mention the quiet financial backing of some other projects (not entirely altruistic, Swarthbeck would be quick to point out, as Eldrick Sloane got a 30 percent return while averting the attendant risk). Eldrick had even been downright understanding about the loss of the hooch—a lot more understanding than some of the folks who'd come to town counting on a bottle or five. But even with those good graces considered, Swarthbeck had a limit to how much irritation he was willing to brook.

"They're taking some more people out."

"So what?" Swarthbeck said. "That's what happens every year. A few knuckleheads get out of line, and they're escorted out. Easy-peasy."

"OK, smart guy," Sloane said.

"You didn't have that big a breakfast, Eldrick. Watch yourself now."

"You ever see ten guys lined up like a damn drill team and marched into the police station?"

The mayor put down the corners of his hole cards. "Hang on just a second," he said to Tut, who looked like he'd welcome the respite. *Breathe while you can, old friend,* Swarthbeck thought. *The whirlwind is still rising.*

Swarthbeck joined Eldrick at the window. Sure enough, Adair had the station door open, and puppy-dog Officer Phil Sakota had the braying herd funneled toward it.

"That," the mayor said, "is unusual."

"I told you."

"Yeah, yeah, OK, Eldrick." Swarthbeck headed back to the table.

"Well, what are you going to do?"

The mayor took his seat again. "I'm going to win this hand, then I'm going to have a few words with Mr. Everly here, then I'm going to go downstairs and shoot the bull, and then I might just walk over and see what Chief Underwood has going on. Will that be satisfactory?"

Eldrick, grim-faced, just nodded.

"And get away from that window," Swarthbeck said. "I don't want a play-by-play."

The mayor turned out to be a man of his word. The flop didn't help Tut, but Swarthbeck got the king to go with his king and ace in the hole. Tut had to stay with the bet because he'd bitten off too much, so he tried to chase the mayor off by shoving in everything. Swarthbeck, with stack enough to play, called. At that point, he figured, he had a moral obligation to separate Everly from his money. At the turn came a five that didn't do anyone any good. Then the river flowed, a useless seven, and Swarthbeck pulled down Tut Everly's everything, and the game promptly broke up. In the hallway outside, after Eldrick and the others had hoofed it downstairs, Swarthbeck cornered Everly against the wall, alternately sprayed in green and white dots from the big sign outside, and he set down the consequences.

"That's fifty grand you're into me for, Tut," he said.

"I know."

"Three thousand tonight, and the rest—"

"I know, John."

"I can't carry you anymore." Here, Swarthbeck moved closer. He liked Tut Everly; he really did. He hated to see it come to this, but he wasn't about to argue with natural selection. "You understand?"

Everly nodded.

"Can you get it?"

Everly wouldn't look at him. "Not by Monday."

"That's the date, Tut. You agreed to it."

"I know. But I can't."

Swarthbeck inched in again, until he was breathing in Everly's ear. He spoke in a whisper. "So you go home tonight and you decide what you're going to tell Marian. You don't tell her tonight. I don't want her down here tomorrow, crying to me about what you've done. But you're going to have to tell her. You follow?"

Everly nodded again. Finally, he looked up at Swarthbeck. His eyes were full.

"My kids, John."

Swarthbeck pulled back and gripped his old friend by the shoulders.

"You should have thought of them before now," he said. "Listen, bud. Is Miles Community College that bad?"

On the street, the mayor found Joe LaMer and got the lowdown. Three or four skirmishes, all of them apparently related to accusations over the dead dog.

"Good Christ," Swarthbeck said. "Why didn't she just throw them out?"

"She wants to make a statement, John."

The mayor mopped his brow. "Yeah, and here's what that statement is: come to Jamboree and land in jail. Doesn't exactly look good on a billboard, does it?"

LaMer shrugged. "She's hardheaded. She's smart, too."

"There's smart and then there's wise. This isn't wise."

"I'll tell you something else," LaMer said. "She's pissed about the cleanup this morning."

"Big deal. Let her go dig around in the Billings landfill if she's so interested."

Swarthbeck waved LaMer off so the deputy could make sure folks headed for bed, or wherever the next party was. You don't have to go home, but you can't stay here and all that. The mayor crossed the street, littered with plastic cups and Indian taco wrappers, and let himself into the police station.

He spotted Roger Simons sitting in the cage. Other men sat on the floor outside it, all of them bound with zip-cuffs.

"Hey, Rog, heard you got your ass kicked by a girl." Simons looked up and mouthed a sarcastic laugh. Blood stained his teeth.

"So, fellas," Swarthbeck said to the group at large, "what did we learn tonight?"

With no answer forthcoming, he cupped a hand to his ear and leaned in. "Anybody?" He straightened up and got serious. "OK, I'll tell you what you learned. You learned not to come to my party and mess it up by being drunk and stupid. Tonight, that lesson is going to cost you the privilege of being here for the rest of the weekend. I catch any of you even sniffing around downtown tomorrow and the toll will be considerably higher. Understand?"

He got nods all around.

"Uncuff them and let them go," the mayor told Officer Sakota.

"But Adair—"

"Phil. Let them go."

Sakota produced wire snips from his pants pocket and set about freeing the men, one by one.

"Anybody in there with her?" the mayor asked, pointing to Adair's closed office door.

"Carl Pollard and some roughneck," Sakota said.

Swarthbeck opened the door, and Chief Underwood stood up behind her desk.

"Hi, Adair," he said. "How you doing tonight?"

"Fine. Busy. I was just—"

"Good. Listen, do you mind if I say something to these guys?"

"I—"

"Good." He pivoted toward Pollard. "Carl, you're a dumb motherfucker. Agreed?"

Pollard tried to scoot around in his chair. "Uh, what are you driving at, Mayor?"

"I'm driving at your dumbness, Carl. It's breathtaking in its scope. Why, I'd go so far as to say that being dumb is your master-work, that you have no peers in the realm of being dumb. Do you follow me?"

"Not really, no."

"Mayor," Adair said. "What's going on?"

Swarthbeck ignored her, turning now to Pollard's sparring partner. "And you, whoever you are, are not much brighter, are you?"

The young guy started to speak, and Swarthbeck cut him off. "My question does not require an answer, son. Both of you guys are going to leave right now, and I better not see your faces again this weekend."

"Mayor—" Adair said.

"Phil," the mayor said.

Sakota came in and snipped the zip-cuffs from the men's wrists. The mayor saw him give Adair a pained look, and that was OK by him. He valued loyalty in other people. Made him think better of them.

When Pollard and the other man cleared out, Swarthbeck took the temperature of his police chief. He figured he'd have to do some damage control, but he'd suspected that before he walked over. She'd have disappointed him otherwise.

"You've got concerns, Adair," he said, taking the seat he'd occupied almost twenty-four hours earlier. "Let's talk."

While Adair Underwood paced through her office and went through her litany of gripes, Swarthbeck tried to keep his smile on the side of bemused rather than an outright smirk. Adair was a big, strong, young woman, and the ferocity of her complaints left the mayor at least as blown back as he was impressed. Simultaneously, he dealt with the notions that he'd hired exactly the right person for the job and someone who would be more trouble than she was worth. A little hard to reconcile that dichotomy.

He'd overstepped? He couldn't disagree with her there.

He'd undermined her authority? Again, probably so. But there was some upside in that, he thought.

He was acting imperial? Whatever. Maybe Adair was reading too many books of high intrigue.

"Adair, sit down," he said.

"No."

"OK, stand up. But I'm getting a knot in my neck following you around the room. Can you just pick a spot?"

She stood at the corner of her desk, a few feet from him. Her mouth was cinched up tight, and her arms crossed.

"Thank you," he said.

"I'm waiting," she said.

"OK, Adair, just let me talk here." He'd reached the end of his patience with the insolence. It was just like a woman to press things when she was pissed off. "I know I said you could run this operation the way you wanted—"

"You said it's my department. That's what you said when you hired me."

"Goddamnit, Adair, just shut up and let me finish, OK?" It was more roar than he'd intended, and Adair lowered herself into her chair. "Ten years ago, Jamboree was almost dead. Nobody really came anymore, and we damn near closed her up. But then Sam took it over, and we got some good ideas flowing, and now you can go to any of these towns around here, and people will say, 'Man, I love that Jamboree.' We're the damn gold standard."

"I still don't see—"

"Adair, please." He slapped her desk, and she clammed up. "Part of the reason we're the gold standard is we don't hassle people. I know we need a certain amount of security. I didn't flinch when you asked for eight men, did I?"

"No."

"But what we don't need is to develop a reputation that we're putting the pinch on people who come here. Mark my words, when those guys sober up, they'll appreciate that we didn't bring the justice system down on them, that they're not facing a couple hundred in fines for drinking too much and being idiots. And they'll also stay away, like I told them to. Which solves our problem going forward, does it not?"

"Yes." She was tight-lipped.

"What I'm saying is, there are 362 other days a year where I won't say boo if you want to run Carl Pollard in for fighting or cite somebody for public drunkenness, OK? It is your department, Adair. I'm just asking you to get with the spirit of this thing for one weekend."

"You still didn't have to undermine me like that. You made me look bad in front of those men and my officer."

The mayor leaned forward, voice a notch lower in conciliation. "Yeah, I suppose I did. I'm a decisive guy. I move fast when I think something needs to be done. I'm sorry, Adair."

She stood again. *A dominion move,* Swarthbeck thought. *I like it.*

"That explain what happened this morning?" she asked. "Decisiveness? Something needing to be done?"

"What do you mean?"

"I think you know."

"Oh, the office?"

"See, I knew you did."

The mayor shrugged. "No need to get all conspiratorial. I just didn't want a big mess down here on the first day of Jamboree."

"You sure that's all it was?" she asked.

"Yeah. Don't you trust me?"

"No."

The mayor stood up and pushed his chair closer to her desk. "And that's what makes you a good cop. Good night, Adair."

SAM

From the trash-riddled center of Main Street, Sam watched the sun peek above the badlands east of town. He looked at his watch: 5:20 a.m. Every year during Jamboree, he went to bed early on Friday night, his ears plugged against the sonic assault, and every year he wondered if he shouldn't be downtown having fun with everybody else. And then, come Saturday morning, every year, he was here at sunrise and thankful for his good sense in bagging some sleep.

His companions on cleanup duty—Eldrick Sloane, Ren Brian, and Chet Mayberry—didn't seem to have quite as much starch in them, having been downtown for the duration the previous night. The owners of the Sloane Hotel, the Double Musky, and the Oasis had promised months earlier to kick in some cleanup help. That was part of Sam's job, getting commitments on jobs like cleaning up and setting up the parade markers. At the time, the business owners no doubt expected that they could saddle an underling with the duty, but in a place where high school dropouts were pulling in thirty dollars an hour for using a scrub brush on oil rigs, the labor pool of peons was turning out to be damn shallow.

"Fellas, if we just divvy the street into quarters, we can get everything swept up pretty quick," Sam said. "I'll run everything out to the dump. We're not aiming for pristine here. Just presentable."

He handed out push brooms to each man. "Smile, Ren," he said. "It's going to be a beautiful day."

"What are you so damn cheerful about?" Brian said.

"It's my favorite day of the year."

"Yeah? Mine is Sunday, when I can count the money and be done with this for another year."

Sam gave him a chuck on the shoulder and sent him off to meet his duty.

The other guys dispatched to their positions, Sam started his sweep at the south end of the stretch, and as he built piles of detritus, he tried to make sense of the conversation he'd had with Patricia an hour earlier. She woke up while he showered, and she'd made him a cup of coffee, a gesture he appreciated.

"What time did you get home?" he'd asked her.

"Ten thirty or so."

"That late?"

"I had a drink with Raleigh."

"Oh."

"Coffee, Sam."

He'd winced at having let it get to him. He wasn't stupid. He knew about her little crush on Raleigh Ridgeley. The way she kept those books close when they came out, like a starving child protecting her food, made it obvious, but Sam had always ascribed that to an innocent fascination with what Raleigh had been able to make of himself beyond the town limits of Grandview. To anyone who stayed, like Sam and Patricia had, Raleigh's life would naturally seem exotic and alluring. But hey, Raleigh came back year after year—by Sam's reckoning, that made Grandview pretty special, too.

He might've cogitated more in that direction if not for what Patricia had said next.

"Henrik was at your mother's again. Samuel saw him."

"Damnit."

"And listen: Samuel, I hope, is going to tell you about this, but in case he doesn't, I want you to know."

"OK."

"Henrik called him a fag."

"He did?" Sam folded his hands into fists.

"Yes. Do you know anything about this?"

That had stung him a bit. He'd snapped the buttons on his shirt to buy time to moderate his reply. "You think I told Henrik about Samuel? Really?"

"Samuel asked if you did."

"Well, that's just great."

His voice must have risen, because she held her hands out, palms down, urging quiet. "You don't get to be hurt by this. Samuel's the aggrieved party. I'm just asking a question."

"No," he'd said. "I did not tell Henrik anything. And I'm getting a little tired of being the bad guy here. Why do you get all the first-hand information and I get all the secondhand questions? Why won't he talk to me about it?"

"Because you were asleep and I wasn't." Here, her voice had gone to a whisper. "And if you'll stop blustering and listen to me, I'm telling you that he wants to talk to you and I told him he should. So if he makes like he wants to, let him. OK?"

"OK."

She'd stood and fixed his collar.

"He wants to go by Norby, you know," Sam had said.

"I know." She'd sighed. "I don't have the energy for any more names. Your son Norby is asleep next door. Your daughter Denise and her husband Randy and their children Chase and Randall Junior are in the basement. They would all like to see you, Sam Kelvig, for breakfast, so hurry home, OK?"

"OK, wife Patricia." She'd smiled at that, and he'd thought that maybe it was a way forward after these weeks of clinging to their own sides of everything—the house, the bed, their interests. He'd puckered up for a kiss, and she'd instead patted him on the chest.

"I'm going back to bed," she said.

Twelve bags full of trash rode in the back of Sam's pickup as he drove home. Breakfast first, dump afterward. He'd see if Samuel wanted to go with him. That would offer an opening for more to say, if his son wanted to say it.

The problem, as Sam had come to view it, was one of perspective. He just didn't see how this was who Samuel claimed to be. When had that happened? In Missoula? God knows, Sam had chafed often during his own time out there, at how little dignity and self-control some of his classmates had shown. California, maybe? Sam couldn't make sense of that place. Norby said he was gay and that was that. "I was born gay," he'd said to his parents, on that excruciating phone call after he and Derek didn't even make it to their flight in Minneapolis. Sam had felt kicked in the teeth on that one, because there he was, trying to understand something that was beyond comprehension, and his own son wouldn't even come look him in the eye.

Sam had his doubts about this "born this way" stuff. The Reverend Franklin had backed him up on that one, talking about the people he personally knew who had been able to conquer their "SSDs." "What's that?" Sam had asked, and the pastor had said, "Same-sex desires." The Reverend Franklin said there was help, that people could beat back the impulses with intensive therapy. "He'll need you to stand by him as he fights this," the pastor had said.

On the ride home, Patricia had told Sam, "That was a mistake. I'm not talking to him anymore." No discussion, no mediation, no attempt to come to a unified idea of what they should do about their son. She'd been unfair, Sam thought. She'd left him out here alone to wrestle with this.

If Samuel was born that way, Sam wondered, *how come he had girlfriends all through high school?* Lidia Faulkner, Janine Cisco, Megan Riley. Those were just the three he remembered. There were more. Sam and Patricia had particularly encouraged him where Megan was concerned. They liked her, liked her family, liked the stock she came from. "The cut of her jib," as Big Herschel was wont to say. It had looked so promising, and then, just like everything else, it fell away and this new person—this Norby person—showed up.

Sam idled in the turn lane off Main Street, waiting for three trucks carrying scoria to pass so he could make the turn for home. He punched the steering wheel. Then he punched it again and again and again.

NORBY

His father's truck rattled up Telegraph Hill, weighted down by the cargo and by the burden of all that had gone unsaid. Every now and again, one of them would look at the other and smile, but nobody dared pop open the conversational seal.

That's OK, Norby thought. *For the first time here, I'm feeling all right.*

The scene at breakfast had been familiar, familial, a grab-it-if-you-want-it free-for-all of pancakes and waffles and fresh fruit his mother had been cutting when he slipped up behind her and kissed her cheek. Randall Junior had sat on Norby's lap, happily popping grapes in his mouth while Denise snapped pictures of them on her phone, and Randy talked of the impending night's adventures, now that Denise was granting him dispensation for one night of fun. Norby had watched his parents—mostly his father, who seemed delighted to have everybody under the roof again. That's when Norby realized he was glad he'd come, and more than that, he was glad to be glad.

The talk with his mom the previous night had gone a long way, he thought, as had what he'd overheard earlier this morning, while still in bed. He'd been relieved that his dad hadn't used the auspices of a private conversation to run him down. He'd been thankful, too, that Sam forswore any knowledge of what Henrik had said. And he smiled now to think that his parents assumed he couldn't hear them. He'd spent his growing-up years in that room adjacent to theirs, the ductwork like an amplifier. They had no idea the things he knew.

The truck had climbed atop Telegraph Hill now, and the turn-in for the dump lay just a few hundred feet ahead.

"You remember the last time I was up here with you?" Norby asked.

"Can't say as I do."

"It's been a long time."

Sam snapped his fingers. "The bike!"

"Yep," Norby said. He laughed. "Never did find it. We tried, though, didn't we?"

"We had to."

God, how Norby had loved that bicycle, a present from his mom and dad for his thirteenth birthday. Chrome plated, with mag wheels. He'd been the instant envy of every other kid in Grandview. For three days, that status lingered, until the bike was stolen from the Kelvigs' garage during the night.

"I've never seen you so mad," Norby said. "I thought you were going to interrogate every kid in town."

"I would've, if I'd had the chance." Sam grinned.

The Kelvigs had gone house to house, asking questions, meeting insolence with guilt-inducing invective. ("See this boy?" his dad had said to one neighbor who'd suggested that all boys' bicycles should be confiscated for the peace of the neighborhood. "His favorite thing in the world was stolen, you moron.") They put up flyers on creosote-soaked telephone poles. They filled out a police report that they knew would do no good, until Sam said, "Maybe somebody dumped it."

That, too, had been a futile effort, unless you counted the three milk pails and the Red Wing crock they found and dragged home to Patricia, who rehabilitated them and turned them into planters that still graced the house.

"That was a good time," Norby said. "Didn't seem like it then, but it was."

They made the turn, and Sam reached over and tousled Norby's hair, just like he would have done in a time when he didn't have to engineer tenderness.

Activity had picked up in town. Folks jammed into Pete's for breakfast, Sam had volunteers marking off the parade route, and Norby was helping his dad put together the viewing stand where Mayor Swarthbeck, Sam, and a few other dignitaries would sit.

"So you saw Henrik again?" Sam said.

Norby grunted as he ratcheted a line of bolts. "Yeah, at Grandma's."

"What'd he say?"

There goes Dad, fishing. Norby smiled. His father knew damn well what his uncle had said.

"He mostly talked about you."

"And?"

Norby finished the last bolt and handed the ratchet up to his father.

"That was it, pretty much. Said you're keeping him from what's his."

"Same old story." Sam went to work on his part.

"What *is* the story?" Norby stood up, and Sam set the tool on the half-finished platform.

"Well, you know about the land, right?"

Norby nodded.

"So there's that. He still hasn't paid me back what he owes. He says he has, but he's lying or confused, same as ever. Add to that the mineral rights, which nobody ever thought of until this damn horizontal drilling started happening, and now he's got dollar signs in his eyes."

Norby set his arms on a crossbar, then his chin on his hands. "How much money are we talking about?"

Sam stretched his arms wide.

"Maybe that's the thing to do, then."

Sam looked stung by that, and Norby noticed and scrambled to make it right. "Sorry. I don't mean to be contradictory. I'm just wondering, you know, from a pragmatic standpoint."

"That would put the wells almost in town," Sam said. "After that, it's all over but the crying. I thank God every day we have those mineral rights so we don't have to exploit them. Other people aren't so lucky, you know?"

Norby nodded.

"We're a haying family. That's what we've been, and that's what we'll stay."

"OK."

Norby knew he'd wandered into a conversational thicket. He just wanted a way out, and his father, perhaps thinking the same thing, provided it.

"Here, son, help me with this front piece."

Norby slid the painted plywood section, complete with the Jamboree logo, into place, and Sam bolted it down to the frame. He knew what his father wanted from him. He'd always hoped that Norby would come home and pick up the mantle from him, same as he'd picked it up from Uncle Rick and Big Herschel before him. And Norby had resisted, first out of youthful contrariness and later because he sensed a bigger threat to his freedom to chart his own life as he saw fit. Now, though, he wondered. Maybe pitching in was nothing more than that. He was happy to help.

"Thanks for that," Sam said. "I'd have been wrestling with that for another half hour if I'd done it alone." They shook hands at the satisfaction of a job done well.

· · ·

By eleven, downtown looked like a different place. Norby and his dad had strung up the bunting on both sides of Main Street, had plugged in and tested the sound system, and had made sure the improvised business loop around town was operating properly, keeping the big trucks moving along without sending them crashing into the works.

With the parade lineup still an hour away, Sam said, "I'm going to do something I never do on Jamboree Saturday. I'm going to take a half hour and buy you lunch."

They settled on Pete's. Norby found himself amazed at how much he'd been craving finger steaks from home. He got a couple of "Good to see ya, Samuel" greetings, including one from Becky Reedle at the front counter. Sam had started to say, "It's Norby now," but Norby reached out and touched his arm and shook his head.

They found a booth in a quiet corner and sank in with a couple of cherry Cokes.

"So it's not Norby anymore?"

Norby fingered his straw. "I don't really know how to explain that."

"I'm not asking you to." Sam took a draw on his drink, still yielding the floor despite the attempt at alleviating pressure.

Norby looked at the top of his hands, resting on the table. He could see the freckle pattern coming in, a little more pronounced each year as his skin soaked in more sun. He'd probably never have the thick, work-calloused fingers his father had, but he was every bit Sam Kelvig's match for Scandinavian skin. He could see a fortune lost to sunblock in the years ahead.

He now looked at his father.

"It's taken me a long time to be—I don't know if 'comfortable' is the right word, because I still struggle with that, so maybe the word is 'accepting,'" he said. "It's taken me a long time to be accepting of who I am."

His father leaned forward in the booth. "But you are, is that what you're saying?"

"Yes. There's still work to do, but yes."

"Work?"

"Explaining myself. Talking to you. Making you understand. Being OK with all that."

Becky showed up with their order, and Sam gave her a grim smile. She took the hint and left.

"I might not. I'm just being honest. What if I never do?" Sam said.

"I—"

"I want to. I want to try, anyway. I'm just a simple guy, though."

Norby scoffed. He didn't come all this way for an aw-shucks-I'm-just-a-country-boy shamble. "Dad, you're not that simple."

"But—" His father stopped, lifting his eyes in anticipation. Norby swung himself a quarter turn in the booth and followed Sam's line of sight. There stood Burt Partain, waving spastically.

"Sam, I need to talk to you," Partain said.

"Well, come on then."

Norby turned himself back around, deflated, as the beet farmer approached on heavy feet.

"Hey, Samuel, good to see you." Partain dropped a hand on his shoulder, and Norby squirmed out from under it. "Listen, Sam, the egg roll truck is venting into Lois Staley's yard and she's raising all kinds of hell. She says she was promised it wouldn't. I checked, and Thuy is where she's supposed to be. Lois says she wants to see you."

"Now?"

Partain looked at his watch. "Quarter after. Problem's only going to get worse once the parade starts. I can't shut her up. She said you promised her."

Sam shot a look to his son. Norby dismissed him with a wave.

"We'll finish this later," Sam said.

Norby nodded. "OK."

As Sam and Partain hustled out, Becky came by with the check.

"You want a box for that?" she asked, waving a finger between Sam's mostly uneaten burger and Norby's untouched finger steaks.

"No."

"Something wrong with the food?"

He smiled at that. So many possible directions to go. "I don't think we had a chance to find out, Becky." He remembered her, sort of. She'd been a sophomore when he was a senior, and a social climber she was. He remembered how much Megan and some of the other senior girls had hated her, as Becky mowed through the guys who should have been theirs alone. He drew a hazy memory of Megan laying out the consequences if he should dabble in those well-known waters, as if that were something he was contemplating (he wasn't, clearly) and as if such preemptive threats were a healthy way to go about a relationship (not that he and Megan would have known much about that).

Now, he caught Becky looking at his bare ring finger.

"You still single?" she asked.

Yes, but you're not, he thought. He wasn't entirely sure of that, actually, but he knew enough. His mother had kept him apprised of the happenings around town, particularly the juicier ones. It didn't come much more luridly interesting than four kids and three marriages by age twenty-six.

"I am," he said.

"You going to the party tonight?"

"Probably."

"Well," she said, "if you see me, buy a girl a drink, OK?"

DOREEN

She stood over the crumpled form of her boy, her eyes narrowed and focused as they took in the length of him. Doreen Smothers held the neckline of her T-shirt over her nose and mouth to fend off the sour-sweet stench of the urine that stained Omar's pants and the wafting scent from the congealed river of vomit that ran away from his outstretched right arm and pooled around the base of the toilet.

"Wake up. You disgust me."

Omar rolled to his right, the momentum getting the better of him, and Doreen reached for him, shouting, "No, no, no."

He now lay flat on his back in his own vomit. His mother, looking him in the eye, spoke muffled words through her shirt.

"You're going to clean all of this up," she said. "Right now. I'm so disappointed in you."

Omar pushed himself off the linoleum, tottering to his feet as clumps of his sick clung to his skin. Doreen, repulsed, made sure she kept eyes on him until he looked away, and then she turned and left.

She'd scolded herself earlier that morning when everything came to light, when she realized that had she obeyed her instincts and waited up for Omar to come home, she could have headed off at least some of this. But he was an adult now, or nearly so, and Doreen had started making peace with giving him some space. A Jamboree Friday night without a hint of supervision had seemed safe enough, and here was where that had gotten them.

Sam's call—to tell her the store was her duty the next couple of days, as if she didn't know that already—had set her to thinking. "I guess some kids snared a case of beer from the Sloane," he'd said in that tossed-off way, like he was relaying the going rate for beet tonnage. "Happens every year, I suppose."

"I suppose," she'd agreed, and once the phone was back on the hook, she listened to her gut and went looking for Omar. A bed check yielded nothing, so she'd checked the bathroom. Bingo, as it were.

Now, she strode back down the hall to the closed door of the bathroom, and she pounded it with an open hand.

"I better not find even a speck in there when you're done," she said.

"Yeah, OK."

She hit the door again. "Yes, ma'am."

"Yes, ma'am."

Doreen returned the way she'd come, to the kitchen table to wait for her boy to show his face, to contemplate again just how nullified she felt by this whole mess. In the space of just a few seconds, she'd considered, and discarded, a handful of options. She could call Eldrick Sloane and offer her apologies and Omar's sweat equity to make things good, but Eldrick would eventually talk, and Omar would get a label he'd never shake, and for that matter, so would she, the single mother who couldn't contain her child. Same deal with calling the coach. He'd run it out of Omar, but anything that brushed up against her son's basketball future wasn't to be trifled with. At last, she alighted on the same answer that was always there: she could take it to Sam. Eventually, that is, but not today, not with everything else on his plate. She sat in her chair and she agitated, and then she gave herself over to the reality of the situation: for the next couple of days, she'd have to carry this alone. She wrapped her hands around her coffee cup and drew it to her lips.

Down the hall, the sound of the shower kicked in.

OMAR

The job done, Omar slipped into the shower and set about shedding the awfulness from his skin. He'd never seen so much puke and piss in all his life, and the idea that he'd come home and upchucked and peed on the floor, in some order or maybe simultaneously, and then lain down in it—confirmed by the contours of his leavings—left him nothing less than astounded at his own stupidity. Why had this held such a mystery for him, his first drunk? It had been about as far removed from exotic as something could be. He drank a beer, hated it, got laughed at by Gabe and the two sophomore girls they'd hooked up with, then drank six more. After that, oblivion. He wasn't sure how he'd made it home.

He dropped his head back under the water flow and let it spray down his neck and back. He hoped the girls wouldn't be there tonight. They were fine, as far as girls went. The shorter one, the one more obviously interested in him, had even let him feel up her shirt, and that had been nice enough, but he hadn't had much time to talk to Gabe. He needed to build some insulation around his coming lie, and he'd decided that regardless of Clarissa's pleas that he keep things to himself, he needed to tell somebody. Gabe could keep a secret, he was pretty sure.

"Are you almost done?" His mother's sharp words cut through the door and found him again. Jesus, but she was pissed off about this. This was her third pass, and each time he assured her, yes, he was just getting clean and he'd be out soon.

As far as tonight goes, Omar thought to himself, *she may have some things to say.* She usually did, and while he tried hard not to disappoint her, he knew the collisions were coming faster. If she had prohibition in mind, he supposed he'd have to give lip service to that. But eventually, she'd be asleep and he'd be out the door, and there wasn't anything his mother could do about that.

A dozen minutes later, he sat at the kitchen table across from her, steadying himself for the brewing storm.

"What did you drink?" she asked him.

"Beer."

"Where did you get it?"

"Some kids had it."

"Word on the street is that it was stolen from the Sloane Hotel."

Omar knew he should just leave it be, just issue a denial and accept whatever punishment was coming, but he couldn't. "You already know the word on the street?"

"Don't get tart with me, young man. The rest of the world has been up much longer than you, I assure you."

"I don't know anything about stolen beer."

She had a bit further to ride on this burst of agitation. "But you just couldn't wait to drink some, could you?"

"I didn't like it."

"Which one? The first can or the twelfth?"

Omar rubbed his eyes. "Don't be dramatic."

Next came the hard slap of her hand against the wood, jolting him out of his disaffection. He wrenched up his face. "Don't you ever, ever presume to lecture me," she said. "I know you're a big man and you don't think you can be bothered with the likes of me anymore, but you will respect me every remaining moment you live in this house. Do you understand?"

"Yes, ma'am."

At once, the hard lines of her face softened, her voice right along with them. "It's so unlike you. And you have so much in front of you. I just don't want to see you make a mistake."

"I know. I'll make better choices." He'd been leaning hard on that phrase of late. It seemed to please her.

Now tears spilled. He tried to smile at her without watching this. It made him uncomfortable, and he couldn't help but think that on some level she was manipulating him. She could always move him where she wanted with her emotions. *We always end up here. Her crying. Every time.*

"That's all I want," she said. And then she stood and moved toward him, toward the hug that she needed and he needed to endure, and with it the less-than-subtle nod to his paternal heritage that she always found a way to bring up, forcing him into deeper conflict about what it meant and whether he was prepared to accept the underlying logic.

"There are people in this town who are waiting for you to fail," she said. "Not because of who you are, but because of what you are. You can't give them that satisfaction, son. You just can't."

THE CHIEF

Adair had come to consider cell phones the root cause of many of her troubles. If she wasn't chasing down some entitled girl— they were almost always entitled, and almost always girls, she contended—who'd run a stop sign while texting, she was confiscating the phone of some oversexed teenage boy who was harvesting titty shots of the sophomore class. (Here, similarly, it was almost always boys and almost always titties.) But this morning, her particular trouble lay in an inability to scare up a phone number she needed, in all likelihood because the person she sought had joined everybody else and ditched the landline for a cell phone. *Easier living, harder investigating,* Adair thought.

She had a buddy from the academy, Jerry Dickson, who was working in Grand Forks County now, and maybe he could zero in on her target, but Adair hated like hell to call in help from the law on a Hail Mary like this one. Dickson would respect her enough not to push, but he'd want some answers before he did too much digging for her. And answers, Adair had decided, were in short supply.

Adair, sitting on her bed, crossed her bare legs and bore down on the computer. A simple Google search had unearthed the name she was seeking: Martha Swarthbeck. She could see from the background-search website that the age was about right. She clicked on the link for Martha's name, and right there, it said "Possible relatives: John Henry Swarthbeck." She half considered ponying up what it would take for the full package—a mishmash of public records—but she hesitated. The whole point of this was to leave as little a trail as possible while she was working out what could be nothing more than paranoia. Every time she even considered what she might say—"Hey, I don't trust your ex-husband"— she felt a flush of foolishness over the endeavor.

She flipped over to the Facebook tab. She'd gotten a couple of likes for her status update that morning: *No rest for the weary at Jamboree.* Jim Fuquay was among them. That swelled her up a bit. Good old Jim. Her post on the Grandview Police Department page—*Have a safe Day 2, everybody!*—lay unmolested after fifty-three minutes.

In the search field, she typed "Martha Swarthbeck" and here it came, Martha Standish Swarthbeck, a profile with one mutual friend. She clicked on it, and the friend in common was Tut Everly. Bingo.

She punched out a message, taking extended pauses between words as she considered how best to shape the message.

Hi . . . You don't know me, I don't think, but I'm Adair Underwood, the police chief in Grandview. I was wondering if I could give you a quick call.

Adair waited. Facebook quickly showed her message as seen, but she saw no immediate evidence that a reply was forthcoming. As the seconds morphed into minutes, Adair again felt the surges of silliness welling up inside. It had been remarkable that she'd remembered the name at all, a snippet of recall involving Joe LaMer and some beers they'd shared during her first week on the job. Curious about the town and its power structure, she'd made innocent inquiries about her boss, and LaMer had told her about

Martha and her mysterious escape to being perhaps the oldest coed at the University of North Dakota.

"Here one day, gone the next," LaMer had said then. "He doesn't talk about her. Nobody else does, either—at least not to him. She might as well have been smoke."

Adair sat up. Facebook indicated that someone was typing on the other end.

Am I under arrest?

Clever. *No, nothing like that. Just want to talk.*

What about?

I'd rather talk on the phone.

John, I'm guessing.

Adair blinked at the screen and lifted her hands from the keyboard.

That's it, Martha wrote. *You were typing eagerly until I said his name.*

Adair went back to it. *Can we talk, please? Just for a couple of minutes.*

She again waited. And then, a single word came back. *No.*

She started to key in a fresh plea, but Martha was typing again. Adair wiped out her few letters and waited for Martha's message to come through.

I earned my right to leave and to be done with that town. It wasn't easy, but I'm here, and I'm happy, and I'm not going to mess with that by getting involved in whatever you've landed in there. I'll just say this—whatever you're wondering, whatever reason you had for bringing this to me, whatever you're worried about or scared of, I have one answer: yes.

Adair looked at the screen, transfixed. A chill ran the length of her, radiating outward.

You got it? Martha prompted.

Adair watched the cursor for a few moments as confusion flushed into her head and then exited. Finally, she typed, *Yes.*

Don't ever contact me again.

Adair drove around town, north to south and back again, repeated loops along the outskirts. When Officer Sakota contacted her by radio and asked what was up, she covered by saying she was just doing a perimeter check.

"Perimeter check?" he'd repeated.

"Yes. I'll be back soon. Those guys get fed?"

"Joe's with them."

"Roger that."

She dumped the contents of her head again, trying to piece things together. *So this is what isolation feels like,* she thought. Martha Swarthbeck, in what she did and didn't say, had given blanket endorsement to any suspicion or fear Adair might have, and she was beginning to think she should start harboring plenty of both.

She didn't see any clear way to go. That was the problem. She could call Captain Fuquay again, but what would that do besides give her another opportunity to hear his rolling laugh and wish she hadn't been so quick to move on? Here, in her cruiser, she could fast-forward to his bottom line: *I agree, Adair, it sounds weird, but stuff that sounds weird isn't evidence. Get yourself something to work with, and then let's talk.* So where did that leave her? She had no confidantes, no sources, no omniscient guide who could speak plainly to her in some fallow field like an agricultural deep throat. She had LaMer, whom she was now inclined to view skeptically after his cryptic warning the day before, and she had Phil Sakota, whose ears she had to towel off daily.

That's some damn thin gruel, she thought.

She made one last loop while she talked out loud to herself. "Eyes open, antenna up, do your fucking job, Adair."

She gripped the steering wheel with both hands and pushed herself ramrod straight in the seat.

"Do your fucking job."

MAMA

Blanche sat on a stool in her bedroom, staring into a mirror at the strange creature looking back at her. She had to concede that Patricia had done good work. Her wispy, unruly white hair had been tamed, first by the brush and then by the curling iron, and now soft curls framed her face. She hadn't wanted the makeup, but Patricia had been deferentially insistent, and a few well-placed accents had brought her into better visage. She still couldn't make sense of that face, though, makeup or not. Blanche was not a vain woman, Lord no, but the toll of the years always caught her by surprise on those rare occasions when she'd look herself over. In her mind and her memories, she would ever remain the redheaded girl who liked to climb trees, was a better fisherman than any of her brothers, and would play catch with the boys in the yard when Big Herschel was too tired to do so.

Patricia stood behind her and to the left, holding up a blue dress Blanche hadn't seen in a moon. "How about this, Mama?"

Blanche shook her head. "There's a white one with a floral print in there somewhere," she said. "That's the one I want."

Patricia turned and went back to digging in the closet.

Something's leaning hard on that girl, Blanche thought. She could guess that Samuel was part of it, but it was more than just that. She'd come in tentative and small-voiced, and that wasn't Patricia by any stretch. Blanche had loved her like one of her own from the get-go. She liked her spunk and decisiveness. Can't raise kids the right way except to be the alpha. Blanche knew this from experience, and she recognized it in her daughter-in-law. The woman who filled her door this morning didn't arrive with that kind of bearing.

Blanche didn't care for the way people were pussyfooting around her. She didn't care for it one little bit. Sam all the time making excuses for Samuel's absences. "He's busy out there in California, Mama." That was pure bullroar, and she knew it. Life's a strange thing. When you're young, they cut you out of everything to protect you. You grow up, and everybody wants you to solve every problem. Then you get old, and they cut you out again. Blanche figured she'd had about enough of this nonsense.

"What are you going to do about this Norby business?"

Patricia whipped around. "What, Mama?"

"Samuel's new name." Blanche paused, waiting for a fresh blast of oxygen. "It's ridiculous."

Patricia held out a dress. "This one?"

"Yes, that's the one."

Patricia walked it over. "This is lovely, Mama. Good choice."

"Don't patronize me."

Patricia laid the dress on the vanity and then set herself onto the bed. "I don't know how we got lost," she said. "Everything is so dramatic. He feels like he needs this. It's not a big deal."

"I think it is."

"Why, Mama?"

Blanche closed her eyes and waited for her lungs to fill again. She'd taken to burning off her mornings with prayers of deliverance. Now, she silently implored the good Lord for the words she needed.

"He has a name. It's a good, sturdy name that tells him who he is and the people he comes from," Blanche said. "You, more than anyone, should know what comes with Norby. You couldn't rid yourself of it fast enough."

"I know. It's just that he's—I don't know, this will sound dumb, but he's trying to figure out his place."

"You mean because he's gay?"

Patricia covered her mouth with her hand.

"You think I don't know?" Blanche said.

"I guess . . . no, I didn't think so. How did you know?"

Blanche laughed, and the phlegm rattled in her chest. "I've always known."

"How?"

"I don't know." She drew in breath again. "I could just as easily tell you how the sky looks blue to me. It just is."

"We had no idea," Patricia said. Her voice dropped, meek. "Is there something wrong with us?"

Blanche laughed again. "Gracious, no. When you're a parent, you like to think you're in control. I don't mean that in a bad way." She waited again for the oxygenator. "It's just that it's sort of in your nature to project things out for your children. You probably figured him for college, for church, for marriage, three or four kids. Does that sound right?" Lord, she was nearly spent. This was more talking than she'd typically do in a fortnight.

"Yes," Patricia said.

"Kind of hard to let that go, isn't it?"

"Yes." She was whispering now. "Much more for Sam than for me."

"I see."

"He's hung up. He says it's wrong."

Blanche closed her eyes. This was partly her fault. She hadn't considered that until now.

"I know what the book says," she said at last, her lungs set for another go-round. "I also know God doesn't make mistakes."

Patricia dabbed at her eyes.

"You talk to that boy."

Patricia nodded, and then stood. She positioned herself behind Blanche and draped the dress across her.

"This is the one," Blanche said.

THE MAYOR

John Swarthbeck figured the walk was his favorite part of Jamboree, every year.

The mayor would begin at the south end of town, where the final parade highlights were assembled—this year, the new Case IH Magnum tractor that Rob Kobuck was pushing down at the dealership. He'd wend his way past the entire procession, shaking hands. Past the Grandview High School classes that had reunited, past the floats for the drill team and the cheerleaders and the Science Club; past the 4-H crew and the Rotary Club and the Toastmasters and the Junior League; past the Knitting Circle, the Lutheran Church, and the Chamber of Commerce; past rusted-out Humvees, tricked-out Cutlass Supremes, and a line of classic cars that could set anyone to dreaming of the fifties. At the head of the line, he'd shake hands with the sheriff and the president of the VFW, mounted on their ponies with the state flag and the Stars and Stripes, and he'd thank them for their service; then he'd cross the street to Clancy Park and make the rounds there before finding his way down Main Street to his perch on the viewing platform.

Did some folks find it an ostentatiously regal display? Yes, Swarthbeck supposed they did. He couldn't find it in himself to care one whit about such pettiness. Jamboree was bigger than anyone's out-of-joint nose, and as mayor of Grandview he considered this time his opportunity to express gratitude on a grand scale for the way the town's heritage was celebrated every year.

As folks milled about in the park, sucking on snow cones and waiting for the parade to start, the mayor zeroed in on a familiar face. Wanda Perkins stood chatting with Alfonso Medeiros, with Larry Grubbs moving around them like a shark, firing off shots from his camera.

"Grubbsie," Swarthbeck said, "don't you have a real job back in Billings?" He took the three of them in with a sweeping look. "Alfonso. Miss Perkins."

"I gotta get back to the truck," Medeiros said. "Nice meeting you, Miss Perkins." He moved away in double time, a single glance back over his shoulder.

"Well, Mr. Mayor," the reporter said. "You certainly have a way with people."

Swarthbeck let it pass. "Nice to see you back in town. How go the travels?"

"Good. Spent yesterday in Watford City."

"Excellent. Nice town."

He really did like her, he had decided. She talked in a set-jaw manner that made even innocuous banter such as this seem like a confrontation.

"Alfonso's a good guy," he said. "Of course, you really ought to talk to Dea, his wife. She's the one who makes that family business go."

"Funny," she said. "He was telling me the same thing."

"What else was he telling you?"

"Oh, Mr. Mayor." She glanced at her watch. "Wasn't this thing supposed to start at two?"

Swarthbeck held her in his gaze. "We're not real particular around here about time. It'll start when I get to where I'm going."

"Well, then," she said, "you better get moving, huh?"

He tipped his cap to her. "Staying for the party?" he asked.

"Wouldn't miss it."

"We'll talk some more then."

Before she could reply or retort—*Smart girl,* the mayor thought, *but she overplays her hand sometimes*—Swarthbeck was on the move again, his hand raking through a little ginger boy's hair, and then he was the recipient of handshakes and backslaps and hoots and hollers. The sidelines swelled now with anticipation as he made his way down Main Street. It wasn't all adoration, of course. He caught the eyes of Tut and Marian Everly, him looking as though his life force had been wrung out and her face drawn and gaunt, and the mayor scrambled for a more charitable place to direct his point of view.

"Are you ready for a parade?" The mayor boomed the question as he drew near to the viewing platform, and a mighty cheer went up from all within earshot. Sam Kelvig waited at the base of the platform, ready to shinny up with him. Big day for the mayor, and big day for Sammy, too. They shook hands, and then they climbed the ladder, the mayor first, Kelvig behind.

Once in place on the platform, Sam took the microphone.

"We're going to get started here in a few minutes," he said as the chatter died down. "First, I just want to thank you for coming out today. The parade, as you know, is pretty much the centerpiece of everything we do this weekend. I want to say, now that I've been director of this thing for ten years, I'm just so pleased that everyone comes out and supports our town in this way. So thank you." Cheers and whistles barreled in. "Now, here's the mayor to get us started."

Sam passed the microphone like a baton and then took his seat.

"Thanks, Sammy," Swarthbeck said. He loved this part, loved being the mayor, loved the chance, here, to burnish his standing just a little more, same as he did every year at this time. He took a moment to calibrate his words to the tiny gap between his saying them and hearing their echo out in the street. "You know, I say something like this every year, and every year I think I won't and then realize I have to. I'm not from here. Some of you know that, maybe some of you don't. I grew up in a little house on the south side of Billings, and I didn't move here until after I left the Marine Corps. But from that day on, Grandview became my home, and will be until the day I die." He paused here, giving space to the cheers he knew would be coming. "I felt like one of you, and you made me feel that, and I've never forgotten it. That's what Jamboree is about. Whether you've lived here all along or you've moved away but come back for this, remember that you're everything that defines Grandview. You're what makes this the best town in America. Thank you for coming."

He leaned over to Sam as the chants began—"*May-or! May-or!*"—and cupped a hand over the microphone. "That's what's called a red-meat speech," he said, grinning.

Now he stood straight again. "So let's have a parade." He drew out that last syllable, until the crowd was at a fever pitch, and here came the sheriff and the man from the VFW, their flags notched into the saddlecocks, and behind them, a car with Barry Bristow's real estate signage on the door puttered forth, hands emerging from the windows to toss candy to the assembled children.

"By god, Sammy," the mayor said, "we have us a party now."

NORBY

A handful of tossed saltwater taffies scattered against the curb, and Norby pointed the bounty out to Randall Junior. "Better hurry, bud." A half-dozen kids descended on the thrown candy even as more came from the next wave of passing floats, and the little boy tromped happily into the scrum, getting his hands on a wrapped piece of candy only to see a larger boy pluck it from his fingers.

"No, you don't," Norby said to the older child. "Give it back to him."

"It's mine," the boy said.

Norby moved up on the boy and snatched the candy from him. He then turned to his nephew and handed it back.

"I'm going to tell my mom," the boy said.

"Do it," Norby taunted him.

The older boy ran squalling down the line to his mother, and Norby took the opportunity to pull Randall Junior back into the crowd just as another sugared volley hit the pavement.

"More," the boy said.

"We will. Just a second."

Norby had enjoyed hanging out with the kid, much to his own surprise. Denise and Randy had done the hard sell back at the house, asking for a few hours alone so they could go tubing on the river with some friends. It had been his mother's suggestion that he take Randall Junior to the park to play while she tended to little Chase. The kid had been game for anything. They'd played ring toss, fished in the duck pond, split a Coca-Cola, and Norby had even slipped the dunking tank operator twenty bucks so he could send Ren Brian into the drink five times without having to throw the baseball. That had been Randall Junior's favorite part, the way the fat man went into the water again and again.

Now he grabbed Randall by the hand and moved up the line a little bit, hoping to avoid a potential clash with the bullying boy's mother.

"You handled that kid well."

Norby looked around. "What?"

A woman in front of him waved a hand in front of his face. "Yoo-hoo. Over here. I said, you handled that kid well. I saw what he did."

Randall tugged at Norby's hand. "I want more."

"Well, go get it, bud."

The boy toddled out to the street and asserted himself this time, getting a rightful share of the Jolly Ranchers that flew out from a cherry-red 1951 Cadillac.

"He yours?" the woman asked.

"No. I mean, yes."

"It's not a tough question."

Norby's cheeks heated up. "He's my nephew."

"I see."

"Yeah."

"You really don't know who I am, do you?" the woman said.

For the first time in his scattered state, Norby took a close look at her. Something there registered, maybe. He couldn't be sure.

"Give me a hint," he said.

"Here's a direct quote: 'I'd be incapable of loving you.'"

"Holy shit," he said.

Randall, now back at his side, chided him. "Bad word."

"Go get some more candy, buddy."

The boy stormed the curb again, and Norby turned back to her. "I can't believe it." And he couldn't. He hadn't seen Megan Riley in ten years, not since an excruciating high school graduation ceremony in which Norby had been the only graduate among thirty-one who was booed in the Grandview auditorium. It hadn't been a unanimous sentiment; he received a smattering of polite applause, too, but in any case, that had been the nadir for him in his hometown. In a few short months of his final year in Grandview, Norby had quit the basketball team midseason and broken up with the girl his parents adored. He'd walked out of his Grandview High days as surely the least popular student council president in the school's history. Maybe in any school's history. Now, here was Megan, with close-cropped hair rather than the ringlets of a decade back, blonde rather than brunette, maybe fifty pounds heavier than she'd been in high school. She wore them well, too. Norby had always thought her too skinny before. She grinned at his confusion.

"Why aren't you on the float?" he asked her.

"Why aren't you?"

"Didn't want to be."

"Neither did I."

As if on cue, the class of 2005 float, carrying twenty-two of their classmates, came into view. Steve Simic, the de facto class leader if neither Norby nor Megan was going to do the job, stood at the edge of the trailer, wearing wraparound sunglasses and holding a Super Soaker water gun. He drew down on a crowd of kids begging for a shot of water, and he drenched every last one of them, Randall included. When it was obvious that Simic had spotted Norby, he used his middle finger to slide the sunglasses up his nose.

"I was going to ask if anyone held a grudge," Norby said. He waved Randall back to him, and the boy returned holding out a piece of taffy as a peace offering.

"Well, I don't," she said.

"Thank you."

"It took a fair amount of therapy to get there, though."

He looked at her, ready to apologize, and she couldn't contain the laughter. "I'm just kidding." And then, her laughter quelled, she added, "I am surprised you're here."

"You and me both."

"Are you going to be downtown tonight?"

"Thinking about it."

"Well," she said, "if you come, I'd love to talk more."

"I'd like that, too."

"OK."

Megan slipped through the folds of the gathered crowd, cutting across the street between two floats and fading into the packed mass on the other side. Norby watched her go, until he couldn't find the top of her head anymore, and he startled himself with a sigh. He'd left here with so many things unfinished or unsatisfactory. Here was one more.

He reached down and took Randall's hand again, and they plied their way through the onlookers to a better vantage point up front. "Come on, bud, let's go. Great-grandma should be coming up soon."

MAMA

This is why you pray for what you really need and, sometimes, for what you really want. Because the good Lord, in his wisdom, will sometimes come through for you in the most generous and bountiful ways.

Blanche sat in her wicker chair on the festively outfitted tractor-trailer and let the sun kiss her face. Her companion, Miss Richland County, took care of the entertainment, waving with unflagging enthusiasm and wearing a stitched-on smile. Aside from the matching tiaras, which Blanche thought the height of silliness, she felt a tinge of sheepishness about all of her fretting and fighting about being in the parade. As it turned out, this was downright pleasant—a nice ride on a sunny day, breeze whistling through her hair. It rather reminded Blanche of her Sunday rides with Big Herschel in those touring cars he always insisted on buying, never mind the complete lack of practicality for their farm family.

Oh, how he would have loved to see this.

Still, it was beyond her to explain how or why she was Queen of the Grandview Parade. Who decides such a thing, and on what basis? In a self-deprecating moment, Blanche might have posited that she had simply outlived the other contenders for the crown, but that wasn't really true. Myrtle Davis, for example, had six years on her and was certainly more deserving, what with all the work she'd done to preserve the town's history. There were others, too. Blanche had even tried to say as much that evening a few months ago when Sam and the mayor had come by to tell her the news of her selection. "But why?" she'd said, and nobody could really say, except that she deserved it as much as anyone did. The mayor had called it "perfect synchronicity," with her coronation and Sam's ten-year mark falling on the same July weekend.

"Mama," Sam had said, "I thought you'd be happy when you found out."

Many times since, Blanche had regretted letting him down that way. She wasn't happy, at least not then, and she couldn't rightly say why, except that she had recently started talking with the Lord and had been asking him to bring her home. That was pure selfishness in her heart, and it wasn't right. She hadn't been happy then but she was happy now, and she resolved to tell her boy so just as soon as she could. She would also remember to thank the Lord in her prayers tonight for letting her see this day. Much as she wanted to go, he had the wisdom to keep her here this long. Glory be.

"Great-grandma!"

Blanche fluttered open her eyes and followed the sound. So many people. Her tired eyes had trouble making solid reads of their faces.

"GREAT-grandma." Now she had a line on him, and there he was, sitting atop Samuel's shoulders and waving to her. Blanche set a kiss on her fingers and blew it out at the crowd, aiming straight at Randall Junior. Such a fine boy, that one, and from all indications his brother was, too. That had been her dearest wish, that goodness fill the hearts of the littlest ones. It had seemed a bit of a long shot, given Denise's general attitude and the profanity of the man she'd married, but here again God had provided. *He is truly wise and generous. Let that never be forgotten.*

The slow putt-putt-putt of the float left the park behind now, and the main downtown stretch came into view. Blanche could hear the amplified, disembodied voice of Sam, calling out the floats and their associations as each passed the Sloane Hotel up ahead. She thought her heart might spring a leak, swollen with pride as it was at her son's careful cultivation of his father's legacy. Could she really be coming up on thirty years without Big Herschel? It didn't seem possible, and yet she knew that the calendar turns with indiscriminate savagery. Were he here today, he would not recognize what his younger son had done with this celebration, but he'd be proud nonetheless. Sam understood what it means to be part of Grandview, and that appreciation had been passed down to him from his father. Sometimes it seemed like nobody was listening to Sam anymore, and that bothered Blanche greatly. It might be a quaint notion today to love your town, but that didn't negate one ounce of Sam's being right and proper for doing so.

Isn't it funny how that works? Blanche thought. Big Herschel could go on and on about Grandview and what made it special. Truth is, he could go on far past the point of Blanche's wanting to hear it. And then he up and died and left her to finish out this life alone, and for all these years she'd have given anything to hear him just one more time.

Sam never forgot a word of it. Everything he's done, he's done for this town.

And now, here he was, just off to Blanche's right on the viewing stand, and he was saying her name. "Blanche Kelvig, my mother, the light of my life, and, I'm proud to say, the Queen of the Grandview Parade for 2015 . . ."

Blanche took a snort of oxygen, feeling it move into her and spread out in her system, like a shot of youth. She stood and waved, and she blew Sam a kiss.

PATRICIA

Baby Chase lay asleep in the stroller, clutching the bottle he'd drained before slumber overtook him. Patricia leaned against the plate glass of Barry Bristow's real estate office, out of earshot of the folks crowding the street to watch the parade, and she talked in a side-mouthed way to Raleigh Ridgeley, who matched her pose— one leg straight and rooted to the sidewalk, the other bent with the foot up against the masonry, butt against the glass.

For the first time all weekend, Patricia was sorry to see him. She would have preferred to leave things as they were the night before, a kiss to communicate all the things she couldn't say, a fluttering run to the door before she could change her mind. To her, that seemed the way of grace, the note that might be struck in one of Raleigh's stories. Here and now in the daylight hours, she was loath to revisit it, but Raleigh had other thoughts on the matter.

"I don't know what you expect," she said, and then she nodded at Raylene Marbury and her daughter, Alexis, as they passed on the sidewalk. Slight smiles came back at Patricia, and she gave the stroller a gentle roll forward and back.

"No expectations," he said.

"Then I don't know what you want."

Raleigh moved a few inches toward her, and she moved the same distance to her right, maintaining the gap between them.

"We don't have to figure it out today," he said.

"I don't know what that means."

"What it means—" He cut the words short. A bystander turned and looked at them. Patricia didn't recognize him.

"What it means," he said, softer now, "is we could start somewhere. Why don't you come to Billings for a weekend?"

"Just like that?"

"Yes. Make something up. You've been to Billings alone. I've seen you there."

She scoffed. "Not for something like that."

"Something like what? What's so scandalous, really? Damnit, Patricia, don't you ever think there might be something more for you?"

She bit her bottom lip, so much did she have to say and so few words did she have with which to say it. She made a quarter turn away from him and moved the stroller in front of her.

"I don't know how to answer that," she said.

"Are you happy?"

She turned back to him now. "You don't get to ask me that question."

"I'm sorry," he said. "I didn't mean it like that." He closed the distance on her again.

"Yes, you did."

"Please—"

"It's OK," she said. "You always choose the right words. That's one of your talents."

"Don't say that."

"It's true."

Raleigh cleared his throat for a fresh reply, but Patricia was on the move now. Something up ahead caught her eye, and now she was pushing little Chase ahead of her, trying to get close enough to see plainly.

He called out to her. "Patricia."

Henrik?

She fell into a dead sprint, the stroller wheels thumping on the uneven sidewalk. Down at the viewing platform where Sam sat, Henrik crested the top of the platform ladder, and the tire iron he drew back glinted in the sun before she could put it all together in her head.

Her scream, when it came, was too late to do Sam any good.

SAM

Some things come naturally, and some take time. For Sam, comfort at being the voice of the Grandview parade had taken nearly all of his ten years in the role. As he read off the roster of floats and cars, he smiled at the memory of his first year up here, his words coming out wobbly and nervous, his jokes either shooting too far or landing too subtly. He'd gone home that first year and told Patricia, "I'm not the guy for this," and he'd believed it. There was no explanation for it. These were his people, folks he talked with on the street or in his store every single day. At a school board or town council meeting, he could lean into the microphone and say his piece with complete confidence. Why had that capability abandoned him here?

It was Patricia who properly diagnosed the situation. "You're putting too much pressure on yourself," she'd said. "You know, Big Herschel wasn't perfect."

And that had been it, really. She'd given him a way to wiggle out from under the legacy, and he'd gone on to make Jamboree his own. Each year, his confidence grew. He started writing jokes and observations on notecards. He got better.

Now, after a decade at the helm, he felt like he was at his best. He'd found that easy middle between keeping the crowd engaged and becoming too much of a presence, and he'd learned over the years that the best joke was a corny one.

Here, then, came the float carrying the Richland County Toastmasters and a chance to show off a new line.

"Well, folks, here are the Toastmasters. They'll talk your ear off if you let them. And, hey, they're looking for new members, so if you want a silver tongue, see Sean Drury. Fair warning from me: If you join up, be sure to eat breakfast before you go. There's no actual toast involved."

That last bit drew the happy groan Sam had hoped for when he wrote it. The mayor, next to him on the platform, gave him a nudge. "Good one," he said.

The class of 2005 float rolled into view, and Sam looked it up and down for Samuel, a vain hope, he knew. He'd wanted his son to take this opportunity to reconnect with his classmates specifically and his town in general, but he hadn't given that hope very good odds. He wished he could transfer the hard-won wisdom he'd accumulated in his fifty-three years and pass it on to his boy, but he supposed that the point of getting through this life was finding out the most difficult things on your own. It should have been Samuel, not Steve Simic, standing up there, leading his graduating class through the first of its many reunions. His son would regret it someday, of that Sam was sure.

The float neared the platform and Sam said, "Class of 2005, folks. These kids are now twenty-seven, twenty-eight years old. Put another way, most of my underwear is older."

A laugh went up, and Simic rewarded the line with a blast of the Super Soaker to Sam's face, which set the hollers into a frenzy. *Little asshole.* Sam took off his ball cap and shook like a dog, then stood up and raised his arms to the sky, and the throng whistled its appreciation.

Sam couldn't bask long in the cheers. His mother's float was next up, and he had decided that whatever he would say here would come extemporaneously, straight from the heart. This last year, in particular, had been so tough with her advancing COPD, and there had been times he wasn't sure she'd make it to this day. That she had, and that she seemed to be delighting in it, gave a lift to his heart. Damn, she looked beautiful and regal, sitting there, taking it in.

"Blanche Kelvig, my mother, the light of my life, and, I'm proud to say, the Queen of the Grandview Parade for 2015 . . ."

Blanche tottered to her feet, a true surprise, and she waved to the crowd. Sam's eyes found hers, her smile brought him in, and she blew him a kiss. At once, though, her face crumbled, and Sam's breath seized up. The tiny hairs on his arms stood erect, a prickling sensation, and Sam thought he heard a voice calling out to him . . .

THE MAYOR

When Swarthbeck saw Blanche Kelvig pitching forward, he had a single thought: get to her. The old gal had gone from radiant to ashen in a single beat, and then her eyes rolled back and she began to crumple.

The mayor planted one foot on the table and made his leap. His stomach took the brunt of the landing as he crashed against the surface of the tractor-trailer. Blanche was down, face against the steel, and Miss Richland County was at the old woman's side, tending to her.

"Stop the truck, Dexter!" Swarthbeck screamed. He pounded the side of the trailer with his open hand. "Stop the goddamned truck!" At that, it came to a lurching halt.

A shrill electronic scream split the air. Swarthbeck scrambled to his feet, looking back at the platform. A huddle formed around Sam, and another group pulled Henrik down into the mass below.

Swarthbeck pulled himself over to where Blanche lay.

"Is she OK?"

The beauty queen dabbed at Blanche's head with the tail of her dress. "She's breathing. Her head's cut." He ran his finger along Blanche's forehead. Blood came from it in surges. He put her nose-piece in place and checked to make sure oxygen was still flowing.

"It's deep, that cut," he said.

He drew himself up to his feet and made a quick scan. Chaos had taken over. The men had succeeded in drawing Henrik off the platform and were working him over on the sidewalk. Eldrick Sloane sat beside Sam.

"Eldrick."

Sloane looked up. "I think he'll be all right, John. He's out, but the damage isn't too bad."

"What did Henrik do?"

"Hit him with a tire iron."

"What?" Henrik was a crazy bastard—everybody knew that—but Swarthbeck hadn't figured him for this sort of madness.

"I know," Sloane said.

By now, Doc Porter had made it through the crowd and had climbed up on the float to get to Blanche.

"She's gonna need stitches, John."

"Him, too, probably," the mayor said, pointing at Sam. "I'll get you a ride."

Swarthbeck hopped off the float and pushed through the crowd to where Henrik lay, subdued by Adair Underwood and her officers.

"Joe," he said. "Take Sam, Blanche, and the doc to the Sidney clinic."

LaMer looked at Chief Underwood, who gave him a nod.

"You got this?" the mayor asked the chief.

"He's pretty beat up."

"Well, I guess you better take him, too, before you book his ass."

"OK."

"I want to talk to him first, though."

"Mayor, I don't—"

Swarthbeck reared back and planted a steel-toed boot in Henrik Kelvig's rib cage.

THE CHIEF

Adair passed a cup of coffee through the bars to the mayor. It's a hell of a thing, she thought, to arrest your own boss. LaMer, Sakota, Eldrick Sloane—the whole lot of them—had looked at her as though she'd lost her damn mind when she slapped the cuffs on Swarthbeck. Adair didn't see how she couldn't.

"That lady from the *Times* sure is interested in you," she said.

Swarthbeck hung his head and stared into his cup. "What'd you tell her?"

"I said I'd be happy to release my report when it's done. Probably Monday. She asked me to e-mail it to her." The chief tapped the business card in her front pocket. "She's leaving in the morning."

"This is silly, Adair," he said. "Let me out."

"Is that an order, like last night?"

Swarthbeck didn't look up, didn't say anything.

"Sorry, Mayor," she said. "Battery is a crime. Even for you."

He sloshed the coffee from his cup, dumping it at her feet. Adair jumped back.

"I tell you what," he said. "Why don't you just ask Henrik if he plans to press charges? Why don't you just see what he says to that?

And after you get your answer, you ask yourself whether you think you can make this stick. Or whether you want to."

The words came out of him calm and evenly paced, as if he were reading a list of ingredients. Adair stepped back.

"Are you threatening me?"

He looked at her, poker-faced. "What do you think?"

"I don't know."

"No shit you don't know, Adair." He ran his hands through his hair. "Fine, we'll play it your way. Get me another cup of coffee, would you, please?"

Officer Sakota radioed in, saying he was coming back to town with Henrik Kelvig.

"What's the damage?" Adair asked.

"Some facial lacerations. Bruised ribs, probably from where the mayor kicked him. They stitched him up and said he was good to go."

"Hear anything about the others?"

"Negative."

"OK, bring him in."

She exchanged text messages with LaMer, and he hadn't heard anything, either. When she told him what the mayor had said, LaMer wrote back, *Well, he's got a point.*

What point?

Henrik won't cooperate.

Why do you say that?

He just won't.

What in the blue blazes is with this town? Adair wondered. She paced the floor, trying to work the angles through in her head. She didn't much care for where she kept landing.

Her phone buzzed. LaMer again.

Listen.

Yeah? she typed.

Let Swarthbeck go.

No.

Now the phone rang. She punched up the call. "What?"

"He isn't going anywhere," LaMer said. "Let him go for tonight. You can always cite him later, if that's what you want to do."

She hung up on him, then resumed pacing. She stopped at the coffeepot and filled the mayor's cup. When she caught Swarthbeck out of the corner of her eye, watching her, she stopped and considered her options, and she realized, again, that she didn't have any that appealed to her. She reared back and threw the cup against the cinder block wall, where it shattered, leaving an angry brown splatter.

The New York Times, *Saturday, August 1, 2015*

That incident, as it turned out, wasn't the biggest challenge Chief Underwood faced during Jamboree weekend. During the Saturday town parade, the centerpiece of the celebration, the proceedings were brought to an abrupt halt when Henrik Kelvig, the 55-year-old brother of Sam Kelvig, attacked his brother on the viewing stand. Sam Kelvig came out of it with a concussion after taking a glancing blow to the head from a tire iron, and Henrik Kelvig was injured in a subsequent attack by enraged townspeople, among them the town's mayor, John Swarthbeck.

Mr. Swarthbeck, 62, a larger-than-life character who has led the town for the past thirty-three years, was cited for his role in the brawl and paid a small fine. A few hours after he was briefly detained by Underwood, Swarthbeck was making rounds during a downtown concert. While declining to go into specifics, he suggested that he was merely acting according to a code widely followed in Grandview.

"We take care of our own, and we take care of our own problems," he said. "If I have a problem with you, I'm going to take it up with you. If you have a problem with me, I'll expect the same."

Asked if he considered that a recipe for lawlessness, Mr. Swarthbeck said, "On the contrary, I think it's a recipe for politeness. That's the problem with the world today: nobody gets called out for the things they do wrong. In Grandview, we'll do that. And we'll still love you afterward. A pretty nice way to live, don't you think?"

SATURDAY NIGHT

THE MAYOR

Swarthbeck sauntered out of the Grandview police station, gave the first gaggle of partiers a stern look that sent them back to their own drinks and their own business, crossed the street, and slipped into the Sloane Hotel. He hooked a hand under Joe LaMer's arm as the deputy passed him in the foyer.

"Alfonso," the mayor said. "He's talking out of turn."

"Gotcha."

"He'll be at the Double Musky. He doesn't wander far."

Giving LaMer his leave, the mayor pushed through the double doors of the restaurant, found Eldrick Sloane, and whistled. When Sloane looked up, the mayor rolled his eyes toward the ceiling, and Sloane nodded.

"Hey, Mayor," a voice called out from the filled tables in the restaurant. Swarthbeck knew the voice and turned to meet it. "Was there a jailbreak?"

A nervous titter moved through the room.

"Eat a dick," Swarthbeck said, and then he left.

Officer Sakota had brought Henrik Kelvig in just as Adair was wrapping up the mayor's paperwork. To move it along and to give Adair a win he knew she was dying for, Swarthbeck had agreed to a disorderly conduct charge and a citation, fifty-five bucks at the county courthouse in Sidney. He figured he could live with that, and he'd noted with some pleasure the relief on the police chief's face that he wouldn't be fighting it.

"Mr. Kelvig, I'm going to have to detain you here while I finish this up, then we'll book you," she'd said, escorting Henrik into the cage.

When she came back, Swarthbeck said, "Can I talk to him?"

"Only if he wants to talk to you."

The mayor had approached the cage on tentative feet. It was a testament to just how erratic Henrik was that Swarthbeck didn't know what response he was going to get. They'd tangled a couple of times over the years, nothing too serious, and if Henrik were in his right mind, he wouldn't put up a fuss about this. But then, who in his right mind attacks a man with a tire iron while a thousand or so people are watching?

"Henrik."

The elder Kelvig brother, his body lithe and hard, like he was made out of barbed wire, kept his head low but acknowledged Swarthbeck.

"Mayor."

"Sorry it came to this," Swarthbeck said.

Adair reared up her head. "You can still press charges if you want, Mr. Kelvig." Swarthbeck yanked around and glared at her. *Dirty pool.*

"No, no charges." Henrik looked now at the mayor. "How's Sam?"

"I think he's OK. A little rattled." They both looked to Adair, who acknowledged the information with a nod.

"I shouldn't have done it."

That drew a chuckle from the mayor. "No shit, you shouldn't have done it. What the hell were you thinking?"

"He's not your lawyer, Mr. Kelvig," Adair said. "You don't have to answer that."

"Adair, please," the mayor said.

Henrik leaned forward and cupped his forehead in his hands.

"I don't know," he said. "It's a long story with me and Sam. Long time. A lot of frustrations and arguments. I just snapped. I shouldn't have done it."

Swarthbeck moved closer, till his ample gut was protruding through the bars. He slipped his hands around them up top.

"Well, don't let it worry you too much," he told Henrik. "You're in a mess, but it's the sort of mess that maybe resolves itself. Do you need a beer or something?"

Adair dashed over, her angry strides echoing through the room. "No, he does not need a beer." She slapped a piece of paper into the mayor's hand. "Here's your ticket. Time for you to leave."

SAM

Sam leaned his bandaged head against the passenger window and watched the beet fields rush past. A slight concussion, the doctor had said. Sam took issue with that word, "slight." He didn't think anyone should be in the business of discounting bruises to the brain. The doctor had smiled, his lips forming two thin lines, and said, "What I mean, Mr. Kelvig, is that you can go home. It could have been a lot worse."

For the life of him, Sam wasn't sure how Henrik had missed with the brunt of the tire iron. Maybe it was just dumb luck. Maybe Sam had moved slightly, or maybe Henrik had lost his nerve. In any event, Sam still didn't see how it qualified as slight. He'd been out, hadn't he? A more precise shot would have fractured his skull, or maybe killed him. A hell of a thing this falling out with Henrik had become. He wondered if he was going to have to watch his back from now on. He sure hadn't seen this one coming.

"I don't feel right, leaving Mama there," he said. Damn, his head hurt, like a cinder block wall had been dropped behind his eyes.

"Samuel's with her," Patricia said. "She's sleeping. They said she'd be OK." He looked at her. She held the steering wheel with both hands, and her fingers fidgeted.

She found him with a nervous glance. "What's happening to us?" she asked.

"I don't know."

"I mean, all of us."

"I know what you mean."

He turned back to the window. They were halfway home now. The doctor had prescribed rest and acute attention to Sam's condition. If one little thing changed, they were to come back right quick. Patricia had been instructed to wake him every few hours and run him through a battery of questions: name, address, favorite book, whatever.

"How's Samuel getting home?" he asked.

"Megan Riley is there with him. She said she'd bring him back."

"Megan Riley." Sam said it with some pep in his voice, a decision he instantly regretted as his head throbbed disapproval.

"Relax. They were talking at the parade."

"This is good."

"Well," she said, "it's good that they're being friendly. I always liked that girl. But I wouldn't get my hopes up."

"About what?"

"About what you're getting your hopes up about."

He nestled into the bucket seat. "You think you know me so well," he teased.

"You have no idea."

He reached for her right hand, pulled it off the wheel. "Don't," she protested, but he'd made up his mind. He brought her hand down to the console and he held it, massaging her knuckles under his thumb.

"When was the last time you drove?"

"When it was you and me?" she asked.

"Yes, silly."

"Because I drive a lot. Every day."

"You know what I mean, silly girl."

She laughed and held his hand, and he squeezed hers tight.

"I'm thinking maybe the Denver trip, a couple of years ago," she said.

"That's right."

Denver. What a fiasco that had turned out to be. A blown water pump in nowhere Wyoming cost them a day and the Neil Diamond concert he'd hoped to take her to. Even back then, he could feel the distance moving into their marriage and he'd glommed onto the trip as a sort of last-ditch play to show her he still cared. They'd come home tired and hot, several hundred dollars lighter, and scraping at each other, and that had continued until, well, now. Sometimes it seemed that some low-boil quarrel was their baseline condition.

She let go of his hand and brought hers back to the wheel. "What are you going to do about Henrik?"

"Not much I can do. He's the cops' problem now."

"Do you think he wanted to kill you?" Her voice wobbled through the question.

"I don't know."

For as long as Sam could remember, that had been the incomplete answer where Henrik was concerned. When you love someone—and Sam figured he did love his older brother, at least in the obligatory sense that being family conveys—it can be much harder to divine his motivation. A stranger comes after Sam with a tire iron, yes, it's attempted murder, plain as day. His troubled brother is the assailant, and he looks—even hopes—for a more satisfying explanation.

But what if this is as good as it gets?

Sam's memory flashed on a night during the winter of his fourteenth year, when Henrik came in from feeding calves. Sam, already asleep in the cramped room they shared, came awake and cursed Henrik for turning on the light. Henrik, in turn, had gouged a finger into Sam's eye, and the melee that resulted drew Big Herschel into the room, squinting, promising to crack the head of the next boy who said so much as boo. That night ended with Henrik whispering threats into the darkness between their beds. He'd always led with his fists, and Sam had always been afraid of him.

Even now, Sam was afraid.

"I wish my dad were here," he said.

They hit the town limits, and Sam told Patricia to stick to the main drag and take him to the police station.

"Are you sure?" she asked as she pulled into a parking spot just beyond the roped-off barrier of downtown.

"Yeah."

"Doctor said you need to get some rest." She put her hand on his arm as he reached for the door handle.

"I won't be long."

Sam waved at some early nighttime gatherers and endured the one-beat-too-long stares at his bandaged head, and then he slipped inside the low-slung building. Phil Sakota leaned against a wall just inside the door, a cigarette vibrating in his twitchy, dangling hand.

"Henrik in there?" Sam asked.

Sakota nodded. "How's your head?"

"Dented. Adair's in there, too?"

"Yep."

Sam grasped the handle of the door.

"Mayor just left," Sakota said. "He roughed up your brother pretty good."

"Yeah?"

"Yeah."

"Good for him."

By the time Sam made it through the door, took the inventory of the place, and fended off Chief Underwood's wave of objections—"Relax, Adair, I'm not pressing charges," he'd said. "Let the county attorney decide"—Henrik was in full hangdog mode. Sam squared a folding chair in front of the pen and sat down.

"Look at me, Henrik."

Haltingly, Sam's brother lifted his angular face. Sam saw not the wild irrationality of the past few days. This was fear and reckoning. Realization. This was Henrik absorbing what he'd done, showing remorse. Sam had seen this look before.

"I'm sorry," Henrik said.

Sam crossed his arms on his chest. "You always are after the damage has been done."

"I'm sorry."

Sam felt his resolve crumble, same as always, no matter how much he wanted to stick it to Henrik. He knew the issues too well. He swallowed hard and steadied himself. There were things to say.

"Mama's down at the hospital. You sorry for that, too?"

"Is she OK?"

"She's an old woman who's had enough of your bullshit."

"I'm sorry."

"So you keep saying."

Henrik pivoted away from his gaze. Sam dropped his arms and leaned back. His head throbbed. Patricia would be waiting, growing impatient.

"Why now, Henrik?"

"Huh?"

"Why'd you decide now that I've screwed you over? Are you taking your medicine?" Sam figured he knew the answer. The biggest losses in Henrik's life coincided with his walkabouts from the pharmaceutical straight and narrow. It had been hard enough to convince his brother to see someone, to get at a reason for his breaks with reality and its demands for proper behavior. But that was only half the fight.

Henrik turned back to him.

"I had the five grand," Henrik said. "I was working a rig around Stanley, and I had it. You came out to pick it up—"

"I never went out to Stanley."

"—and we were going to be square, and you didn't do what you said you'd do."

"I never went out to Stanley, Henrik."

"Where'd the money go, then?"

Sam threw his hands in the air. What kind of question was that? It could be anywhere. It might never have existed. Henrik's fleeting acquaintance with his right mind made for a constellation of possibilities.

"I never went to Stanley," Sam said again. "You never gave me any money."

"That's—"

Sam put his hands on his knees and leaned forward. "Don't you get it? It didn't happen. Just like Joanna never stepped out on you, Dad never tried to get you fired, and on and on. It didn't happen, Henrik. Have you been taking your medicine?"

Henrik ran a hand down his face, squeezing at his eye sockets. "Don't remember."

"Well, goddamn you for this."

They made it home, Sam telling the tale with silence. Patricia parked the car and prodded him to get inside and lay his head down.

"I gotta be downtown tonight," he said.

"The hell you do." He flinched at how pissed off she was at that idea. "You want me to tie you down to that bed? I'll do it."

He clutched her around the waist. *"Rowr,"* he purred. "That sounds like an offer."

"Don't be silly. That's definitely on the restricted list until you heal up." She laughed, though. That was a good sign.

"Thank you for today," he said.

"For what?"

"For being there."

She wriggled out of his grasp. "Where else would I be? Now get to bed."

MAMA

I'd sometimes sit in that old house, just me in the recliner, listening to the white noise of the television, and I'd stare straight into the ceiling fan, my eyes sinking into the white glow of the lamp underneath, the whipping blades casting shadows around the room, and I'd fixate on it, until my eyes started to play tricks on me. The lamp would melt, seeping down walls and across the ceiling, and the fan blades would distort and wilt like the clocks on the branch in that painting.

It never occurred to me, Lord, that you were giving me a glimpse of what lay beyond—a way of recognizing it when my time finally came, according to your boundless wisdom and grace. I thought I was just an old, bored woman, but you've shown me now that you had a plan and a time for me, and that my worldly wishes would not move you to it until you were ready for me. Thank you, Lord. I, too, am ready, and I can hear you saying, "Grandma, I love you . . ."

Her eyelids flickered and then lifted, and a young man's face came into sharp relief.

"Samuel?"

"Hi, Grandma. We were just leaving."

A young woman peeked out from behind Samuel and waved to her.

"Who's we?" Blanche asked.

"You remember Megan. Megan Riley."

"No," Blanche said. "I don't. Forgive an old lady, my dear."

"No problem," Megan said.

Blanche grunted and tried to slide herself into a sitting position on the hospital bed. The effort left her expended, and she waited for piped-in renewal from the nosepiece. As her breathing settled and the room came into greater focus, she could mourn the unfairness of it all. A dream about the light, the first she could remember in her waking hours, was just a tease. Here she was, still in a world that didn't hold much for her anymore, still an old lady with a compromised set of lungs, still an afterthought—and one who had to suffer such mean-nothings as "no problem," on top of it.

Even as she cataloged her grievances with the status quo, the immediate past began to reboot.

"Where's your father?" she asked.

"He went home."

"Home?"

"Yes. He's dinged up, but all right."

"And your Uncle Henrik?"

"Dinged up, too. And in jail."

With no time to catch herself, Blanche began weeping, and the girl, Megan, came and sat down beside her, holding her hand. Samuel stood his ground and rubbed his hands together. "Do you know what happened, Grandma?"

"Yes. I saw it."

"I can't believe it. Nobody can."

Blanche raked her bottom lip with her teeth and said nothing to that. What could she say? She hadn't seen it coming, either, and she alone had been privy to Henrik's most frightening tirades these past few days. She could now rue her own sense of self-importance, the hubris that she'd somehow be able to control him and veer him away from his self-destructive impulses. When he'd fallen at her feet, crying, she thought she'd found a way to get at the thinking part of him, a way of making him see the trouble ahead if he kept pushing. She'd read that badly wrong, and now the situation was infinitely more complex.

"Your Uncle Henrik has a sick mind," she said at last.

"To say the absolute least. He got messed up pretty good. Mayor even got in a shot. Kicked him in the ribs and broke one of them, I heard."

"That's not exactly something to celebrate, is it?"

"No, ma'am."

Blanche changed tacks. "What time is it?"

Samuel opened his phone. "Quarter after seven."

"How long have I been asleep?"

"A couple of hours. Doctor says he wants you to stay a few days."

"That's preposterous," she said. "I'm fine."

"Just telling you what he thinks."

"Well, I'll take it up with him, believe me." She gave Megan a wink. "Now do me a favor, would you?"

"Of course," he said.

"Go find me a pen and some paper. If I'm going to be stuck in here, I ought to at least entertain myself."

"OK." Samuel stepped out of the room on his errand, and Blanche took up matters with Megan.

"Now tell me," she said. "Are you and my grandson friends?"

"We were, I guess. A long time ago. I used to date him back in high school. I've actually met you, you know."

"I know. I remember now. You came to my house for Thanksgiving."

"Yes, that's right."

"You've changed."

"Well, it's been nearly eleven years."

"Yes," Blanche said. "I suppose it has. You'll forgive me being direct with this—"

"Yes?"

"I'm wondering what your interest is in him now."

"I haven't thought about it."

"Oh?"

"Not really. I only saw him again today."

Blanche waited for a fresh shot of air. Samuel returned before she could get to it.

"Nurses had some paper. But they want you to sleep, too," he said.

"I will. Now you two get on back to town. I'll be fine."

"You're sure?" he asked.

"Yes. Go."

Samuel opened the door and motioned for Megan to join him. She pushed herself up, and gave Blanche a quizzical look.

"You children have fun."

Once they were out the door, Blanche went to work. She hefted the dinner tray across her lap, fashioning a writing desk, and then she began to put words to paper. She'd gone as far as vanity could take her with Henrik, and that hadn't served anybody—him and Sam least of all. She was an old, foolish, vain-hearted woman, she told herself, and she should have stepped into this years ago and made a clean division of it. She'd do that right now, while she still had the time.

One last detail occurred to her, and Blanche pressed the nurse call button on her bed.

The door opened presently.

"Yes, Mrs. Kelvig?"

"I'm sorry to bother you," Blanche said. "Do you have an envelope I could have?"

"Of course. I'll get you one."

Blanche turned back to the job at hand.

She began to write: *In the event of my death . . .*

NORBY

Norby and Megan settled into a couple of plastic chairs on the sidewalk outside Jordy Rusch's tattoo studio, far enough down the street that the warbling from the rhinestone cowboy up on stage didn't crowd out their conversation.

They'd ridden back from Sidney mostly in silence, the only deviation into conversation Megan's question about coming downtown. Norby figured that would be preferable to sitting in the house another night, listening to the stamping of little feet on the floor and enduring another viewing of that Pixar flick with the theme song he couldn't shake once it got in his head.

Now, they drank beer from plastic cups, courtesy of the Double Musky, and swatted at interloping mosquitoes. Megan picked at the edges of conversation.

"She asked me what my intentions are," she said.

"Get out of here."

"Seriously. Am I supposed to have intentions?"

Norby took a pull from his cup. "It would probably be better if you didn't."

"What does that mean?"

"Nothing."

She pitched forward in her chair, demanding an audience. "Don't give me that."

Norby drained his cup, then he held it up and stared into the bottom, as if he might have missed a drop.

"Do you want to go for a drive?" he asked.

They leaned against the fence at the edge of the Grandview railroad bridge. Across the river, the water-colored badlands faded in the dusk light, while swimmers below plied the evening waters of the Yellowstone. Norby breathed in, letting the aqua flush of the river bottom sweep into his nostrils.

"Do you remember when I came back from basketball camp that last summer we were in school?"

"Yes."

"We came up here that first night I was back. Do you remember that?"

"Vaguely."

"I remember it well." He tightened his grip on the fencing and leaned back. "That's the first time I tried to break up with you. I was too chickenshit to do it."

Megan's voice caught, as if strangled at the source, and then she released the words one by one. "OK, I remember. You were acting weird. You wouldn't kiss me."

"I didn't want to kiss you."

"Don't be mean."

"I'm not trying to be mean. I'm trying to tell you something."

He began to explain himself, but she cut him off.

"I knew," she said.

"You did?"

"Well, no, not then. Then, I was invested in a different idea. But you know, Samuel, I've had a lot of time to think about—"

"Norby."

"Huh?"

"I go by Norby now."

"Why?"

"Not for any good reason. Let me tell you a few things, OK? I want to."

"OK."

So began the unloading and unpacking of things Norby had held close for a decade.

"We were in Salt Lake for basketball camp," he told her. "Rich Buckner and I were roommates. Some things happened."

"What things?"

He looked at her, purse-lipped.

"Oh."

"It was my first time," he said. "But I'd known for a while, you know? I just didn't know what I knew, if that makes any sense."

"So Rich was—"

"No, I don't think so. Not like I am. He was curious, and we did some stuff, and when we came back, I thought, *well, how do I deal with this now?* I don't want to make it bigger than it was, but it was like a part of the world I didn't know existed had opened up to me, you know? I didn't want to go back to how things were."

"I see. So I represented a big problem for you."

Norby looked at her. She was stung. No denying that. She was also standing there, waiting for him. She was a good friend, then and now. He wished he'd recognized that sooner.

"I thought if Rich and I could, I don't know, come out together, that would be easier. I wasn't stupid. People were going to have stuff to say no matter what. But everybody liked Rich, so I thought . . ."

"Yeah. I can see that. But come on. In Grandview? I don't see it."

Norby turned and rested his back against the fence. "Anyway, it didn't happen. Rich got mad when I asked him. He said what happened in Salt Lake—hell of a place for that, huh?—was just what it was. He told me he'd kick my ass if I said anything, so of course I didn't. And then, you know . . ." He trailed off. A few years after graduation, Rich had been on a cargo plane that crashed in Afghanistan, and was among the twenty-nine losses. He had a hero's funeral in Grandview, and Norby's story got buried with him.

"What did your parents say? I mean, you have told them, haven't you?"

"Yeah."

"What did they say?"

"Not much. Dad, I don't think he wants to believe it. He's trying, you know, but it's just surface stuff. Mom gets it, I think."

"Moms usually do."

Norby knelt and worked a stone out of the long-abandoned rail bed. He threw it overhand, hard, out across the river, and it landed with a satisfying *kerplunk.*

"I'm not sure why I told you all this."

"Funny," Megan said. "I'd say you owed it to me."

He looked at her. She smiled, but he could see she wasn't kidding.

"Maybe I do," he said. "Yeah, yeah, I do. I don't know that, if I could go back in time, I'd do anything differently. I don't know. Maybe I wouldn't have just quit playing. I didn't think I could be at basketball practice every day with Rich, knowing what happened, knowing I couldn't say anything. It seemed like the path of least resistance."

She reached out and touched his arm.

"Was it, though?"

He turned back to the water. He didn't have an answer to that—at least, not one he cared to give flight. She leaned into him, and he slipped his arm across her shoulders.

On the drive back to town, he gave an account of Norby and came to a decision: it was time to let that go, too.

"I plucked it clean out of the air," he said. "When I left for Missoula, you know, I was all about new beginnings, new definitions, all that stuff. It was a name other than the one I'd had my whole life. And then, honest to God, it just sort of became what I responded to. I wonder if that's how it works with celebrities. I mean, Cary Grant." At the invocation of the name, he growled like a cat, launching Megan into a peal of laughter. "The guy's name was Archibald. At what point did he stop turning around if somebody said, 'Hey, Archie'? That's the way it was with me. If somebody had said 'Samuel,' I don't know if I'd have even realized it was my name."

"I worked with a guy in Billings named Dikran," Megan said.

"Mmmmmmm. Dikran," he said, punctuating the first syllable and growling again, and she punched him in the arm.

"Armenian guy," she said. "Nice guy. Went by Greg. As would anybody."

"So, this Dikran, is he single?"

"Shut up, Norby."

OMAR

The sophomore girls lost their interest in Omar and Gabe when they heard that there wouldn't be any beer, and Omar stood firm on that point, because his mother had made the stakes clear enough: If she smelled even a whiff of alcohol on him in the morning, he could kiss any unsupervised time good-bye for the rest of his natural born life. "You think I can't make you go to MSU Billings?" she'd said. "Come home stinking of beer and I'll show you what I can do. You won't get any closer to Los Angeles than your TV."

He had to take notice of the threat, no matter how much he thought she might be bluffing, because LA was continually on his mind. He hadn't heard from the Bruins coach lately, but they were in what the NCAA called a "dead period," where contact with recruits was verboten. The coach had said he'd stick to the letter of the law, but he'd winked when he said that. Omar was getting a lot of e-mail from people outside the basketball program—alumni and other people who had some connection to UCLA—telling him what a great place it was. "I looked you up on the Internet," they'd say. "Hope you come play for the Bruins." They weren't the only ones doing it. He heard from alums at Duke and Syracuse and a lot of other places, too. And he'd talked to his coach in Grandview, who told him to play it cool, like he was trying to get the cutest girl in school to go to prom with him. Let the teams make their pitches, he'd said. Omar knew he'd probably go to New York and North Carolina on official visits, just to keep things interesting and fun, but he also knew he'd already cast his heart for LA.

"What do you want to do?" Gabe asked as they stood outside the Country Basket. "You want to go back to my place?"

Omar shook his head.

"What then?"

Omar wasn't sure. He just knew that he was done with the ordinary. He'd had this sense, in a way he couldn't articulate to Gabe, that nothing was going to be the same after he climbed down from the railroad bridge with Clarissa. About the only thing the beer had been good for was giving him a reprieve from thoughts of her and what was coming Monday. Gabe had been a reliable friend. He'd even said he'd borrow his parents' car and drive out to Fort Peck on Monday, just so he didn't cross paths with Omar's mom. But Omar figured everybody had his limits, and he didn't see Gabe as someone who would understand the complexities of Omar's mind. Even Omar himself didn't understand it. He wanted to be reckless and wild and outside the boundaries that had been erected for him, and still he kept being returned—or returning of his own volition—to the roles he'd rather reject. The dutiful son. The helpful ex-boyfriend. The steadfast friend.

John Rexford's Mustang, jammed full of a quorum of football players, sped by on Main Street, then hooked a left into the houses on the west side of town.

Omar pointed after them. "Let's see what those guys are up to."

"No way."

"Don't be a chickenshit, man."

"I'm not," Gabe said. "There are four of them and two of us. They've got a car, and we don't. It doesn't sound like much fun to me."

"Whatever, man. I'm going." Omar started to jog in the direction Rexford had taken. He crossed the street, then turned and jogged backward a few paces while he looked at Gabe, imploring.

"Shit," his friend said, and then he ran to catch up.

Rexford had the horsepower, but even in a small town like Grandview, he was stuck with operating on established roads. Omar and Gabe faced no such restrictions. By cutting through alleyways and backyards and moving through the neighborhoods at diagonals, they managed to triangulate the football players' heading and plant themselves in a burned-out ditch on the western edge of town, maybe fifty feet from where Rexford and his friends were picking their way through a grown-over backyard.

"What are they doing?" Gabe whispered.

"Shhh. Let's get closer. Stay with me."

"Omar, no."

"Yes."

Omar crawled on his hands and knees through the ditch, first alone, and then with Gabe trailing him. The residue from the recent burning clung to their hands and the smell of charcoal leavings filled their lungs. At the intersection with the alley, Omar popped his head up and took inventory of things. They were behind Rexford and his friends now, facing their backs, and considerably closer. Omar figured they could chance creeping up just a bit. He moved forward, low to the ground like a soldier climbing under the concertina wire, and he motioned for Gabe to fall in. They pressed up against the chain-link fence. Night had dropped fully in, and Omar wasn't sure he could pinpoint the individual positions of Rexford and all his buddies. He'd managed to peg them all once he got a second look at the car—Rexford, Jimmy Nolan, Allan Terhune, Robert Sizemore. These guys were the heart of the football team, and the situation had quite the makings of a scandal if they were up to no good. Given the hour and where they were, Omar didn't see how it could be otherwise.

Rexford did the bulk of the talking.

"He's on the other side of the fence."

Terhune: "John, no."

Rexford: "Nobody will miss him. He's a fucking yard dog."

Sizemore: "Don't be a pussy, Allan."

Nolan: "I'll get him."

Omar leaned into Gabe and whispered in his ear. "Go get somebody."

"Who?"

"Sakota. LaMer. They're both down there. Just go."

Gabe quietly shuffled backward to the ditch, while Omar flattened himself on the ground, hidden by weeds. Unease spread through him like an advancing tide. He felt like he wanted to retch.

Rexford retreated to the car and popped the trunk. He reached in and fished out four aluminum cans, which he passed around.

"A little liquid courage, fellas."

Omar hunkered down. Truth was, he'd begun to feel the same kind of creeping fear Gabe must have sensed. He didn't have much truck with these boys. He didn't play football—hated everything about it, in fact, and had clear back to eighth grade when the coach looked at him and had visions of a star flanker—and that was these guys' specialty. Rexford, Terhune, and Nolan were on the basketball team with Omar, but it was a different dynamic there. Omar was the unquestioned star of the team and had been elevated to a status where he rated his own story line. He'd developed the sense that the town's interest in him—indeed, his teammates' interest—lay only in whether he could deliver a state championship. If he did, he belonged. If he didn't, he could go off to LA and never be heard from again, for all they cared.

Terhune was talking again. "It's somebody's pet, man."

"So what?" Rexford said.

Asshole, Omar threw in silently.

"Stuff is getting insane. My dad said there was a fight downtown about the stupid Chihuahua."

"You really are a pussy, Allan." Sizemore, again.

"I'm not doing this."

"Gimme a *P*. Gimme a *U*. Gimme an *S*—"

Terhune made like he was walking away, and he came right toward Omar there in the weeds. At the moment Omar decided he'd have to make his presence known, a pair of headlights swept over the other boys from the side. They dropped their beers.

"Let's get out of here," Nolan said.

Rexford grabbed him by the arm. "Relax. We haven't done anything."

Officer Sakota stopped the cruiser and climbed out. Omar craned his neck to his left and found Gabe sitting in the front seat of the police car.

"What are you boys doing?" Sakota said. He cast his flashlight beam on each of their faces.

"Nothing, Officer," Rexford said.

Sakota pivoted the beam downward, picking up a glint off one of the beer cans. "You been drinking?"

"No, sir."

"Looks like you have."

"Those aren't ours, Officer," Nolan tossed in. "Lots of people drink here, though."

"I see. So you're not up to anything?"

"No, sir," Terhune said.

"So you won't mind moving along, will you?"

"No, sir," they all said.

Omar kept his face down.

"OK, move along," Sakota said. "Don't let me find you out here again."

"Yes, sir."

Sakota ducked back into the cruiser and made a three-point turnaround, then waited for the other boys to get back in the Mustang and clear out. Once the lights and the noise receded and blackness fell again on Omar, he pushed himself up and ran like hell back toward downtown.

THE CHIEF

Adair was behind her desk, winnowing her e-mail, when Sakota came in.

"Hey, Phil, listen to this." She tugged her glasses down her nose until she had the right angle.

Chief Underwood: We've had a look at the dog your man fished out of the river. We dug two .22-caliber bullets out of the carcass. Looks like we have a different problem. Will advise when we know more. Please pass on our condolences to the owner.

"Somebody shot that dog, Phil."

She looked up. Sakota's face looked as if he'd swallowed sour milk.

"What?" she said.

Sakota walked closer.

"I wasn't going to say anything about it," he said.

"What?"

"I was just up by the old Zelnov place—you know, up by the irrigation canal?"

"Yeah," Adair said.

"I was making rounds through the neighborhood and Gabe Bowman comes running up, flagging me down," he said. "He said there were some kids up there looking to steal a dog."

"Who? What kids?"

"Wait a second," Sakota said.

"Where are they now?"

"Adair, wait." Sakota mopped his forehead with the back of his hand. "I went up there. They weren't doing anything. I mean, I think they were drinking, but I couldn't have cited them for anything. I just, you know, tried to throw a little scare into them and told them to clear out of there. Which they did."

"Who?" Adair said.

Sakota spat out the names.

Adair came around the desk. "So what's this Bowman kid's story? What was he doing up there?"

"He said he was just sneaking around, you know, having some fun, and he overheard these kids talking about grabbing the dog."

"He was sneaking around alone?"

"That's what he said."

"You believe that?" she asked.

Sakota shrunk a bit at the question. "Well, shit, Adair, I didn't really think about whether I believed it or not."

"Maybe he has something against these boys."

"Maybe. I don't know. Bowman's pretty well liked, from what I understand."

"You know," Adair said, "I see him running around with Omar Smothers a good little bit."

"There wasn't anybody up there but me, Bowman, and those four boys," Sakota said.

"Yeah, yeah, yeah." Adair paced the floor, looking for answers in the ceiling blocks. "I don't have a good feeling about this. What about you?"

"I'm sweating like a whore in church, Adair. You know I don't feel good about it."

She liked the answer. On the general subject of Officer Sakota and his readiness to cop to fear and unease, she remained undecided. That could be a real liability for a police officer. But it made him a good, forthright person. She'd take that, for now.

"I want to talk to that Rexford kid," she said.

Sakota shook his head as though he were trying to clear water from his ears. "No. Come on. On what basis?"

Adair had to give him that one, although she suspected it fell more in the area of concern about who Rexford's daddy was than it did her lack of probable cause.

"OK," she said. "I'll talk to Bowman."

Sakota exhaled in a short blast. "Well, good luck. He was pissed. I drove him home and he was all, 'I shouldn't have said anything. I should have minded my own business.'"

Adair sat across from Gabe Bowman in his basement. His mother and father stood in the doorway, observing. Adair ran her eyes along the walls, noting the Marvel Comics posters. In the corner, by the TV, sat three kinds of game consoles. On the other side of the room, an electric guitar stood lonely in its stand. The tools of exquisite distraction. At once, she felt all of her thirty-four years and the crushing quaintness of how she'd filled her own teenage hours with sports and visits to the public library.

She'd already gone round and round with the boy. He'd said maybe he was mistaken, maybe he only thought he heard what he'd reported to Officer Sakota. She'd coaxed him, pressed at the soft spots of his story—"Are you sure you were alone, Gabe?"— but he'd held steady. Only once had he shown some indication of where his fear might lie. "You know, those guys saw me in the car. They know who turned them in." That stung her. Dumb move by Sakota. He should have just sent Gabe on his way.

"OK," Adair said. "I'm going to let you get back to it. If you think of anything else, let me know, OK?"

"Yeah, OK," Gabe said.

The Bowmans walked her upstairs to the front door. Fred stepped outside onto the porch with her.

"What do you think?" he asked.

"I think he's scared."

"Yeah."

"I think there's probably not much more I can do than keep an eye on the Rexford kid."

"He's holding something back," Fred said. "But you have to understand. Gabe is a good kid—"

"I don't doubt that, Mr. Bowman."

"Let me finish. He's a good kid, but he's a little out of step here, and that's hard in such a small place. There were almost three thousand kids at my high school. It was impersonal, yeah, but you could find your crowd. Gabe doesn't really have a crowd. And there's this other thing."

"He's black," she said.

"Yeah. I'm not the kind of guy to hide behind that—can't change it, wouldn't want to, gotta deal with it. But I hear things. I see things. You can bet Gabe does, too."

"Sure. Of course."

"If some kid is killing dogs, I hope you can stop him. I'm just saying that it's asking too much of my son to help you. Understand?"

Adair made the loops in town, looking for Rexford and his hot new Mustang, a show of his old man's ostentatious ways if there ever was one. Grandview's leaders had made the decision long ago to outsource legal matters, and Pete Rexford had been there to pick up those nuggets at his usual rate, plus anything else he could drum up through his private practice. By Adair's reckoning, that gave him a pretty sweet deal. On most matters, Pete Rexford held the only opinion about whether he was in conflict between his public and private duties and so far, she'd observed, he'd found in his own favor.

This alignment of players put her in a particularly delicate spot now. She supposed that if additional information emerged and she could put more attention on John Rexford, she'd have to go down to Sidney and see the county attorney. In the meantime, she figured, she'd send a subtle yet unmistakable message: she was watching.

Sakota's voice broke in over the radio.

"Adair, you better come down to Clancy Park."

"What's up?"

"Somebody's beat the hell out of Alfonso."

She pulled into the dirt driveway at the Kelvig farm, backed out, and pointed the nose of the cruiser toward town. She tore out of there, pushing sixty on the back roads.

"I'll be there in a second," she said.

NORBY (SAMUEL)

Samuel and Megan were carrying Indian tacos across Main Street toward the Double Musky when Alfonso Medeiros staggered out of the shadows of Everly's Welding Service and leaned against the streetlamp.

"Holy shit," Samuel said. He handed his food to Megan and sprinted across the street to Alfonso, who'd slipped down the lamp pole and dropped his ass onto the sidewalk. Someone had pounded Alfonso's face into misshapen rawness. Both eyebrows had been split, spilling blood that stained his T-shirt. His left eye was like an eight ball, and his nose bent right at an impossible angle.

"Jesus," Samuel said. "What happened?"

"Fell down." A bloody bubble formed on the outside of Alfonso's nostril and popped.

"Bullshit." Samuel knelt and looped Alfonso's arm over his shoulder. "Come on. Let's get up. We'll get you across the street."

Samuel bent his knees sharply, then extended his legs like pistons, driving the heavier man up. He struggled with the dead weight of Alfonso, inching him across the street in haphazard lurches.

"Go tell Dea," he said to Megan, who set down the food and ran toward the taco truck on the other side of the park.

A murmuring enveloped them, and Samuel for the first time saw that some of the crowd had peeled off from the festivities down the street to check on the commotion. He spotted Steve Simic, still in sunglasses this deep into the night.

"Come on, man," Samuel said to him. "Give me a hand."

Simic handed his drink to a buddy and loped over. He slipped under Alfonso's right shoulder, and together the long-ago friends found a pace and hoofed him across the park. A few others fell in, following them.

"What happened?" Simic said between grunting breaths.

"Somebody beat the hell out of him."

"Fell down," Alfonso said.

"Nobody's going to buy that," Samuel said.

Simic looked down at his own shirt. "He's getting blood all over me."

"Just hold him. We're almost there."

Dea was out of the truck, waiting for them, her wails of "*Dios mío, Dios mío*" growing louder as they approached.

Samuel and Simic turned Alfonso around and gently sat him on the steps leading into the truck. His head seesawed on his neck, and Dea let out a cry. "*Querido Dios en el cielo, mi marido.*"

Samuel looked at Megan. "You have your cell?"

"Yes."

"Call the cops."

"They're coming," said somebody in the pack of onlookers.

"Alfonso," Samuel said. "What happened?"

"Fell down."

Dea dabbed at his brow with a towel that came back bloody. In the better light, Samuel found welts all along Alfonso's jawline.

"Don't give me that. What happened?"

"Fell down."

Dea dropped her head onto her husband's shoulder, sobbing.

Samuel looked up at Megan, as if he could find an answer there.

• • •

Officer Sakota arrived first, and after staggering around a bit and letting loose with "oh, shit, man," he put out the radio call for Chief Underwood and the ambulance crew, which would have to come in from Sidney.

Dea's quick work had her man less bloody, at least, but the sweeping away of the plasma brought the full extent of his injuries to greater light. Samuel's amateur assessment had Alfonso fitted for plenty of stitches and a heroic dose of morphine to keep the pain at bay.

"Joe, you out there?" Sakota said into his radio.

Feedback shot through Sakota's speaker. "Yeah."

"You gonna come down here and take a look?"

Chief Underwood's voice broke in. "Hold your position, Joe. I'm almost there. Keep an eye on things around the concert, OK?"

"Roger that."

Seconds later, the lights on Chief Underwood's cruiser sprinkled the park in alternating surges of blue and red. Alfonso had lain down in the grass outside the truck while Dea beat back the insurgent blood. Sakota knelt beside Alfonso and held his hand as he waited for the chief to get there.

"Ambulance is on the way, Adair," Sakota said.

Underwood also went to bended knee beside Alfonso and took hold of his arm. "Who did this to you?"

"He's not going to say, Chief," Samuel said.

"Come on now, Alfonso."

"Fell down."

"Baby, please." Dea looked at her man, tears streaking her cheeks.

Alfonso looked up at her, his features jumbled and mournful. "Fell down."

Adair rocketed to her feet. "What is with this fucking town?"

• • •

237

They huddled around Alfonso and his crying wife for fifteen minutes or so, waiting for the Sidney ambulance. When it at last arrived, Sakota waved the driver onto the grass so the technicians could get at Alfonso more easily. While the crew bundled Alfonso up and put him on a stretcher, Dea micromanaging the entire affair, Samuel broke off from the group and found Chief Underwood.

"Tough night, I guess," he said.

"Yeah."

"I'm Sam's son."

Chief Underwood shook his hand. "How's your dad doing?"

"OK, I guess. Sleeping, Mom says."

"Good. Glad to hear it."

"Anyway, I just wanted to introduce myself," he said. "I found Alfonso over by Tut Everly's place. Be happy to talk to you for your report, if you need me."

"Not going to be much of a report if he's not talking."

"I guess not."

She turned to him. "You think he fell down?"

Samuel blurted a laugh, which he quickly smothered out of respect for the gravity of the situation. "I was born at night. But not this night."

By the time the chaos cleared and folks migrated back to the downtown scene, Megan looked as though she'd had enough many times over. She said she'd just as soon go home, and Samuel offered to walk her the three blocks before cutting across town to his folks' place.

"You going to be around tomorrow?" he asked.

"Yeah. I might hang close to the house, though. Not sure I can take more partying."

"No party," Samuel said. "Just a pancake breakfast and the Raleigh Ridgeley thing. I guess I'm in charge of cleanup now."

"When are you heading back?"

"Monday night. I'll stay in Billings, then fly out Tuesday morning."

"Well," she said. "No pancakes for me. And definitely no Raleigh Ridgeley. Read him in college. That guy lives in his own asshole."

Samuel snickered. "My mom loves his stuff."

She did an exaggerated eye roll. "Whatever. But listen, I'd like to hang out a bit more. Tomorrow afternoon?"

"That'd be great."

She reached for him, a hug in the offing. Samuel let himself relax into her, and he breathed in the scent of so many long-ago summers.

The thump from the band downtown found Samuel's ears as he zigzagged through the neighborhood between Megan's house and his parents', marking time and memory by matching houses with occupants, past or present. He'd surprised himself the first night in town, as he tried to remember the names of everybody who'd graduated in his class. Such a small group, it shouldn't have been difficult, but Samuel couldn't do it. He finally had to consult an old yearbook to put the names together. He'd lingered over Rich Buckner's photo, the consommé of what might have been and what came to be almost too much to contemplate.

Now, his phone buzzed, and with it another piece of his past came calling.

When u coming back?

He checked the time. 12:18, 11:18 back in California. Not too early for Derek to be drunk texting.

Not for a few days.

Hurry back. I miss u.

Revulsion and despair collided in Samuel's gut. At once, he wanted Derek again, and then in the next beat he didn't want anything more to do with him. For preservation's sake, he stuck with the second blush.

Don't fuck with me.

I miss my Norby.

Norby's dead.

Now the phone rang.

"What?"

"Oh, it's you," Derek said. Samuel listened closely. He didn't detect any slurring.

"Of course it is."

"You said Norby's dead."

"Figure of speech."

"Oh, OK."

"What do you want, Derek?"

"I want you to come home so we can talk."

Two women, maybe early twenties, came veering up the sidewalk at Samuel. He nodded and moved aside so they could pass. Their alcohol-tinged air hung like a cloud as he pushed on.

"Nothing to talk about."

"Don't be mean," Derek said.

"Don't be manipulative."

"Don't you want me?"

Samuel brought himself to a dead stop on the sidewalk. Now there was a question worth pondering completely. And, as it turned out, it was a remarkably quick job.

"No, I don't."

"But why, Norby?"

"Samuel."

"Who?"

"Never mind. Just shut up, OK?"

"Don't be mean."

Samuel ran a hand across his face, forehead to chin. That gave him just enough time to let his impulses settle and the right words queue up on his tongue.

"I don't expect you to understand it, Derek, and I couldn't explain it in a million years. So let's just be honest, OK?"

"OK."

"I don't want you. In fact, I want you to fuck permanently off. Clear enough?" He pulled the phone from his ear and ended the call.

Nobody had left the porch light on. Samuel fumbled with his keys before getting the right one in the lock.

The door let out a moan as he stepped through, and he immediately hit a soft spot in the floor, the sharp creaking of the underlying wood cutting through the silence. He rued another bit of memory lost. He used to know where all the noisy steps were and could dance around them like a teenage ballroom swinger. Now, every step betrayed his position.

"Have fun?" His father's voice found him from the kitchen.

"Yeah." At once, he felt foolish for going with the pat answer rather than the honest one. "What are you doing awake? Where's Mom?"

"Your mother is not here." Sam fingered the rim of a half-full cocktail glass.

"Where is she?"

"I don't know." His father took a slug of whiskey. "I was hoping she was with you."

"No. She's not." Samuel shrugged and tried to pass it off with nonchalance. A flailing attempt, he figured. This wasn't like her.

Sam threw back the remainder of the booze.

"Well, that's curious, isn't it?"

• • •

The New York Times, *Saturday, August 1, 2015*

If a single self-proffered theme emerged during Grandview's Jamboree weekend, it was the one struck by Mr. Swarthbeck: this is a special place, different from and better than the average small towns that dot this corner of Montana.

On the surface, this might be viewed as a debatable claim. Once you get east of Billings, Montana is mostly empty space, and the towns that do exist are not unlike Grandview. The demographics are older and white, most cling to some central identity, and most are led by people who wonder where the next generation of leaders will come from. Most, too, are suffering from a steady loss of population as Montanans, much like their contemporaries in the country at large, migrate toward urban centers. What separates Grandview, and its larger neighbor Sidney, is the proximity to oil. Thus, the town is growing, and in ways that put traditional community values and the uncomfortable aspects of the present at odds.

"I couldn't wait to get away from here," says the town's only famous son, novelist Raleigh Ridgeley, who sets much of his award-winning fiction in the part of the state known as the Big Empty. "As a young person, I didn't see what a place like this held for me, or someone who saw the world the way I was beginning to."

Now, Ridgeley returns every year for Jamboree, where he holds a discussion of his books and the larger themes of his fiction called, informally, The Raleigh Ridgeley Book Club. The author, 53, splits his time between houses in Billings and Scottsdale, Ariz.

"You have to understand the people. These folks come from ancestors who looked at this vast, empty, brutal landscape and saw opportunity," he says. "That's not an easy vision now, even with the oil, so you can imagine what it was then. That kind of relationship with the land toughens you up in ways that are hard to explain. You learn to take a punch. You learn to find optimism you didn't know you had."

SUNDAY

PATRICIA

Once Patricia settled her mind on the question of what she wanted, she slipped into the night-black bedroom and found her husband's snoozing, swaddled head, and she kissed him on the cheek and she said, "I've never stopped loving you." He stirred a bit, and she swept back his surrendering hair to calm him.

She might have stayed at his side if not for the subsequent realization of why. That's what sent her into the night to ensure that there would be no further misunderstandings.

Now, she sat alone on a stool at the Top Hat in Sidney, draining a beer that she'd have never chosen were she here with friends or with Sam, trying to sort out in her own head the explanation that she figured she would be compelled to offer. The reasons made sense to her—for the first time, it all made sense from the outside and the inside—and yet she could fixate on no system of language for communicating it to someone else, least of all to Raleigh.

Yes, she loved his work. Yes, she envied his life. Yes, she wondered. Yes, she fantasized. God, yes, she fantasized. No, she did not want to grab his proffered hand and take a leap with him, tempting as that might have been in the moment he suggested it. Yes, she still loved Sam. God, yes, she loved him.

She finished the last of her drink and sized up the room. She figured she was the oldest here by ten years, at least, and one of only three women. The bartender asked if she wanted another, and she said, "No, thank you, I have somewhere else to be." She set a ten on the bar and made for the door.

The interior pep talk continued in the car on the way to Raleigh's motel, and she wondered now if she were trying to convince herself rather than him. She didn't think so. She just wanted to be precise, so that her clarity could also be his once she'd unpacked it. Raleigh had been kind and attentive, and that had gone a long way toward opening her lonely heart. She didn't want to lose the friendship or the anticipation of the many Jamborees to come, the many books to come, all of which she would cherish.

She pulled into the Lazy Z parking lot and counted the doors to number eight. He would be impressed that she'd remembered that tossed-off bit of information from two days ago, given all that had happened in the hours since.

The lights were off. She considered stepping back into the car and going home and leaving this errand behind. And then she found a reserve of gumption and stepped forward.

Two crisp raps on the door set off audible motion on the other side. She smiled as she pictured Raleigh, fumbling about in his underwear and looking for his glasses, his horseshoe of hair whipping this way and that.

The curtains peeled back a bit from the window, then fell back into place.

The door opened far enough for Raleigh's bewildered head to peek out.

"Patricia."

She ran her hands down her hips, as if she could wipe away the oddity of the hour or the audacity of her reason for being there. "Hi, Raleigh."

"What—"

"I really need to talk to you. I know this is strange. But it can't—"

"What are you doing here?"

Patricia might have answered, until an arm coiled around his midsection and a voice broke into the clear. "Baby, come back to bed." Patricia leaned her head in and recognized the server from the coffee shop.

Raleigh looked at Patricia, and his color emptied out.

"Oh," she said.

"Wait a minute."

"No. I'm going to go."

"Wait."

"I can't."

In her shame, Patricia drove first for the eastern hills, crossing the river, and stretching the run into barren North Dakota, until sensibility returned to her and she realized she had nowhere to go out there, and that she would have to bury her embarrassment—and, yes, her anger—somewhere between here and home. She turned around on an oil-well access road and drove west toward the Sidney lights, and then, at last, north toward Grandview.

As she passed the Lazy Z, she wanted to avert her eyes but couldn't help herself. Number eight was lit up, her interruption of Raleigh's evening continuing even as she wished she could just teleport back to the other side of midnight and stay by Sam's side.

She pressed on. She felt foolish. Stupid. What did she care, anyway? Had she not gone to tell him that the notion of a future together was a dead end?

Well, yes, she told herself, that much was true. Also true: he'd bagged the first piece of ass he could after she'd left him to attend to Sam. All those pretty words, and they meant nothing.

She whipped the car to the side of the highway and pulled her phone from her purse.

A text message from Samuel: *Where are you?*

Be back soon, she texted back.

She scared up the number of the Lazy Z and placed the call. An automated answering service let her punch through to Raleigh's room.

"Hello?"

"I'm sorry," she said. "I shouldn't have come."

"Where are you?"

"You are an asshole."

"What?" She sensed exasperation from him, and that sent her emotions tumbling again, to sorrow and rage and shame, at once.

"I'm sorry. It's not your fault. But you are. You're a fucking asshole." The words came out clipped and heavy, each one a hammer. "That girl, she's what, thirteen—"

"Twenty-three."

"I'm not being literal, you idiot."

"Come back," he said. "Come back and we'll talk."

"No."

"Please."

"I can't."

She hung up.

She then set the phone in her purse, dropped her face into her hands, and allowed herself to cry. She lifted her head and looked at the clock, glowing in the silent dark. She would give herself two minutes, and then she would dab her face and put drops in her eyes, and then she would go home and she would be done with this forever.

That's what she would do. Life is about plans. She had one. Simple as that. Just do it.

Her head dropped, and she let herself go.

SAM

When at last Sam heard the car idle and then settle in the driveway, he stood from the kitchen table and made his way to the foyer. He wanted to be the first person Patricia saw. She would have to deal with him now, in the moment, not later, on her own terms. The hell with his drumming head and his pain. He would do this now and do it right.

She came silently up the outside stairs, her head down, and he thrilled when she jumped back upon seeing him there on the other side of the glass, like some bandaged-up Bela Lugosi. *Good evening.*

Samuel had rooted her out by sending a text message. "Dad, she said she'll be back soon," he'd said, and that was all fine and dandy, but where had she gone and why? He could think of no good place and no good reason, and he'd told his son to go ahead and turn in, that nothing and no one would be served by a mass interrogation. He'd said the same to Denise when she came upstairs for a glass of water. "Just go back to sleep, baby. We'll see you in the morning."

Patricia, her senses gathered about her, opened the door. "You're awake," she said.

"I realized I was alone."

"I stepped out for a bit."

"I'd like to know why."

"It doesn't matter," she said. She tried to move past him, but he stood, immobile.

"It does. To me, it does," he said.

She lowered her head, then brought it up again. He thought she'd been crying. She looked as though she might start again.

"Fine," she said. "Let's go in the bedroom."

As she unburdened herself, he found no satisfaction in having predicted all of it. While the minutes she was gone had piled up, he'd sat silently in the kitchen, even after Samuel came to keep him company, and he'd slowly unfurled ever more scurrilous reasons that she should be absent. The worst and most likely was that she'd had a rendezvous with Raleigh. Sam knew things—more than he let on, and more than she seemed to give him credit for knowing.

"So you love him, then," he said.

"No. No. I love you."

"Which is why you were with him."

She reached for his hand, and he pulled it away from her.

"I wasn't with him. I went to him, to tell him something."

"What?"

"That I love you, and that I couldn't be with him."

Sam knew well the feeling of being hollowed out. Losing Big Herschel just when he'd pretty much convinced himself his father would live forever—that was hard. Losing his own son by degrees, by cuts and nicks and blemishes and misunderstandings—that was brutal. Having no way to reach his brother's shore—that was tragic. But this was something else, a swamping emptiness that carved him up from the inside.

"So you thought about it," he said.

She again reached for him, and again he denied her. "Sam, we've been at this too long for me to try to sell you something that isn't the truth. Yes, I thought about it. Don't you get that? Haven't you ever thought about it? It's been thirty-two years. Isn't it just, I don't know, natural?"

"I have never thought about it," he said, defiant, and he knew it was a lie, but the anger was coming out faster than he could process it now, sliding sideways, reckless. He wanted to say something that hurt.

She'd been crying since they sat down on the bed. Weeping. This was a night for sorrow. And now, Sam felt his own eyes spill. He wiped the leavings away.

"Have you kissed him?"

He watched her intently, and she matched him. "Yes."

"You're a slut." He was reaching wildly now, he knew, for the extremities of what he could say that would hurt her the most, and he dove toward those.

She bit her lip. "If that makes you feel better."

"How many times?"

"Twice."

Sam felt his air leave him. "I wish I were dead."

"I'm sorry."

"I don't love you anymore," he said, and the dagger effect he'd intended for her buried itself in him instead. Behind it, anger cascaded in again, a river looking for a sea to empty its load.

"I'm sorry."

"I don't. I don't want you in this room. Get out."

He lay back on the bed and turned until his back was to her. The inside of his skull felt as though his brain were being wrung like a dishrag. He closed his eyes, and he listened, and he offered nothing but abject silence until she got up, gathered her nightclothes, and left the room, latching the door behind her. He opened his eyes again and watched his own fuzzy shadow cast against the wall in front of him, and listened as the blades of the ceiling fan cut away at the suffocating air.

SAMUEL

Samuel lay in bed and took in every syllable of the awfulness playing out a door over. More than once, he thought he ought to retrieve his earbuds and cue up some music on his phone, and every time he squelched that plan in favor of continuing to eavesdrop. He didn't want to know any of this, and yet he figured not knowing would be worse.

His phone buzzed. He checked it. Denise, downstairs.

Can you believe this bullshit?

No, he wrote back.

We're leaving in the morning. Shame on Mom.

Nobody is coating themselves in glory tonight.

You should go, too. Maybe you had the right idea.

No. I'm staying. It will look better in the morning.

Suit yourself.

He heard the door open and then close. Footfalls across the hardwood. The creaking of the couch as his mother settled in.

He turned on his light and went to the closet, rooting through the boxed-up remainders of the life he'd once had here, until he found the stack of blankets she always stored for the winter nights that left his room, facing north, so much colder than the rest of the house. He chose a thin one, a lightly woven wool, and he carried it into the living room and lay it across her.

"Thank you," she whispered, and she reached across the distance. He put his hand out and grasped hers.

"It's going to be OK," he said.

"Promise?" She said it with a hopeful lilt.

"It's going to be OK. I love you. Good night."

MAMA

When her beginning and her end collided in the same moment, Blanche Kelvig couldn't have imagined where she would be. Not with Big Herschel on the farm, raising up two boys they loved—one who made them proud, and one who seemed to live for confounding them. She was not at the center of her weekly knitting social or helping Sam with his mathematics or fetching Henrik from some bit of trouble.

No, she opened her windows and she looked out across an expanse of McKenzie County bottomland, lush and radiant and clear and bright on a late July day. She pegged the calendar by the height of the corn, she twirled in the gingham dress her mother sewed for her by hand, and she looked out again to see her father coming up the lane, for once his day done before the sun went down. The smell of boiled ham and potato dumplings rode on the air currents of the farmhouse, finding her nose, and she raced downstairs to see Pap and Mommy, and to set the table with softened butter and maple syrup, just the way Pap liked.

They all sat down together—Pap and Mommy and John Henry and Blanche and Benjamin—and they said grace, to thank the good Lord for his wisdom and generosity and the blessing he offered that they might have this moment. Peace, happiness, and love—every bit of love that had ever come her way—settled on Blanche, and then the roof of the farmhouse rocketed skyward, blown to pieces that evaporated into the blue sky, and she was not afraid. She ascended from where she sat, riding on a cloud, and she was not afraid. She rose until she could see nothing except the boundless wonder of infinity, and she was not afraid.

And when Big Herschel reached out, clasped her hand, and said, "Walk with me, won't you, my love? I have someone you'll want to meet," Blanche mouthed her final words:

"Oh, wow. Wow. Wow. Wow."

SAM

The Kelvigs huddled in a semicircle under the relentless fluorescents. The early-morning phone call from the hospital had roused an uneasy house, and though their alliances were frayed, they made the trip together in the predawn mist. Now, in a hospital foyer flickering like a dream, Randy sat in a plastic chair and held Chase, while Randall Junior's sleeping head slumped against his father's shoulder. Samuel and Denise and Sam and Patricia looked at the letter Sam held, the one the nurses had found under the dead hands of his mother. Sam read aloud while the others followed along.

> *In the event of my death . . .*
> *I'm too old and too tired to be anything but direct. This is what I want.*
> *I want to be cremated and my ashes spread in the places I loved. That's the farm where Herschel and I raised you boys, and the river bottoms in North Dakota where I played in my young days. You know the places. I've shown them to you many times before. I want no services or memorials. You know I was here, and that's enough.*

I want the house razed and the farm sold or otherwise disposed of. Get what you want out of the house and let it go. I know you will. Let the land go, the mineral rights, too, and be done with it. It's just soil and trees, and it's been divisive for too long. Get rid of it, and go on with your lives. This is what I want.

Forgive your brother. Maybe you can't forget it, and maybe you shouldn't, but there's nothing you can feel about him that will make things worse for him than they already are. The best thing you can do is remove some of his burden. Do it, please. For me, if not for yourself.

Accept your son. Completely, everything he is. If you have a hardness in your heart because of what you think the good book says, then I have failed you. The older I got, the more I believed in God, and the more I believed that what I could know of Him from words on the page was a mystery beyond my comprehension. The mystery and the beauty are all that count, anyway. This is your boy, your flesh and blood. Love him. This is what I want. It's what God wants, too, or my life has been squandered on believing.

I have seen what is coming for me. I have been wishing for it for years now, and I believe Providence and I are on the same page now. I do not fear death. I welcome it.

You've been a good son, you've turned into a fine man, and if your life is all I accomplished with mine, I've done a very good thing, indeed.

I'll see you again.

Love,
Your Mama

Wet eyes and dry mouths beheld the moment. Sam folded the letter, taking care to use the creases his mother had already made, and he tucked it into his shirt pocket.

He looked at his son, his daughter, and his wife, with love and anger and hurt and desire and hopelessness percolating in his gut.

"Well," he said, "that's that."

THE CHIEF

Sleep never came for Adair Underwood.

She finished her evening in the early-morning hours by handing out her deputies' pay packets and thanking them for their service. "There'll be jobs for all of you in a year, if you want an encore," she'd told them, and she found it curious that she received only noncommittal shrugs right down the line.

She made it back to her trailer just after three in the morning and had a staring contest with the digital clock. She remembered the words of Captain Fuquay from her first year in the department: "A tired cop is a compromised cop. Compromised in judgment. Compromised in readiness. Compromised in usefulness." She didn't figure she could make a living second-guessing someone with Fuquay's credentials, but it still left her stumped: What can you do about it if you've already fallen into the tired trap?

Judgment? *That's debatable,* she thought. It probably wasn't her wisest move ever to track down and follow the Rexford kid the night before. After a while, she hadn't even made a secret of it. She saw him coming out of the Country Basket and tipped her hat to him. Later, up on Telegraph Hill, he'd slowed down to a few miles per hour below the speed limit, baiting her. She just tailed him to the Frandsen ranch, where he executed a perfect three-point turn-around in the access road and went back to town.

Readiness? She sure as hell hadn't been ready for what happened to Alfonso Medeiros, nor for his seeming nonchalance about what had brought him to such a sorry state of affairs. She also didn't much like what she was thinking. She couldn't forget Sakota's face, the utter revulsion at what he'd seen. Sam's son, too. A couple of the deputies-for-hire had walked down, and they, too, registered at least some physical reaction to the beating Alfonso had taken. These were hardened men, from the big city. But LaMer, after Alfonso had gone to the hospital, when she'd finally caught up with her deputy and filled him in? Joe had nodded impassively and said, "Seems like Alfonso's always getting himself into some trouble."

Usefulness? Adair was beginning to wonder. By her count, she had, at minimum, a kid who might or might not be killing dogs, a mayor who might or might not be undermining her at every juncture, and a deputy whose alliance might or might not be with her—and with whom she might or might not be infatuated. And she was nowhere near being able to put any of those problems, or herself, to bed.

And now she could hear Fuquay's voice in her ear again. "Nice work, Underwood. Tell me, are you a natural-born fuckup, or did you take a class?"

Around five, she gave up on a notion so quaint as rest and went into the kitchen, hauling out cookie sheets and all the makings of some homemade chocolate chip cookies, save for the chips themselves, which she ended up fetching from the Country Basket while wearing a pair of gym shorts and last summer's ratty flip-flops. "No Twinkies?" Berry Fagan asked her, and she rewarded his tepid joke with a middle finger that sent him rolling off in peals of laughter. Crossing the parking lot to her cruiser, she waved at Sam

Kelvig, who passed by on Main Street with a full car. As she wondered what he was up to at this hour, she figured she might as well swing some breakfast by the jail for his brother. *Hell of a weekend,* she thought. *The people I was gung ho to arrest got turned out, and this poor bastard Henrik looks like he'll be in there awhile.*

She reversed course and headed back into the store to heat up a couple of breakfast sandwiches. Berry, all three hundred freckled pounds of him, wandered back from the stockroom and said, "Hey, Adair, what do you call a cop who jacks off too much?"

The microwave ding signaled her to remove one sandwich and put another in.

"I don't know, but I'm sure you're gonna tell me."

"Pulled pork," Fagan said. "Get it?"

Adair closed her eyes and silently begged for the microwave to finish its business.

"Adair, do you get it?"

Ding.

She scooped the sandwich out and put a fiver on the countertop for Berry. "I get it," she said. "I'll be back later to arrest you for crimes against humor."

Berry horse-wheezed out a laugh. "Good one."

"I'm serious, Berry. Quit for your own sake."

At the station, when she saw the flash of white higher on the wall than any such thing should be, she knew, certain as she stood there. She didn't need to see the bedsheet that had been fashioned into a rope or Henrik's purpling face or lolled-out tongue or the puddle below his stocking feet where he'd wet himself in his convulsions.

The brown paper bag hit the floor, and Adair broke for her office down the hall on a dead run so she could get her key and bring Sam's brother down. Every movement was frantic and disjointed, every thought sharpened for collision with the next one, every panicked impulse immediately offset by an admonition deep within her to slow down and proceed with deliberation.

Once inside her own door, she forced herself to sit until her breathing leveled out. There was nothing she could do for Henrik now that a few minutes would compromise. At last, she tested her breath and tested her voice, and then she placed the calls to the emergency response team and the county coroner.

And as she did so, as she gave the rote, even-keeled account of where she was and what she'd seen, all Adair could think about was the oven back at her trailer, set at 350 degrees and waiting for her to come home.

A tired cop is an unfocused cop.

THE MAYOR

Swarthbeck sat at the Kelvigs' kitchen table and took in the faces twisted in pain. He met every one of them by looking them in the eye. That's damn hard to do when there's a world of hurt dropping down onto things, but it's the respectful approach. He'd come here, to their home, to give them the bad news about Henrik, and he intended to honor their pain.

"Hung himself?" Sam said for the second time, as if the question might get a more palatable answer if he gave it another whirl. Nobody else was doing much talking. Junior was looking down at his laced hands. Patricia, strangely distant it seemed to Swarthbeck, sobbed into a napkin. The girl, Denise, and her family hung back a bit.

"Yeah, Sammy. I'm really sorry."

Swarthbeck really was sorry, and not just because he was here piling more bad news on a family that had plenty of it already. He hadn't gotten the word about Blanche before arriving at the Kelvig house, so when he'd opened things by saying, "Sorry I'm coming by so early on a Sunday," Sam had blurted out, "We just got back ourselves. Mama died." That had made Swarthbeck's subsequent words all the more difficult to say.

That's grief sometimes, Swarthbeck thought to himself as he gave Sam a pursed-lip smile. It doesn't stop at kicking in your door. It'll kick in your teeth, too, just for good measure.

"Do they know when it happened?" Sam asked.

"Not yet. Coroner's on it. He was a little cheesed off, truth be told. Said Henrik should have been in county lockup, which is probably true. But hell, it was the weekend. Adair figured she could just move him Monday when he got arraigned. Can't blame her for that."

"No, of course not." The words dragged out of Sam in a diffused way, like maybe he hadn't even heard what Swarthbeck had said. Understandable, the mayor supposed.

"And listen, Sammy, you all stay up here and take care of each other," Swarthbeck said, unable to keep himself from fixating on Sam's bandaged head. "We've got two things left, a breakfast and this Ridgeley thing. We can get people to cover for you. Hell, Eldrick Sloane's never read a book in his life, but he can set out some folding chairs in the park for Raleigh."

Sam's boy looked up. "I'll help out at the breakfast."

"I'll be at the book club," Sam said.

Patricia started to speak. "No—" Sam cut her off with a look drenched in a kind of nastiness that caused even Swarthbeck to move his chair back a few inches.

"Sammy," he said, "maybe she ought to do it, considering—"

Sam short-circuited him, too. "She's not going to be there."

Swarthbeck figured he'd seen enough of this, and figured the town had seen enough, too. "You're not going to be there, either," the mayor told Sam. "You've got plenty of work right in this house, looks like to me. You got that?"

Sam chewed hard on the inside of his cheek and said nothing.

"You got that, Sammy?"

"Yeah," Sam said at last, too mocking by half. "I got that."

• • •

It was a curious scene, one that gave Swarthbeck plenty to pon-der as he drove back to Chief Underwood's office to do what he'd already had on his agenda before the coroner called and changed his plans. He'd come loaded for bear on his first pass through the office, ready to sit her ass down and deliver the facts of Grandview life if she fought him about going out to see Sam and his family. Other than showing mild surprise that he knew about Henrik—and he cleared that right up by saying Coroner Keith Goodnight wouldn't piss in Grandview without mayoral permission—Adair had been accepting of his presence and his offer to break the news to the Kelvigs. That bought her a reprieve, but not a pardon.

Now, he strode into her office and found her there in full uni-form, ready to get back on the job. He closed the door behind him.

"I thought you weren't working today," he said.

"Henrik Kelvig kind of changed my plans. Figure I better be around."

"Good idea." Swarthbeck poured himself into the chair oppo-site her.

"How's Sam holding up?" she asked.

"He's tough. You know his mom died, too?"

"That's what Goodnight said."

Swarthbeck pitched himself forward and put his hands on Adair's desk.

"I didn't come for the small talk," he said.

"I didn't expect so."

"What are you doing, Adair?"

"Talking to you."

His hands still clasped, Swarthbeck brought his forefingers to a steeple and pointed them at her. "Sassing me is not going to work."

"I thought I was being funny. Tell me your issue."

The mayor never broke his gaze. "Why are you harassing a teenage boy?"

"Excuse me?"

"John Rexford. You know what I'm talking about."

He watched her fingers as she shuffled some papers on her desk. A little quiver to them. Not much, but enough.

"Well?" he said.

"If you know about that, then you must also know what we heard about him."

"You mean what some kid who was skulking around town last night said?"

Adair cleared her throat. "Yes."

"That's not exactly evidence, is it?"

"No."

"And you're not exactly Sherlock Fucking Holmes, are you?"

Her voice quavered. "You don't have to curse at me, John."

He slapped his hand on her desk, and the sound of it jarred her. "Oh, believe me, I'm exercising great fucking control here, Miss Underwood. This is a gross misuse of your duty, Chief." She winced and he was glad, because he intended to mock her. "We hired you to run a little police department in a little town, not Scotland Fucking Yard. You harassed the son of this city's lead attorney. Do you think that was wise?"

"I think—"

"That's not a question that needs an answer. Henrik's dead because you couldn't be bothered to take him to county—"

"Wait a minute. You told me yesterday—"

"Shut up, Adair. Just shut your goddamn mouth. You're still in your probation period, aren't you? One hundred and twenty days. Do you think I'd have any trouble at all getting the votes on the town council to shit-can your ass tomorrow? Do you? You might as well have killed Sam Kelvig's brother. Which way do you think he's going to vote, if it comes to that?"

Tears made their way down the foothills of Adair's nose. She said nothing.

"You better decide what kind of police chief you want to be, Adair. Things can get very uncomfortable for you here very quickly."

He stood and looked her over, and she seemed to shrink in his presence. He considered whether he'd overplayed it a bit. Regardless, he'd succeeded in bringing her to silence, and experience told him that would lead to compliance. He headed for the door.

"John?"

He grasped the doorknob. "Yes?"

"Are you threatening me?"

He let go and turned to face her.

"It doesn't matter. The question you should be asking is whether I have to. Have a good shift, Adair. It's almost over now."

OMAR

Omar Smothers fidgeted in the pew, fixing his attention on the missionary donation cards, the tithing envelopes, the spines and right-angled corners of the hymnals, and the dust on the pencil holders. As he used a fingernail to gouge off a piece of hardened eraser, his mother reached over and set her hand on his, and he withdrew it.

He closed his eyes tight and then opened them again, and he tried to pick up the thread of the Reverend Franklin's sermon, something about love and forgiveness, topics number two and three on the pastoral hit parade, right behind sin. The genial old pastor's words found his ears again and then morphed into meaninglessness, and Omar was back inside his own head, pulling up the carpet and looking under it.

He hated this church. Well, not this church so much as church itself, but this was the only one he'd known. He hated the sitting still during the sermon when he'd rather be home shooting hoops or playing *Call of Duty* with Gabe. He hated the old guys who slapped him on the back and talked to him about nothing but basketball, as if he was the vessel for the dreams they'd once had for themselves. He hated the eyes that followed him for just a little too long. He hated the whispers that were a little too loud.

His mom nestled closer to him and slipped an arm around his shoulders. She seemed to carry none of his burdens, and to boot she had been in a fine mood this morning, at least until the news of Mr. Kelvig's losses had reached them. She'd been thrilled to see him come home at a sensible hour, and not a whiff of alcohol on him. She'd asked him to sit with her on the couch—"We'll watch anything you want," she'd said—but he'd said he was tired and went to bed.

Rest had not come as easily as lying.

He thought now about how he'd gone over to Gabe's afterward, to find out what the cops had said to him. He'd stopped cold in the street, seeing Chief Underwood's cruiser there, and he figured he'd better move right along. As he headed for home, he passed the Country Basket, and there John Rexford sat with his buddies on the hood of his car, eating a burrito.

"Hey, half-breed," Rexford had said. "You tell your friend Bowman we're gonna get him."

Omar had tried to play it cool.

"For what?"

"He knows."

Omar shuddered now in the pew. Damn cowardice. He'd balled up his fists last night, but there was no percentage in taking on Rexford there, with his three friends at the ready. He'd had to slink home and pretend to sleep, all the while piling up his resentments in neat little stacks.

The Reverend Franklin droned on. Omar looked left, across his mother's lap, to the emptiness of the pew. Mr. Kelvig and his family hadn't shown up, the first Sunday in forever that they'd been absent—and certainly the first Jamboree Sunday that they'd missed. "I hope he's all right," Omar's mother had said. "The poor man, losing his mother and his brother today. We'll have to take them some food." The unoccupied space left an abscess in the church, and everyone had moved away from it.

Omar went back to playing with the pencil, and his mother reached out again.

"What's wrong?" she whispered.

"Nothing."

When at last the Reverend Franklin let the air out of the sanctuary, with a call for peacefulness and contemplation, Omar was up and out of the pew.

"Honey, don't you want to go to the breakfast?" his mother called after him.

"I'm not hungry."

"Where are you going in such a hurry?"

"I have to go see Gabe." The first of his lies floated to the surface; there'd been many since. "We're going to go through his tackle box and get set up for tomorrow."

"Well, come by the store for lunch, anyway."

"I will."

Omar pushed and squeezed his way through the narthex, past well-wishers and wistful old men. Once clear to the street outside, he turned south and sprinted full-on toward his friend's house, his questions fairly spilling from him. What had the cops said? What about his parents? Was he in trouble? Did he tell Chief Underwood that Omar was there, too?

He zigzagged through alleyways and backyards, paved streets and sidewalks, four blocks of sprinting harder than he ever had on a basketball court, his lungs engulfed like wet sponges, until at last he pulled up at Gabe's place and saw his friend's father kneeling in a flower bed. The strangeness of the scene took a second to register with Omar. The boxy off-white house, one he'd seen nearly every day and pretty as could be with a manicured lawn and a newly built wooden porch, sat before him, and spray-painted on the front of it, in rising, sloppy, red letters were the words "WE WILL GET YOU."

Gabe's father dabbed at the marks with a brush of too-white paint, just beginning the job of blotting it out.

"Don't have the right color," Mr. Bowman said as Omar approached. "Will have to get it tomorrow. Maybe I'll just repaint the whole thing." He spoke with deliberation, in a flat tone—as if it were somehow disembodied—that shook Omar. Mr. Bowman, always quick with a joke and a kind word, seemed beaten and mournful.

"Can I talk to Gabe?"

"He's inside."

Omar stepped toward the door.

"Omar?"

"Yes?"

"Were you with him last night?"

Omar braced for something. He wasn't sure what. "Yes." He watched Mr. Bowman from behind, waiting for a reaction that wasn't going to come.

"Your house is plaster, isn't it?"

"Yes, sir."

"Mind it, then. It will be harder to paint over than wood."

After a grim welcome from Gabe's mother, Omar found his friend in the basement, strumming discordant notes on his guitar.

"You saw what they did to the house?" Gabe said.

"Yeah."

"Why couldn't you go get the cops if you were so interested in it?"

"I'm sorry."

"Yeah. Whatever."

"I am."

"What good does you being sorry do me?"

Omar sat down on the couch, at the far end of it from Gabe.

"I don't know," he said. "What did the cops say?"

"Nothing much."

"What did you say?"

"Less than they said."

"Come on, Gabe."

Gabe struck the guitar with a downward chop across the strings, and they screamed at the assault. Omar shrank. "The fuck you care? They didn't ask about you, if that's what you want to know. I think the chief suspects, though. She was asking if I was alone. Who else was I going to be with?"

Omar tried to patch himself back together. "I'm sorry I got you into this."

Gabe went back to picking at the strings. "I didn't even want to be there."

"I know."

"Nobody's going to mess with you. You know? Big basketball hero. This time next year, you'll be out of here. I'm gonna have to watch my ass every second."

Omar softened his voice. "Come on. This will blow over."

"You think?" Gabe's voice dropped in register, too. A sullen quality infused it. "This isn't insults in the hallway, dude. They spray-painted my house, threatening me. Do you get that?"

"Yeah, I get it."

"I don't think you do. My dad looks at me like I'm a coward. Terhune's dad is on his crew, and he can't say anything to him about what he's done. The cops won't be able to do anything about it, because they can't prove it, just like I couldn't prove they were gonna kill that dog. It's over for me here, and you made that happen. You didn't mean to, but you did."

"I'm sorry."

"I don't care. So there's that."

Omar walked down Main Street toward home. Past the Country Basket, past the hole where the mayor's office used to be, past Mr.

Kelvig's Farm and Feed, past the Sloane Hotel, which had survived another Jamboree weekend. Sadness lapped at his insides. How was it that life as he knew it three days ago seemed so much simpler than what he saw ahead of him now, with its infinite complications?

He could count on no help from Gabe tomorrow. That much was certain. Also certain was the fact that Omar had made a promise to Clarissa, and now he had even more motivation to see it through, to keep another friend safe from John Rexford's menace. The lies and deceptions—and the consequences should he be found out—were the price of doing the right thing, he figured.

Clancy Park came into view, in front of it Omar's turn toward home. He'd lie low today, and tomorrow he would do what he'd vowed to Clarissa. He broke into a light jog, and then, just as quickly, he came to a stop.

At the corner, Rexford's Mustang idled. The rising sun glared off the windshield. The Mustang's engine revved, and the tires left a rubber scratch in the intersection as Rexford made a right turn up Main Street, a middle finger dangling out of the open driver's-side window.

SAMUEL

First in a trickle and then in a steady stream, the people of Grandview covered the two blocks from the Lutheran Church to the serving line in Clancy Park. They came on foot and by car and by medical scooter and bicycle, the alphabet generations and the boomers and the pensioners, in their Sunday best and flip-flops and cutoff jeans. One by one, they took a plate from Maris Westfall, plastic knives and forks from Marlene Wolters, coffee or juice from Nancy Drucker, and pancakes from Samuel at the griddle—"One or two, your call," he'd tell them—and then found suitable spots to sit in the grass and along the bandstand.

There had been inquiries, of course. Nobody much expected Samuel's father to be there, what with the injury and the recent sadness, but all the busy biddies wondered aloud about Patricia. "Oh, she's not feeling well," Samuel had said, simply enough, and that had brought about much cooing and invocations of "oh, dear" and a few who got to the most salient question of all: "Is she going to miss Raleigh? That would be such a shame."

She would, indeed, miss him, and Raleigh Ridgeley was hard to miss. He sat alone by the microphone stand where he'd soon be holding forth. He ate the pancakes in small bites, daintily, nibbling at the tines, not like the other men in the park. Not like anyone who still knew what it was like to be from here.

Samuel watched him and molded bad thoughts from the wet clay of his mind. He wasn't entirely sure what to do with them, though. It wouldn't be fair to say he considered Raleigh a friend; until recent years, Samuel hadn't considered him at all, but he'd reread *The Biggest Space* out in California and had found wisdom there that he hadn't seen the first time around, in his own callow youth. He and Raleigh had settled in at a restaurant after a book signing in Mill Valley and had talked into the evening, two Grandview expats sharing what they'd learned in their exposure to the wider world beyond the beet fields and the oil trains. So maybe they weren't friends, exactly. Compatriots? Absolutely. As such, and as a son standing outside the triangle Raleigh had formed with his folks, Samuel felt a gnawing at his gut that he couldn't quite define and didn't care to endure.

From behind, hands slid across his eyes, blacking out his vision.

"Guess who."

He cracked a grin. "Andy Warhol."

"What? Andy Warhol? He's dead."

"Houdini?"

"Deader than Warhol."

"Rush Limbaugh?"

"Well, his career is dead, anyway."

Samuel broke into a rollicking laugh, and Megan let him loose.

"You look like a natural," she said. "You sure you don't want to come back to paradise for good?"

"Maybe," he said.

"Really?"

"Maybe not."

She brushed a slap against his shoulder, and they laughed together again, and Samuel thought now that he'd given short shrift to what it meant to him to have a friend. It had been a long time and a lot of intense, futile energy poured into Derek at the exclusion of all others. For the first time, he felt something—in his heart and in his mind—akin to breaking the surface.

"Have you eaten?" he asked.

"No," she said. "Starving. I was waiting for you to ask."

He turned to the helpers down the row and asked if he could be excused. Maris Westfall shooed him away, saying, "You love-birds go have fun," and that set off a whole new stratosphere of laughter. Oh, the many things Maris didn't know would blow her damn doors off.

Samuel flipped a couple of cakes onto a paper plate for Megan, and they headed off into the gathering crowd on the park lawn.

As Megan ate, Samuel recounted the bad news, each piece of it catching her by surprise. That, in turn, surprised him, though he knew it shouldn't have. He'd spent his first eighteen years in this place, and he knew well the inconsistencies of what information got laid bare for everyone's consumption and those things that could rest shrouded in open view. The news simply hadn't found Megan yet, even as they were surrounded by people who knew that Blanche and Henrik were gone, and who cast excruciatingly sympathetic looks and nods in Samuel's direction.

"I'm surprised you're here," she said.

He shrugged. "Staying away wouldn't change anything. Grandma definitely would have wanted this to go on."

"Your uncle, though."

They sat atop a picnic table, and Samuel leaned forward, arms propped on his knees, hands cupped under his jaw to hold his head. "I didn't know him, not really. I think maybe my dad is feeling more than he's letting on, though. I don't know. It's a lot to process."

"Even after yesterday?"

"Maybe especially. You know?"

She set down her plate. "No."

"I don't know. I'm kind of scattered. I was just thinking, though, it's his brother. I think it would be cool to have an older brother, don't you?"

"I never really thought about it."

"Well, yeah," he said. "You're an only child. You wouldn't want the competition."

She play-slapped him again. "Shut up."

"I'm just saying," he said, "maybe there's something Dad wanted to say, or maybe he hoped things would get better. Now?" He let the question hang there.

"Yeah," she said.

He pushed on through. "I used to think I hated my sister—"

"You *did* hate her. I remember."

"OK," he said, "yes, in that narrow teenage sense, where anybody who isn't glorifying you is the enemy, yeah, I hated her. But the truth is, I just didn't know her. Still don't. And maybe we never will figure out how to be friends, but here's the deal: I'm getting to know her sons. My nephews. I love those little guys. And that makes me want to know her, too."

They sat awhile. Sunday had come in warm but not choking, a slight breeze tickling the grass from the west, the kind of mottled purple-gray sky that provides cover without threatening, even as the suggestion of rain plays at the nose. Samuel brushed his eyes across the faces he knew and the ones that had shoved into his town in the decade since he'd had a stake here. Unless you counted the bank, white-collar jobs didn't exist in Grandview. Everyone—man, woman, and child—had the look of having earned what they had, and that included snippets of happiness like breakfast in the park. For the first time, he realized that he missed it, the satisfaction of a life claimed from the surrounding squalor.

He looked at Megan. The rims of her eyes had gone red.

"You broke my heart, you know," she said.

"I know. I'm sorry."

"I forgive you."

"Thank you."

He crab-crawled down from the tabletop, lowering himself to the bench seat. She followed him there and closed the distance, and they watched as the plastic seats that fanned out from the bandstand began to fill with matronly posteriors.

RALEIGH

Before he cleared his throat, before he said a single word, before he began his teardown of this idea that the West was anything different or special, Raleigh Ridgeley found the empty seat amid a sea of Grandview's fine women, and an entire scene filled his head with such florid detail and forthrightness that he wished he could stop and write it all down.

In it, a man has come to an uncertain alliance with the notion that the object of his quest sits back in the one place whose dust he's spent a lifetime shaking off his shoes. She's a fixture of the remembered life that he's fled in quiet desperation. And now that he's come to the end of this bitter negotiation with himself, he badly wants to tip his heart over and see what spills forth and invite her to challenge her assumptions about her own life, the simpler course she chose that really isn't so simple at all.

How, then, does he do this? It mustn't be melodramatic. No public declarations in the square, as the townsfolk cheer and the husband who's never cherished her sits and stews, an object of pity and scorn. That's the stuff of Hollywood and its cheap manipulations. No, this man would not swim the waters in such a way. He might say nothing at all and simply return to his place, perhaps after standing in the rain in the middle of her street while she watches from the garage. That old Western archetype, the strong, silent sufferer.

No, it mustn't be that, either, not in light of what Raleigh has come here today to say. Perhaps, instead, it's a conversation under a streetlamp in the blackest pitch of night, a kiss on the hand, and a long wave good-bye—reminiscent of Raleigh's own recent experience, minus the wrestling match against the garage. Or maybe it's a letter sent from a safe distance, with no return address and no signature, yet she would surely know whose hand wrote it. Maybe he'd let that seep in awhile and then open his door one day and she'd be there, unable to beat back the currents of a life she no longer wanted.

Closer. He was drawing closer. Something open-ended yet inevitable—now that would do the trick nicely. It would take the right words, arranged in the right way, vivid and yet deathless, the kind of words Raleigh Ridgeley would have in his quiver.

Damn, but he wished he could go to the laptop now and get this down, before the purity of it all blew away.

He fumbled a smile, and the ladies sat forward in their seats, ready to hear him.

"So," he said, "who's read *Squalid Love*?"

In unanimity, hands shot skyward.

He spent an hour and a half with them, the first sixty minutes of it pleasurable as he deconstructed the mythical West and cast its compromised parts aside. He fairly shook the roof of the bandstand as he inveighed against the robber barons of regional literature, those simple fools who'd plundered the legends for their own gain, repeatedly giving us laconic sheriffs and drunken Indians and tripe for dialogue that amounted to no more than a fat splash of tobacco juice.

"The West is what you're making of it, what I'm making of it," he intoned. "We have the same problems and the same desires and motivations as anyone else, and I'm sick and tired of cartoon characters made of granite who speak either with their fists or a gun. It's hackneyed, and we—you and I as readers—deserve better."

He expected some pushback on that, and he got it. Marge Fleener said her husband enjoyed a good horse opera, and she didn't see the problem with that, as Elbert wouldn't read anything else but the St. Louis Cardinals box score if he didn't have those old dime paperbacks.

"My dear Marge," Raleigh said, taking her hand, because he knew she'd like that, "the problem isn't those old books. The problem is that they've been repackaged again and again, under the banners of new writers with new titles who say the same old thing, over and over. I ask you, how many borderline-personality small-town sheriffs with a fleeting acquaintance with ethics do we need in our books? Whatever the number, we've doubled or tripled it. Meanwhile, we have damn few Western books in which anyone orders takeout. I wonder why. Too realistic?"

Raleigh played all the notes, pure and tonal and beautiful. He told of book critics in Europe and writers' workshops in Peru, of seeing his own face on a poster in Signoria Square and wishing he had Groucho Marx glasses so he could hide behind them. He told of standing off set in Hollywood, watching the hot new actor with the killer abs make an absolute mockery of Shakespeare, because if there's anything they like to give hot new actors to establish their bona fides, it's the works of the Bard. He brought them to tears as he replayed the feeling he gets, every time, when his flight banks hard left and comes in over Billings and he sees the sandstone bluffs and knows he's coming home again. "Don't believe what you read," he told them of the breathless accounts of his life on other shores with his most recent girlfriend. "This, the very ground I stand upon today, is home." They swooned when he said that.

The harder slog came in the final half hour, as the members of the book club slung their questions at him and pined for answers that Raleigh would have rather left to the spaces between the words or their own imaginations.

Nancy Drucker wanted to know why, in the book, Marisol would leave Jefferson for that nothing of an extra on her film. "It doesn't make sense," she said, to which Raleigh replied, "Does anything ever when it comes to the heart?"

The question-neutralized-by-a-question ploy seemed to work with the others, too. Barbara Perrigrine was mystified by Jefferson's burning of the 365 drawings he made of Marisol. "All that money," she said. Raleigh waited a dramatic beat and said, "What value would you be willing to accept in exchange for everything you ever wanted?"

On and on he batted back their queries with oblique answers and rote lines, and he became exasperated only once, when Tana Myers asked him if Jefferson and Marisol would be getting back together, maybe in another book. Her question, delivered earnestly enough, irritated him, for he and Tana had enjoyed a more intimate time a few years back, and he had talked about these things with her, and he thought she had listened.

"I can't imagine so, no," he said.

"They seemed so in love," she said.

"That's not enough, is it? Does anyone here think that's enough?"

Nobody said anything. His voice had gone shrill.

Later, after signing the books and posing for the pictures and after the Grandview women had floated back to their homes and husbands, Raleigh helped Mayor Swarthbeck stack the chairs and took their solitude as an opportunity to unload what was weighing on him.

"I don't think I can keep doing this for free," he said as he hefted two more chairs onto the tower they were building.

Swarthbeck didn't break his pace. "You think anybody gets paid for this?"

"I think you do, in a manner of speaking." Raleigh bit off the last word; it was an overstep, a bad one, and he shouldn't have gone there. It's just that the damn words sometimes came faster than he could corral them.

Sure enough, Swarthbeck stopped his work and stood there, his gaze penetrating any armor Raleigh might have. He knew the mayor had silently chafed at his fictional depiction in *The Biggest Space*, the way Raleigh had borrowed wholesale Swarthbeck's arrival in town as a twenty-one-year-old out of the Marines, one who set about worming his way into civic matters first as a bar owner and then as a consolidator of indeterminate breadth, with his interests silent and overt dangling into nearly every aspect of town life. It had been anything but a flattering portrayal, but then the book took off, and people actually made pilgrimages to town to drink with the real-life Mayor Engmar Bentsen, and Swarthbeck began to see the upside of his ancillary fame.

"In a manner of speaking," Swarthbeck said, "you do, too. Look, Raleigh, if you don't want to do this anymore, just say the word. We'll retire it. Next time around, I'd be just as happy to get rid of the Sunday stuff altogether. But don't come here and try to extort—"

"Extort?"

"Yeah, extort." Swarthbeck moved in on him, and Raleigh backed up. The mayor stopped and smiled.

"We all know you're speaking tonight at Dawson Community College and how much they're paying you, Raleigh. That's half a year's wages for some sorry asshole here, so don't insult me by poor-mouthing. Every year you come here, you don't buy a single meal or a single drink, and you get all the pussy you want." A wicked grin accompanied the last bit, and Raleigh's stomach turned on him. He just wanted to go, to leave it be, but Swarthbeck had revved his engines now.

"Nothing wrong with a little pussy, of course, although I prefer to accumulate—how should I put it—more *concrete* assets. My point being that you get exactly what you want from this weekend, so let's not sully this thing with craven talk of money, OK?"

Raleigh tried to find his bearings. He set a hand on the bandstand and waited for the scene to clear.

"We done?" he asked.

The mayor stacked the last of the chairs. "I think so. Just one more thing."

"OK."

"My daddy told me this once. Took me a long time to figure out what he meant."

"OK," Raleigh said again.

"Don't shit where you eat. You know what I'm saying?"

"Vaguely."

Swarthbeck chuckled. "I have a feeling Sam Kelvig wouldn't mind clarifying it for you. I'm letting you know that as your friend. Have a safe trip home, Raleigh. And let me know about next year, OK?"

PATRICIA

Sam sat across from her in the living room, same house, different worlds. Just for the sake of comfort, Patricia might have preferred that he not stare at her with such ugliness in his heart, but she could not blame him for wanting to keep her pinned down in the house, under his watch. Had it been Sam with the faltering heart and the wandering eye—and she had never suspected such a thing—she would have played it exactly the same.

The part that got to her, the part he'd never understand no matter if she spent her remaining days trying to explain it, was that she had no interest in being where Raleigh was. As she turned it over in her mind, she almost wanted to laugh. Almost. If anybody needed a way of tracing just how much things had changed, there it was: Three days ago, she'd fantasized about Raleigh. Two days ago, she'd felt his tongue against hers. Today, now, this very minute, she wanted a reset. How was that for seismic shifts?

Denise and Randy and their brood were gone, a frozen storm heading out the door. Denise had kissed her father and snubbed Patricia, and they'd backed out of the driveway without even a wave. Patricia did get to kiss the children; she'd caressed their little heads and told them how much she loved them, while Denise stood with rigid arms outstretched to receive her babies, her body pitched at an acutely angry angle.

Samuel was gone, off to spend more time with the Riley girl. Patricia's mouth turned upward as she thought of this, and of the answer he had given early that morning in the hospital when she'd asked about Megan just to have something else to talk about, and perhaps with a lilt too hopeful that there might be more afoot with her son's old girlfriend.

"It's just really good to have a friend, Mom," he'd said. And then came the bit she'd have to get used to, somehow. "I'm still sexually attracted to men. Real talk, as the kids say."

"What's so funny?" Sam slung the words into the space between them.

"Nothing."

"My ass, nothing."

She clammed up. Nothing good could come of a defense on these grounds. Sam had walked the house like a caged bear all morning, all stress and menace and searching for a fight. Patricia didn't see a way to deal with that—wasn't sure, in fact, that there was one—but she had wits about her enough to know that escalation would end badly.

"You've ruined everything," he said.

"I'm sorry. Sorry you feel that way."

"I don't feel any way. It's just the way it is."

"I'm sorry."

"No, you're not."

Again, she stifled the urge to engage. She clasped her hands and squeezed them.

"I should've been at the park," he said.

"Samuel and the mayor had it covered."

"Not the same."

How many times had Sam lamented Samuel's ongoing absence from the place that once cradled him? How often had he talked about the legacy—honestly, a bit of a stretch in the case of Jamboree, a Big Herschel invention of recent-enough vintage that Patricia well remembered the first one—and the shame of their son not being there to continue it?

Damn, the fool's gold of yearning. Were they not here, staring at each other across a widening gulf, Patricia and her husband might be talking about how dreams they never dared give breath were now within taunting reach. Samuel had come home, and had even reclaimed his name in his tossed-off way. Blanche had made it to her Jamboree parade coronation, and despite the difficult circumstances of her final hours, the doctors had assured them that her fall was not a complicating factor in her death. She had, simply, come to her end, one she'd been praying for and one they could accept. Henrik? Henrik was a different matter, a true tragedy, but it would be a lie to say they'd never considered the possibility he'd remove himself from the picture. At any rate, Sam's attentions were clearly elsewhere.

They talked of none of those things. They only looked at each other. She only grew sadder at the wasted time. He only grew angrier—at the fact that he couldn't make himself feel better by making her feel worse, she suspected. The whole sorry circumstance hung in their house like stale air.

He looked at his watch. She looked at the wall clock above his head. It would be over now, the book club meeting in the park. She let out a breath as if she'd been holding it the entire morning.

Sam found his feet and jangled the keys in his pocket.

"Where are you going?" she said, standing up herself, compelled to do so by some foreboding sensibility that had crept into the room.

"You know where. You could draw me a map." He strode for the kitchen, for his boots, for the wallet he kept on the kitchen counter because it was apt to go missing anywhere else.

She fell into step, on his heels. "Don't do that."

He wiggled feet into boots she bought him in Billings a year ago, on his birthday. Why would she notice that? She shook her head, clearing the tangent.

"Sam, don't."

He lunged at her, and she backed herself up to the refrigerator. He stood there, in perfect symmetry with her, inches away, and he pointed a long finger at her nose.

"No," he said. "You don't get a say in this. Not now." His words came direct and straight and quiet, so soft that despite their content they wouldn't have been menacing in the least if delivered without the accompanying visual.

A leak sprung in her resolve. Her chin dimpled and quivered.

"Please," she said, her voice shaken.

He left her there, curled into herself in the kitchen, and she heard the door close and the quick steps on the concrete and the truck engine gun to life, the low, angry yell of it fading into nothingness as he drove away from her and toward Raleigh.

SAM

The timing was exquisite. When Sam's truck came to a rolling stop where Ellison met Main, Raleigh's Lexus dissected the intersection and headed south, toward Sidney. Sam let another pickup, Elbert Fleener's, slip past before he fell in. He'd watch this play out from an actionable distance.

A mile out of town, Elbert, hauling potable water, took the right turn Sam knew was coming, and then it was just him and Raleigh in the visible portion of the southbound lane. Sam didn't move up to close the distance. He turned the radio off and settled into the white noise of the truck's tires against asphalt.

Back in town, Raleigh had passed him without even a glance, and Sam couldn't be sure whether he'd know the truck, anyway. No matter. He would hang back, a silent stalker, and he would go where Raleigh led. And there . . .

Well, that was a good question, wasn't it? Sam hadn't exactly given that much thought. Patricia sure had the fear in her eyes, though, and he had been all too willing to let her think he was going forth with the worst of intentions. She'd tried to sit there, serene, while the ceaseless waves of anger and hurt had pounded on him, and he'd turned that around right quick by getting up and leaving. She was slumped and broken when he left, and that served her right for what she'd done.

He wouldn't mind throwing a little fear into Raleigh, too. Sam shifted in his bucket seat and fastened a harder grip on the wheel. Nobody respects a commitment anymore. That's what it comes down to, Sam figured. If Patricia had been inclined to wander, then she was weak. If Raleigh proposed to be there to scoop her up, then he was opportunistic. Neither quality was worth bragging about. *Maybe,* Sam thought, *I can keep this guy away from some other poor bastard's marriage if I can scare him a little.*

Piece by piece, then, the course of action came to Sam, the workability of it just as evident. He tightened up again, anticipating, committed. He flipped the radio back on and the voice of the old crooner Jim Reeves floated into his ears, delivering an apt tune for the occasion:

He'll have to go . . .

When Raleigh turned into the Lazy Z parking lot, Sam registered a sliver of surprise. It's not that Sidney could boast four-star accommodations, but the Z couldn't even dream about such plaudits. At its best, it was an overnight stay for travelers seeking wider horizons. At worst, it was a flophouse. Whatever the case, Raleigh and his snooty attitude and his new Lexus fit the scene bizarrely.

Sam idled into the parking lot and backed into a space across the lot from where Raleigh stood at his trunk, retrieving his notes and his laptop case. Sam watched from the cab, sizing him up, for he'd never before looked at this man, someone he'd known since he was a kid, and tried to ferret out the best way to kick his ass. Sam's mouth went to cotton as he looked Raleigh up and down. For the first time, Sam noticed that he was actually a bear of a guy—maybe six four, probably 210, 220. Big hands. Broad shoulders. Sam had always dismissed Raleigh as a sissy, someone lost in pretty word swirls that didn't amount to anything worth talking about. Now, here, he looked a hell of a lot more formidable than that.

"Nerves," Sam told himself. "It's the nerves, damnit."

He forced himself to stick to his tossed-together plan, and now he reached under the passenger-side seat, his blind hand coming across the thick forged steel he'd been certain he'd find there. He found his grip and drew it out, eighteen inches of monkey wrench, the vise jaws gone to casual rust since their last use. It would do. Small enough to handle easily, big enough to threaten damage—or inflict it, if necessary.

He opened his door and brought his left foot to the pavement. He stood erect, and the right foot followed. He shut the truck door, which responded with a creak, and Sam froze. Raleigh, unbothered, continued sorting through his papers in the trunk. Sam crept forward, his left arm at his side, his hand holding the wrench.

Sam took steps slow and deliberate. He licked his lips and swallowed the saliva pooling in his mouth. As he approached, his shadow swept across Raleigh's open trunk, and that's when Raleigh finally turned around. Sam pulled himself up to a stop.

Raleigh looked him in the eye first, and Sam tried to fashion a poker face out of the moment.

"What are you doing here?" Raleigh asked. His eyes moved now to the object in Sam's left hand. "Is that for me?"

Sam's body stiffened, his mind locked in a stalemate with his motor skills. His limbic system engaged, screaming out orders to start swinging. His hand, however, loosened the grip on the wrench.

"You're a piece of garbage, Raleigh," he said at last.

"I've been called worse."

The nonchalance. The sheer gall. Sam hadn't felt in his right mind since Henrik had gone after him, and now the only thought that bubbled up was one cloaked in incredulity. How could Raleigh be so unaffected by what he'd wrought?

Sam dropped the wrench at his own feet.

"I figured," Raleigh said. "You don't have the guts."

Sam held his gaze. "You're not worth it. You're a piece of garbage who takes advantage of other men's wives."

Raleigh closed the trunk of his car and adjusted the box of papers under his arm.

"I have sex with a lot of married women," he said. "Guilty. Maybe husbands ought to ask themselves why that's happening. I've never taken advantage of anyone."

"You took advantage of Patricia."

Raleigh sat back against his car. "Ah, yes. Well, Patricia is someone special, isn't she? She's not like the others. Two things about that. First, I didn't have sex with Patricia. Second, last I checked, she went back to you, although for the life of me I can't see why. This isn't really about her, though, is it?"

"Rationalize all you want," Sam said. "You've put my marriage in jeopardy."

"Simple truths simply aren't truthful. You put it in jeopardy, long ago, with your inattention and stupidity."

In the staring contest that ensued, Sam tried to find a shore he could swim toward. Anger at Patricia. At himself. At Raleigh, no doubt. But the encounter left him shaken, too, because he hadn't expected Raleigh to be so matter-of-fact or dead in the eyes. The violence Sam hoped to marshal relied on an equal, opposite reaction from the object of his rage, and Raleigh offered nothing there. *He's a sociopath*, Sam thought. This man, with a seemingly boundless capacity to suss out empathy and human motivation, was an empty vessel.

Sam hung his head. Raleigh pushed himself off the car and brushed past him.

"Next time," Raleigh said, "don't bring a wrench if you're not prepared to use it. Makes you look like a schmuck."

Sam waited till the receding steps fell fully away and the opening and closing of the door signaled that Raleigh was inside. Then, he knelt, picked up his wrench, and went back to his truck. Once out of the parking lot, he turned the nose of it north toward Grandview. Home. Or what home used to be, anyway.

THE CHIEF

If anything, Alfonso looked even worse. Adair sat at his hospital bedside, Dea across from her on the other side, holding her husband's hand. The swelling in Alfonso's face had cut off the oxygen to his burst capillaries, leaving the bruises morphing from red to blue. He sucked water from a Styrofoam cup through a straw, and then he handed the cup to Dea and smiled. He'd been smiling the whole time Adair had been there. It was unnerving.

Adair tried again.

"Alfonso."

He turned his head her way, and Adair got a fresh look at the deep, stitched-up cuts on his cheekbones and the jagged line along his brow. It was as if he hadn't defended himself at all. She looked at his arms and hands. Nothing there. None of it made any sense, and Alfonso was no more inclined to shed light on the situation now than he had been hours earlier, in the park.

"Alfonso," she said again, "I'm going to level with you. I think I know who did this."

"I fell down," he said. The words came out malformed.

"Bullshit." A sharpness she hadn't intended infused the words, and Dea let out a squeak, then fortified her hold on her husband.

"I fell down," he said.

Adair shook her head. She looked at the Medeiros children, all four of them, ranging from age four to twenty. They held up the wall across from their father's bed, long-faced and sullen.

It was Dea who finally spoke.

"We don't want any more trouble," she said. "Alfonso's sorry this happened, aren't you, baby?" Alfonso turned his head and looked at the ceiling, sad-eyed. He nodded.

"*You're* sorry?"

"Please," Dea said. "We don't want any more trouble."

The exodus of RVs and cars with plates from elsewhere passed Adair southbound as she drove back to Grandview. The gathering she'd obsessed over and planned for had disbanded, and by the evening, there'd be little evidence the crowds had ever been there. She remembered, now with a damning perspective, what Swarthbeck had told her after her first Jamboree planning meeting. "It's gonna be a whipsaw. You'll think it's never gonna end, and then it will be over like that. The damnedest thing." She wondered now if he meant it as an advisory or a warning.

At the Country Basket, as she was coming out of the store with an energy drink, she met Sam Kelvig coming in. They lingered outside the glass doors silently, facial contortions filling out the meanings for which words were insufficient.

"I'm sorry," she said finally.

"I know."

"Do you hate me?"

"No," he said. She took note of the deadness in his eyes and words, and she didn't feel better.

He pushed through the doors to get inside the store, and Adair exhaled.

Back in the car, she fished her phone from the console and punched in a text message.

Where are you?

She sipped her drink and watched the screen.

North end. Sup?

Meet me on Telegraph Hill. Need to talk. Five minutes.

K.

On the hill above Grandview, Adair sipped the last of her drink and set the can on the hood of her cruiser, next to Joe LaMer. She was tired. Every blessed inch of her.

She telescoped her gaze across the valley. The afternoon had rolled in overcast. Spotlights punched holes in the cloud cover and illuminated patches of the town below. Beautiful. The kind of day people don't appreciate the way they should.

"You look tired," LaMer said.

"Yeah. I am."

He crossed his arms and tried to find the spot on the horizon that had drawn her attention. "So what's up?"

"I need to ask you something," she said.

"Shoot."

"What happened to Alfonso?"

LaMer took off his cap, holding it in his right hand while his left scratched at his dampened hairline. "Got beat up."

"Who did it?"

"I don't know." LaMer put himself back together. "Why?"

"I think you do know."

"No, I don't. But you have a theory. Let's have it."

Adair set her jaw. She had no cards here—just whatever amount of gumption she could muster. All she had was the fact that Alfonso's beating, so repellent to everyone else, hadn't seemed to move LaMer, and she wanted to know why.

"I don't have a theory," she said. "Just questions. Gut feelings, maybe. What if I told you I don't trust you anymore?"

LaMer got a faraway look about him. It was the one she'd seen in Pete's on Friday, as though he wasn't really with her.

"I guess I'd say I was sorry to hear that. I trust you."

"Sure you do."

He said nothing.

"I don't think we can work together," she said. "What if I asked you to leave?"

"I'd say no."

"You can be on a rig tomorrow making a lot more than we're paying you."

"No."

They were squared off now, each dug in and unyielding.

"I'll keep pushing," she said. Her heart revved.

"Swarthbeck will put me right back on the job. You have to know this. You're in much more jeopardy than I am, Adair."

She felt her knees go, as if someone had sliced the tendons. She caught herself and held steady.

LaMer only looked at her. He didn't need to do anything else. The meanings and the intimations were clear enough.

"You disappoint me," she said, turning and heading back to the door of her cruiser.

"Sorry," he said.

"No, you're not."

She dropped into the driver's seat of the cruiser, fired it up, then spit gravel in LaMer's direction as she raced out of there, back to the highway, down the hill, into the cold cradle of the town below.

PATRICIA

She'd managed to fill the big suitcase, the one they'd bought at that outlet store outside Denver, with enough clothes to last her a week, which was about as long as she imagined Nancy and Mel Drucker would want her staying in their basement. They were good people, the Druckers, but a week was the outskirts of anyone's toleration of visitors, and so Patricia had her mind set on that marker as a time for her to leave before she trampled the welcome mat.

After that? Well, that's uncertainty for you. The Druckers lived two blocks away, and she figured she could stand that distance from Sam and the house and everything she'd managed to claim in this life. If a week and a two-block walk couldn't put a damper on this rage she'd unleashed, if Sam couldn't find a place in his heart for her anymore, she'd have to face up to some choices she never thought she'd have to make.

A rap at the bedroom door. "Mom?"

"Yes."

Sunlight sliced the darkened room as Samuel slipped past the door and found her at the chore.

"No," he said. "You're not doing this."

She lugged the suitcase off the bed and onto the floor. "It's for the best."

"It's not. It's madness. Where's Dad?"

"I don't know." That was the truth, as far as it went. She'd braced herself for some indeterminate calamity, but there'd been no sign of it. No sirens or phone calls or footsteps at the door. No Sam, either, and that frankly terrified her.

"Well, come out into the living room and sit down until he gets here."

"I should just go."

"Mom," Samuel said. "Sit down and talk to me."

Patricia mostly listened, rapt, as Samuel laid bare the notions she'd been considering in ways that she hadn't examined. He told her of his talk that morning with Megan, how he'd bent her ear about happiness and how slippery it seemed. Megan had said, simply, that she no longer sought happiness but fulfillment. When her marriage ended and her job went away and her mother died, compelling her to return to Grandview and take care of her father, she didn't figure happiness was something she was likely to see again. She was wrong about that, he said. Happiness comes and goes, all the time.

"It's transient," he told Patricia, in Megan's words. "It's driven by circumstance. And I sat there and I said, 'My god.' I mean, my god. I thought if I changed this or that, or went somewhere new, I'd find it. It doesn't work. For me, it hasn't worked. I think I'm looking for the wrong thing."

Patricia nodded. Her eyes filled.

"You love him," Samuel said.

"Yes."

"He loves you."

She nodded.

He put his arm around her and pulled her in, and she folded herself into his shoulder, and she buried her burden there.

• • •

Nighttime fell, and they were alone in the house. Almost as if on cue, Jamboree had ended and the first cool, wet day of the summer slid into its place, dropping a gully washer on Grandview.

Patricia and Samuel dined on soup, the quickie potato kind that she'd often made for him and Denise when they were kids. She mostly let him be; it was clear he was chewing on something inside. Their talk had been a catharsis of sorts, but now she wasn't sure for whom. Her tears had dried and her jumbled insides had sorted themselves out again, and for all of that she was thankful. Samuel, on the other hand, had drawn inward and quiet, and she knew that well. When he was a little boy, it had bothered her to the point of worry, that someone so young could seem so serious and self-contained. The pediatrician in Billings had told her not to stress out about it, that Samuel was a normal, healthy boy in all of the measurable ways. Now, that stoicism fit him better. He was considered and kind, a full-grown man.

When Sam breached the front door, drenched and distant, his bloodied bandage askew on his head, Patricia and Samuel were up and tending to him.

"Dad, are you OK?" Samuel guided him to a seat in the living room.

"Yes. Fine."

Patricia reached for the bandage, and he looked at her a bit bewilderedly but allowed her to remove it in a slow unfurling.

"Where have you been?" she said.

"Around. Been thinking."

"Tell us," Samuel said.

Patricia disposed of the soiled bandage and went to the hall closet to find a fresh dressing. She came back and nodded at Sam, and he tipped his head forward so she could wrap it.

"I saw Mel Drucker at the Double Musky. He said you're moving in."

"Not moving in," she said, her voice a whisper. "Just . . . I don't know."

"I wish you wouldn't."

Patricia completed the job, and she slipped her fingers under his chin and lifted his head. His eyes were ringed in red.

"OK," she said. "I won't."

Sam leaned back. "I've been thinking about what Mama said. I think I'll move over there while I'm closing up the house."

"OK," Patricia said. She clamped down hard on what was coming up from her.

"Just temporary. We'll see how it goes," he said.

She nodded.

"I'm sorry," she said.

"I'm sorry, too." He reached out, and she set her hand in his. Samuel, from his seat next to his father, found Sam's shoulder and gave it a squeeze. Patricia closed her eyes and tried to hold the picture in her aperture for as long as it could last.

The New York Times, *Saturday, August 1, 2015*

On this particular weekend, optimism seemed in short supply. The brother-on-brother violence that marred the town parade took a grisly turn when Henrik Kelvig ended up dead in his jail cell, apparently a suicide by hanging. The Richland (Mont.) County Coroner's Office said a complete report won't be available for several weeks.

"We had an inexperienced police chief who didn't follow protocol," Mayor Swarthbeck said by phone. "We've corrected that." Calls to the erstwhile police chief, Underwood, were not returned, and it's unclear what became of her. Swarthbeck said he didn't know and that any official information about the chief was "a personnel matter."

For some, the event called Jamboree may simply be a victim of the times, a small-town celebration squandered by a gold-rush mentality and all that comes with it.

"It's a big moneymaker for us," said Alfonso Medeiros, whose family parks a taco truck at Jamboree every year. "But it's not as fun. You used to know everybody. Now you don't. There's not as much trust."

MONDAY

THE CHIEF

The final, indisputable calculus for Adair Underwood lay in every-thing she hadn't done. She hadn't unpacked the boxes she lugged into the single-wide trailer three months earlier. She hadn't put anything on the walls. She hadn't spent a night in Grandview that wasn't preoccupied with her job or LaMer, and what disasters those two had turned into. She hadn't even signed a lease: Eldrick Sloane just let her pony up half the monthly rent every paycheck. Why wouldn't he? He knew where she lived.

Those being the circumstances, it was easy enough for her to take the boxes back out and load them in her ancient Suburban, park her cruiser under the weather-worn carport, then leave an envelope stuffed with cash—enough to cover the month, which should have been plenty for Sloane—on the foldout kitchen table. She left her badge there, too. She had little doubt that John Swarthbeck would find it, maybe even before Eldrick Sloane did.

She took the gun, though. "Let them requisition it after I'm safely to where I'm going," she said aloud as she finished moving out.

She wasn't paranoid, she told herself. *A prepared cop is a good cop.*

In one of her last acts in Grandview, she called Captain Fuquay. The clock said he'd be into his third Scotch after the night shift. She could count on that, regardless of what his doctor might have told him was the prudent course.

"Well, yeah, Underwood, you can probably come back and get your job," he said after a coughing fit of surprise at her question. "You sure? This was a big step for you, running your own show."

"I'm sure. I liked your show."

"Want to tell me why?"

"Yeah. After I get there."

He grumbled phlegm into his end of the connection. "Well, come on, then. No guarantees. Gotta get it through the county commission. But you were a good hand, and we need somebody, and they usually give me what I ask for."

Adair clutched the receiver in both hands. "That's good enough for me," she said.

The spitting sound of tires on gravel pulled Adair out of the dull trance of mopping the kitchen floor, her last act of compliance. It wasn't as if the absurdity was lost on her—she was leaving a hell of a mess, and she knew it, but she couldn't stomach sticking Eldrick Sloane with cleanup of his trailer on top of it.

She moved to the window and pulled the curtain aside, letting in a slice of moonlight. Joe LaMer slipped out of his pickup and looked toward the window. Adair narrowed the gap and held her gaze. He wore street clothes, a white T-shirt and jeans. Sakota would be home asleep by now, she figured. Grandview had entered an eight-hour period without a police presence, an occasional, and regrettable, concession to the clock and limited manpower.

LaMer moved toward her Suburban. He cupped his hands against the glass of the back window and peered in. He'd know now. Inconvenient, Adair figured, but also inevitable. She'd have been found out as soon as she didn't show for work, and truth be told, she didn't really expect a clean getaway. Maybe she didn't even want one. She knew only that she saw no way to stay here, and no way to explain that to anyone.

She slipped the gun into the waistband of her sweatpants and took the direct route, banging out the front door and startling LaMer, who stumbled back from the Suburban.

"Why are you here, Joe?" She looked down on him from the landing.

"Came to see you."

"Here I am." She shifted from one foot to the other. LaMer slipped his hands in his pockets and tried to effect nonchalance.

"You going somewhere, Adair?"

She came down the stairs. She hoped he might retreat a piece, but he held his spot.

"Clearly," she said.

"Why?"

"You know why."

LaMer stepped toward Adair, and she stepped back, keeping the distance.

"This is silly," he said. "You don't want to do that."

"Yeah, I do."

He stepped forward again, and she backed against the fuselage of the trailer.

"But what about *Star Wars*?"

"You're kidding, right?"

He took the hem of her T-shirt between his thumb and forefinger. "No. Come on, Adair." He went to lift the shirt, and her hand found his, stopping him.

"Not here," she said.

"No?"

"Let's go inside."

In the end, it was all surprisingly easy to take down Joe LaMer, with his own bravado and stupidity doing most of the work. He went up the stairs ahead of Adair and entered the trailer as if he were the lord of the place. She followed, digging out the gun from the back of her pants, and planted a foot in LaMer's back in the living room. He spilled onto the floor, and she put the gun on him before he could make sense of what had happened.

"Why Alfonso?" she said.

LaMer held his hands up. "Come on. Put that away."

Adair shoved the barrel against his nose. "Tell me."

"Swarthbeck."

"Why?"

"He talks too much. That's what John said. Something about the way he talked to that reporter lady. You know John. It's all gut feelings. Alfonso talks too much."

"So do you."

Adair pulled the gun back, then smacked LaMer in the head with it. The first crack got his attention. The second turned out his lights.

Adair closed up the trailer and locked the door. Her place sat at the end of the last residential street in town, tucked into the curve where Montana meets North Dakota. When she left, she followed the road out past Clancy Park, to where it joined Main Street. The corner sign on First Bank said 12:03 a.m. Grandview was finally, blessedly silent, moonlight shadows over downtown, not a car moving.

Adair turned right and pointed the Suburban toward the Dakota line, just a few hundred feet away. Maybe she could make Minot before she needed to rest. She had cash enough to get where she was going, anyway. No paper trail. Not with what she'd left behind. She figured that message would be delivered soon enough by LaMer's compromised condition, and she could only hope she'd removed any incentive to chase her down and push the issue.

When the tires touched North Dakota asphalt, she let her breath go.

SAM

In fits and starts and bursts of energy propelled by supplemental oxygen, Blanche Loretta Kelvig spent the final year of her life cataloging and inventorying the artifacts of two families.

In the room where Sam and Henrik fought, slept, and conspired as boys, she had set out the things that belonged to Big Herschel that the boys might want, along with filled-out sheets from a yellow sticky pad that put details into the gaps. They would know Herschel's white cowboy hat, gone to light brown from the years of dust, toil, and sweat and the days under the sun. But the spurs he wore in the Brockway Dairy Day Rodeo in '55? That was before the boys were born, so Blanche's uptight blue cursive pointed the way:

> *Your daddy won the all-around that year. He thought he*
> *was the king of it all. I told him that I wasn't about to ride*
> *in a pickup from rodeo to rodeo and that he needed to come*
> *home and do right by me. And that's what he did.*

Over the washer and dryer, which Blanche wouldn't accept until Sam insisted during Samuel's senior year, were file folders with copies of every tax return on the farm, clear back to its purchase, a paper testimony to just how many times she and Big Herschel had managed to muscle the farm into solvency by the skin of their teeth. Along the tops, she had made note of the seminal occurrence of the year. Save for the boys' birth years, the observations tended toward the meteorological and agricultural:

1963: The flood.
1971: We lost the breeding bull.
1978: Drought.
1979: Drought.
1980: Drought.
1981: Plenty of water, praise the Lord.

All over the house, Sam found these guideposts to his history. His grandmother's clothes iron, with the addendum that Grandma Kelvig *could have scared the clothes straight with her cackle.* A picture of Sam and Henrik that he didn't recognize, the two of them standing in a mud puddle with their arms around each other, Henrik towering above Sam by head and shoulders. *See? You guys did get along.* Sam broke down when he found that, everything he'd tamped down after Henrik's death coming up and through him, and he knew he'd never be able to put those regrets to rest. A paper tablecloth from his and Patricia's wedding reception sent him into a fresh round of tears. The yellowed newspaper clipping of his Uncle John Henry's obituary even got to him. John Henry had come home from Da Nang in a box and gone into the ground, and nobody had said anything else about him. But Mama had kept the hard record of it.

The breaking of morning shone through the east-facing windows, and Sam stood in the half-light, awash in his own memories and those he'd have to co-opt as the eldest Kelvig man standing.

He fell back to his mother's favorite chair and set his head into his hands, and he waited for his will to regenerate.

The mayor came around at about seven. Sam didn't notice that the house had been breached until Swarthbeck was standing in the kitchen. Sam was on his knees, packing dishes into a cardboard box.

"Need some help?" Swarthbeck said.

"No. I've got it. Didn't hear you knock." He put the best hard gaze on Swarthbeck that he could muster. Everything was an irritant now.

"Yeah, sorry. Blanche's door was always open, you know?"

"I know." Sam pushed to his feet, the rarely used muscles across his back and shoulders scolding his neglect. "What can I do for you, John?"

Swarthbeck stepped aside, clearing the path back to the living room, Sam's hobbling destination.

"I was going to ask the same question of you," the mayor said. "You doing all right?" He followed Sam's lead.

Sam settled into his mother's chair and motioned Swarthbeck to take the one opposite.

"I don't suppose I'll have much truck with 'all right' for a while," he said.

"I know, Sammy. Hell of a thing, this weekend."

"Hell of a thing," Sam agreed.

His eyes found the ceiling, and still he could feel Swarthbeck staring him down, waiting for an opening. That was always the way with the mayor. Always an agenda. Sam wasn't much inclined to give him a clear landing, the way he usually did. If Swarthbeck wanted something, he was going to have to be direct.

"Sammy," Swarthbeck said, "this isn't official or anything, but I want you to know I'm sorry about what Adair did with Henrik."

Sam moved forward in his seat. "What did she do?"

"You know, not moving him to county lockup."

"Oh, hell, I'm not worried about that."

"It was against regulations, Sammy."

"It wasn't going to change anything." Sam slumped back into the chair again.

"Well, I have to say, you're being pretty magnanimous about this," Swarthbeck said. Sam noted at once that the mayor sounded almost disappointed, and he figured the time had come for his own declaration.

"Listen, John, I'm done, all right?"

Swarthbeck clasped his hands and pitched forward a bit. "Done how?"

"Jamboree. It's time for someone else to take it on."

Swarthbeck smothered a dismissive chuckle. "Listen, things look pretty bleak right now, I get that, but—"

"I've been grinding on this awhile, John," Sam said, a clear lie, yes, but one that served his purposes now. "I've got bigger fish."

"Patricia?"

"Who told you?" Anger rose up in Sam.

"Sammy, come on."

Sam swallowed. "Yes, Patricia. My kids. My business. This town. My attentions have not been where they should be." He pursed his lips, cutting it off there. He had more he could say, about pride and forgetfulness, love and complacency, and how he wasn't going to lose anybody else he loved to his own shortcomings, but Swarthbeck wasn't entitled to any of that.

The mayor considered his watch. "I gotta go," he said. "Keep your powder dry, OK? We'll talk about this some more."

"My answer isn't changing, John."

Swarthbeck rose and made for the door. "We'll see."

PATRICIA

Patricia emerged from a night of audacious dreams and marveled at her eagerness to see these days through. Lord, she'd missed Sam's contours in the bed next to her. No denying that, and as her senses came into sharpness, she again felt the tinge of fear that he might not want to come back. She pushed it down with resolve and got herself dressed.

She found Samuel in the dining room, finishing off a bowl of the sugar-bomb cereal Denise had brought for her kids and left behind. He gave her a guilty grin. "I love this stuff."

She tossed him a reproachful smile and then took note of the duffel bag on the table, packed tight with his belongings.

"Leaving today?"

"Yeah." He grabbed the bag by the handles and brought it to the floor. "Drive to Billings tonight. Fly out in the morning."

"Billings?"

"Yeah. I—" He stopped. His face contorted. "Oh. I'm sorry."

"You didn't fly into Bismarck?" she said.

"No."

"And the point of this lie was?" She wore a smirk, and he picked up on the intent behind it.

He laughed. "I don't even remember anymore. Can you believe that?"

"Probably not," she said, the banter she'd so missed returning to her. "But I'll accept it. The slate's clear. But we're not doing this anymore. Any of us. You got that?"

She cooked Samuel a proper breakfast and filled in the sleep-addled bits of her epiphany, and when he slid the puzzle pieces of his own plans to the middle of the table, she could see that it all fit together.

"You want to come to California?" he said.

She nodded. "Later this week. I want to get some things squared away for your father."

"You can ride back with me in a couple of weeks," he said. "Megan gave me a line on a job in Billings. I'm thinking maybe I could make a go of it there."

"You wouldn't mind your old mom helping to pack you up?"

"Mom, no. I'd be thrilled to have you there."

When her eyes welled, she turned away from him, the old, familiar stoicism holding on. "I want to do something fun," she said. She swallowed hard. "I want to know that I'm not all worn out yet."

"You're not." He stood up and went to her. "I promise."

He held her by the shoulders. She turned into him.

"Your father will be so happy that you're coming back."

He dipped his head, forced her to look at him. "Yeah?" he said. "Well, I'm not doing it for him. And I'm not doing it for you, either." Then he laughed, and she wrapped her arms around him and held on.

THE MAYOR

Promptly at 8:00 a.m., John Swarthbeck walked out of his temporary office on the ground floor of the Sloane Hotel, crossed the street to the Oasis, and turned right. Eight doors and two blocks down, the sidewalk delivered him to Everly's Welding Service. Tut had the main bay open, just as Swarthbeck had requested.

Getting to the request had been a quagmire. Marian Everly had come into the Sloane the night before like a summer squall, all histrionics and sideways threats, Tut hanging on to the tail of her shirt like she was an unruly child, the mayor closing the door and telling Tut to get control of his damned woman like any self-respecting man would.

So began the playing of the cards, and the figurative didn't go any better than the literal did for old Tut. Marian said they were mortgaged to the hilt to get the new equipment that was getting them in on some Bakken jobs and the fifty grand just couldn't be raised right now, not with nuts to make. Swarthbeck set down the trump card, a signed contract with Tut on the amounts due and the consequences of nonpayment. "We'll have to pull the kids out of UM," Tut had said, no more convincingly than in the stairwell at the Sloane a few days earlier. And while Swarthbeck thought it a damn shame that the burden was shifting to the kids, he didn't see how it was his concern. "So you'll be motivated to make this good," he'd said.

Marian, by then, had looked thoroughly defeated. She'd grabbed her husband's arm and pulled him toward the exit, regret writ large on her face.

Swarthbeck held the door for them. *Degenerate-ass gamblers. They spew misery.*

Now, Tut stepped through the bay opening and said, "Let's get this over with."

Swarthbeck approached and lifted his T-shirt, a show of the revolver tucked into his waistband.

"Jesus, John."

"I just don't want there to be any questions," the mayor said. "This'll go better if we have complete understanding."

He moved into the dark coolness of the garage, his steps echoes in the steel building. Tut kept a clean work space, a point in his favor. By the time Swarthbeck would be ready to head back to the Sloane, he'd have the full scope of the place.

"Where's your crew?"

"Gave 'em the morning off," Tut said. "Didn't want anybody to see this."

"Good thinking." Swarthbeck ran a finger along the top of a brown acetylene canister, then brought it up for inspection. Nothing. Clean place.

"OK," he said. "I want an inventory of everything. Anything still being financed, I want to see the paperwork on that, and don't try to tell me you don't have it. I want to see the deed on the property and the building, and I want your tax records."

"Tax records?"

Swarthbeck turned around and faced Tut.

"You misunderstand 'everything'?"

"No."

"It sounds like you did."

"No, I just—shit, John, tax records? They're up at the house."

"I want 'em. Today."

"Jesus."

Swarthbeck leaned in on the smaller man.

"The son of God ain't your fifty percent partner, Tut. I am. Get me what I want and stop wasting my time."

It was the little edge of intimidation Swarthbeck needed to get his reluctant partner moving. Tut scurried out of there to rev up the truck and head up the hill to Marian and a fresh round of her wrath.

When Swarthbeck was sure he'd gone, he turned and started his count. He knew a guy who could get him seventy cents on the dollar for the canisters, and that would be a start.

Later that morning, back at the Sloane Hotel, Pete Rexford came through the door. Swarthbeck looked up from his pile of Tut Everly's paperwork—a treasure trove, he'd already discovered—and took in the sight of his old friend. Absent were the pressed Western slacks and fine boots Rexford usually wore. Before Swarthbeck stood a sweaty, dirty, bewildered man.

"Jesus, Pete."

"Where are your goddamn cops?" Rexford advanced on the mayor's desk. "Can't get a one of them on the phone."

Swarthbeck stood. "What happened?"

"Damn debacle, that's what. My boy's car is sitting out in front of the house, burned to nothing."

Swarthbeck came around the desk and closed the distance between them. "Burned?"

"Firebombed. Something. Where are your cops?"

"Day after Jamboree, Pete. I imagine they're home sleeping." *Or something,* he added to a thought he'd just as soon keep to himself for now.

"Who'd do this?" Rexford said.

Swarthbeck pushed past his friend and headed for the door. He figured the answer was clear enough to anybody who'd been paying attention. Adair had overstepped for sure this time.

Joe LaMer came through it all right, all things considered. He had stiff legs and a sore ass, the products of nine hours handcuffed to the oven in Adair Underwood's abandoned kitchen. He had a knot on his head from the butt end of her revolver, and when at last he could speak again, he complained of a hell of a headache as residue. And he had the indignity of waiting on John Swarthbeck to read the note on the kitchen table before the mayor fetched the key and freed LaMer and pulled the duct tape from the deputy's mouth. The mayor hoped that hurt most of all.

Swarthbeck pushed the note at the officer, who took his time climbing back to his feet.

"This all true?"

LaMer didn't take the offered piece of paper. "Yeah."

Swarthbeck pulled it back and read again.

> *John,*
>
> *I know about Alfonso, I know about the explosion, and I know some other things, too. LaMer here can tell you all about that.*
>
> *You make it right with Alfonso. I'll be checking in with him, and if you don't, I'll bring the fight back to you in ways that will really hurt. You make it right with him, and you leave me be. Those are my terms.*
>
> *Your man gave it up without a fight. I threatened to make him a gelding, and he spilled it all. You might want to choose your henchmen a little more carefully.*
>
> *Adair*

Swarthbeck crumpled the note and stuffed it in his pocket. LaMer, rubbing his dented head, said, "John, I . . ."

The mayor hunched over and took a powerful step forward, driving his fist into LaMer's nuts, and the younger man fell again.

OMAR

Omar scanned the horizon, from the bald knobs on his right to the sloping valley on his left that met the Yellowstone off in the distance, running along the scoria stacks. He did it again, as if he weren't aware of the bleakness—both in the landscape and in the situation. It was him and Clarissa and the grasses in the summer wind and the occasional big rig and a whole mess of trouble, as if there weren't enough of that already.

He'd told her—*told* her—that she should stop and have the car looked at when he saw the engine light, and Clarissa had said, "No, it's fine, it's just an electrical short," and she'd kept her foot planted damn near to the floorboard on the drive between Grandview and Glendive. Not more than twenty minutes after they'd joined the interstate headed west toward Billings, the car had hocked up a god-awful noise and had lain down and died on the road's shoulder.

"What are we going to do?" Clarissa now asked him, that tremor again in her voice. He wanted to wheel around on her and tell her to stop crying about shit and just deal with it. This was her show, her decision—her decision from way back, when she'd tossed Omar to the side as if she could just deny what had been welling inside him.

"We have to call someone."

"No," she said.

"We have to."

"We can't."

He brought the fingers of his right hand to his nose and breathed in, same as he'd done intermittently since they left Grandview. He still couldn't believe it, the way John Rexford's car had erupted in flames. He'd shoved the gas-soaked kerchief into the tank and lit the end, same as he'd seen Javier Bardem do in that movie. The petroleum scent was a delicious reminder that maybe he wasn't completely inept, a bit of assurance he needed just now.

"Clarissa," he said, his voice rising into the wind, "it's over. This isn't a flat tire. The car is dead." He knew this not because he had a particular way with automobiles—he did not—but because even Omar could push his head under the front end and see the cracked pan and the flood of life-giving oil spreading across the asphalt.

She sat in the open door frame, set her face into her hands, and sobbed, and he'd had enough of that, too. And yet he made his way around the car and stood beside her, gently clearing his throat to let her know that she should calm down and join him in the moment.

"I can't just go back," she said at last, the sniffles muffling her words. "Can't we just give it a little bit? Maybe we can catch a ride into Billings, right?"

He crossed his arms and then turned to her.

"What about your car?" He didn't see any way around it now. When the car got dealt with, so would they, and so would the lies about where they'd gone today.

"I don't care," she said. "We can call someone after."

Omar considered that and found the answer worked for him, too. For all he knew, Gabe was gallivanting around Grandview now, blowing Omar's already-thin cover. And then, of course, there was John Rexford and his car, both problems for another time. Maybe by now Gabe would know about it, too, and maybe he'd even consider that Omar had done what he could to set things right.

He moved against Clarissa, forcing her over, and he shoved in next to her and waited. For something.

The sun made its push toward the high point in the sky and beat down on them, and Omar crawled into the backseat and lay on his back, his knees bent into acute triangles and very nearly brushing the headliner, and he dreamt of basketball and all the opportunities that were on an inexorable march toward him.

His body twitched. The basketball dreams were pure dopamine, a place where the ball was always small, the basket always vast, and his moves always correct. He chanced to dream of final-second shots and championships and victory parades on teammates' shoulders.

And then Omar's eyes fluttered open. The car seat smell and the sweaty stench from his lying in the sun flooded his senses. Perspiration leached into the shirt on his back.

"Clarissa." He turned onto his side and saw her in the driver's seat, her head dangled off to the side.

"Clarissa."

She lurched forward. "Huh?"

"Somebody's here," he said. He sniffed his fingers again.

Tires rolled along the rumble strip behind them, the crunch of gravel accompanying, and then came to a stop.

"Who is it?" she said.

Omar tried to pull his knees in while simultaneously shoving his torso upward so he could get a look out the back window. The confines of the car left him precious little room to move.

Outside, the sound of a door opening and then slamming shut. Footsteps on the pavement. Long strides from the sound of it.

"Oh," she said, "it's that guy."

"What guy?"

"You know, that author guy. From Jamboree."

The sound of the steps fell off. A shadow loomed in Clarissa's open window, and then a face peeked in.

"You guys need some help?"

SAMUEL

He found his father in the old tack room, a pencil in Sam's chewed fingers taking inventory of what had been left behind. There hadn't been a horse on the spread since before Big Herschel spun off into the cosmos, and there hadn't been anyone keen to deal with the detritus until now.

The door to the shack had lain open, and Samuel found his way in without rousing the old man. He figured he'd just stand there a spell and wait for recognition to register. Might even be able to throw a scare into his dad, and that would be a nice reversal from the many years when Sam had lurked around darkened corners after a scary movie, ready to separate his son from his sense of security all in the name of a good laugh.

On and on it went, Sam counting riggings and horseshoes and time-beaten boxes of nails and the rest of it, quick jots in his notebook. Samuel held still and silent, and then he whinnied, deep and throaty and loud, like an old draft horse, and Sam's notebook went flying as he whirled around to fend off an intruder.

When he saw his boy, his face moved through surprise, confusion, anger, and then relief in about the space of a breath.

He listed about, Fred Sanford-style, and said, "The ol' ticker hasn't got many of those left in it," and then he smiled, and Samuel knew he'd hit the mark.

He brought his forefingers to a point and thrust them forward at his father. "Gotcha," he said.

At the house, Samuel poured two glasses of Coke and carried them into the living room. Sam sat stretched across the sofa, Blanche's window unit blowing frigid kisses his way.

"You got it all accounted for?" Samuel asked. He handed his father one of the sweaty glasses.

"Just about. Some good stuff. Lots to keep, but some things to get rid of, too. Make for a nice weekend sale this fall."

Samuel took the seat across from him and savored a sip.

"And the rest?" he asked.

His father sat up straight, snapping his fingers. "Forgot about that. Talked to the guy today." He leaned forward and fished in his back pocket for his notes. "So we're thinking conservation easement, all right? The two farms adjoining this one don't want the rigs here, either, and they've got their mineral rights. In fact, they came to me, because they were nervous I'd cash the place out."

Samuel wrinkled up his nose, confused. "So no sale?"

"I'm giving it away," Sam said. "Satisfies what your grandma wanted, and it keeps those things"—he waved in the direction of the east wall and the rigs that rose in the distance beyond it—"at bay for a while."

Samuel watched his father as he talked. He couldn't tease out whether it was an idea driven by inspiration or anger. He supposed it didn't matter, at that.

"Sounds like you're solid," he said.

Sam nodded. "I am. I really am." He smiled, and then it crumbled. "How's your mother?"

"You should ask her yourself."

"Come on."

"You should."

Sam sat up farther and drained his glass, then he pushed himself erect and grabbed his cap from the hook beside the door.

"You have some time before you go?" he asked.

"Yeah, a little."

Sam reached for the door. "Well, come on, then."

RALEIGH

Raleigh kept checking the rearview mirror and the human cargo in the back. Funny kid, this Omar Smothers. Raleigh hadn't even realized he was there, in the car now far in the distance, until he heard the rustle and tumble of thrown weight as the kid got himself upright. When he'd offered them a ride, the Smothers kid—Raleigh knew him on sight; this kid was a big star, or soon would be one—had told his friend to take shotgun, that he wanted to go back to sleep. And sure enough, he'd dropped off into slumber inside of fifteen miles.

Raleigh looked again and marveled anew at the size of him. Not many men towered over Raleigh, but this kid qualified, and one look at those hands suggested he wasn't near done with the growth. Raleigh might have had trouble even taking him for a kid if not for the baby face—*life'll beat that out of you soon enough,* he thought—and the wispy mustache that he was trying too hard to grow.

He shifted his gaze now to the girl, and he smiled at her, and she looked at her lap. She'd been stealing glances at him since he picked them up. He could feel the surreptitious stares. She had questions, and she was just trying to decide how to get them out. He got that a lot.

"You sure you don't want to call your folks?" he said.

"No, it's fine. I'll call later."

"You can use my phone if you want."

"No, thank you. It's OK."

She glanced at him again and then looked away. Nervous. Raleigh wasn't so far removed from his own adolescence that he didn't know what this was about. They were getting away and didn't want anybody to know, for whatever reason. He rolled his left shoulder against his cheek to scratch an itch. None of his business. If Billings is where they wanted to go, he figured that's where he'd take them.

Now he looked at her again, and this time she struggled to meet his gaze. "What's it like to be famous?"

"I wouldn't know."

"Yes, you would," she said.

"Well, I'm not movie-star famous."

"I didn't say you were."

Smart girl. A little more on the ball upstairs than he'd been inclined to give her credit for initially.

"It's a drag," he said. "Or, in your nomenclature, it's totes lame."

He gave her another smile, and she parted ways with a courtesy laugh.

"What's nomenclature?" she said.

In Forsyth, a hundred miles to go, Raleigh left the highway and tooled into the main drag to the Town Pump. He had to piss, and the girl—Clarissa, he kept reminding himself—said she wanted something to drink.

"You want anything?" he said to Omar, still prone in the backseat.

"Beef jerky."

"You got any money?"

"No."

"No worries," Raleigh said. "I'll get it." He slammed the door shut. Little fucker. Giant fucker. Whatever. It was hard to see what that girl saw in this kid.

Inside the store, he grabbed some jerky for Omar and a cup of Colombian for himself. At the register, he pulled a copy of the *Billings Herald-Gleaner* from the stack and set that on the counter, too. When Clarissa queued in behind him with a fountain drink, he waved her up and paid for everything.

"Thank you, Mr. Ridgeley."

"It's Raleigh. And you're welcome."

By Custer, fifty miles to go, they were fast friends. Clarissa had extracted from him a promise to do a video chat with her English class, and Raleigh had painted anecdotes for her that amplified and exaggerated his travels. From time to time, he'd watch the boy in the back, who'd cracked open his bag of jerky, taken a couple of small bites—and let that god-awful stench of animal flesh into the car—and then gone back to snoozing.

"Are you a cheerleader?" he asked her.

"No, I hate those bitches." She caught herself. "Sorry."

"It's OK. When I was in school, being a cheerleader was just about the most important thing in the world to a girl."

"How old are you?" she asked.

"Guess."

She passed a discerning eye over him. Raleigh sat up straight and tried to suck in his gut.

"I don't know. Forty, maybe?"

Raleigh laughed.

"What?" she said.

He waved his right hand in a tight circle. "Nothing," he said. *Forty? Sweet Jesus. She must think anything north of that is dead.* "I like your answer. We'll go with that."

They drove on a few miles. Raleigh just smiled. *Forty. Unbelievable.*

"You know," she said, "it doesn't matter. You're cool."

"Thank you," he said. He looked at her, and she smiled. "So are you."

In the final few miles, Raleigh did what he'd been thinking of for a while, and he made his insurrection. They were talking about something—he'd lost the thread—and he slipped his hand across the console and set it on her thigh, just below the line of her shorts. She didn't look, didn't acknowledge his touch, but he felt the tightness in the muscle and the rigidity of the skin. He pulled back and she looked at him, and he tried to strike a look that offered conciliation. He put both hands on the wheel, and Omar thumped in the backseat as he adjusted his position.

Billings now slipped into view, the east-end industrial area dappled in the sun.

"Where do you want me to drop you?" he said. "Or do you need something to eat or—"

"Just the mall," she said. He listened closely for clipped words, for iciness, but it was hard to tell. The move had been unwelcome, in any case. Regret was thoroughly his, and his stomach roiled.

He left the interstate at King Avenue and drove into the West End. A few turns and it would be done. He'd planned to ask if he could help them out somehow in getting back to their car, but he wasn't going to do that. Get them out and get gone.

In the backseat, Omar now rose to a seated position. Raleigh watched him through the mirror as he blinked away sleep.

"Hey, sleepyhead," he said.

"Hey."

They crested Twenty-Fourth Street, and the mall loomed into view.

"Where?" Raleigh said.

"Anywhere." Clarissa didn't look at him.

He pulled into the Dillard's lot, the first one available, and he came to a stop. "This good?"

"Yeah," she said.

While the kids clambered out, Raleigh pressed the button with shaky fingers to release the trunk lid so Clarissa could retrieve her stuff. *Come on, come on, come on.* He drummed fingers on the steering wheel. Next, finally, came the slam of the trunk, hard, and Raleigh engaged the window button and said, "No need for that."

Omar's shadow crossed his face, and Raleigh looked up to see the man-child looming over him.

"Forget something?"

The punch came like a stroke of lightning. The force of it broke the bridge of Raleigh's nose, and before he could get his finger back on the window switch, Omar's massive hands had hold of his shirt and were pulling him through to the ground below. The force of the fall knocked the air from his lungs.

The next shot, to Raleigh's right eye, broke the orbital bone, and he heard the girl screaming, "Omar, no!"

Dazed, and with one good eye to see it, Raleigh watched the boy's bloody fist rear back again, giving him just enough time to ponder the possibility that if somebody got this kid off him in time, before too many more shots, this all might make a good story one day.

DOREEN

The sadness began for Doreen Smothers when she saw Gabe Bowman walking up the sidewalk in front of the Farm and Feed. She gave Elbert Fleener his fifty and his sack of rabbit feed, and she moved along the big front windows, shadowing the boy, until she reached the door and opened it.

"Gabe?"

The Bowman boy turned to her, and his face betrayed a forgotten detail.

"You're not at Fort Peck?" she said. "Where's Omar?"

Gabe slumped, and then he told, and then Doreen made intimate acquaintance with silent terror.

Doreen closed the store and drove to Sam Kelvig's house, and her heart quivered when she didn't see his pickup out front. He'd called that morning to ask her to please mind the store just one more day, and of course she had said yes. In deference to his pain, she had stifled her own request, that Sam might try to find a way to reach Omar on that older-man-to-younger-man level she couldn't scale no matter how much she tried. It could wait, she'd figured.

And now . . .

Patricia met her at the door, red-eyed and apologetic. No, she said, she didn't know where Sam had gone. "We've had some sadness here," Patricia told her, and Doreen had pursed her lips, at once not wanting to intrude but also figuring, lady, there's trouble enough for everyone.

"Thank you just the same," Doreen had said to Patricia's "Is there anything I can do?" Doreen knew the direction the kids had gone and the destination, and she knew she wouldn't close the gap by standing on the Kelvigs' porch and explaining the inexplicable.

Badlands and beet fields and a ribbon of river mark the path to Glendive, where Interstate 94 comes shooting through on its barren east-west run. Doreen was a few miles into it, anxiety and adrenaline rising as she pushed the car to eighty-five and then ninety, frantically doing the math of how long it would take her to cover two hundred-some miles.

In the passenger seat, her cell phone lit up, an unrecognized number with a 406 area code, and she reached for it.

"Yes?"

"Doreen Smothers?"

Here came the sinking. "Yes."

"Sergeant Wexler, Billings Police Department."

She guided the car to the shoulder, the entirety of her given to trembles, as if on a blood-sugar crash.

"Yes?" she said again.

"I have your boy here. He wants to talk to you, and then I'm going to need to talk to you a bit more, OK?"

"What's happened?"

"We're still figuring it all out, ma'am. Somebody's hurt bad, and your son is involved, and we're still trying to sort it out. Here he is, OK?"

"OK." Doreen looked south to the sunbaked sloping prairie, and she wondered how you brace yourself for the vagaries of violence when your son—your child who would never willingly hurt anyone—is involved.

"Mom?" came Omar's voice, the first time Doreen had heard his little-boy lilt in years.

She straightened her legs and pushed her back into the bucket seat, and she said, "What did you do?"

The spill came in sniffles and chokes and hysterics, and Doreen became convinced in frantic increments that the dreams she'd harbored on his behalf were fracturing, one by one.

SAM

Sam stood next to his son atop Telegraph Hill, and by rote he made his customary post-Jamboree scan of the town, a little bit of theatrical closure he allowed himself every year. It had never looked like this before. And then, at once, he thought that assessment too simple. Does anything ever look the same?

"Swarthbeck blowing up his own building was the most normal thing that happened," he said. The incredulity stretched his voice into thinness that came across as exasperation. Sam knew better. He was on the damn verge of melting down, all the time now.

"Never a dull moment, right?" Samuel said, nudging him. Sam didn't acknowledge that, and didn't say anything else. Samuel cleared his throat and settled back on his heels.

"I'm going to be back, Dad," he said. "I'm going to be back soon. And we're going to do better from now on. All of us. OK?"

Sam swallowed what was moving up in his gullet, and he blinked. Reset. Focus. Stand and deliver.

"And your mother?"

"You talk to her. I'm not ferrying messages between the two of you, OK? I'm not going to do it. But I think that's her intent, yeah."

"Intent." Sam rolled the word around on his tongue before expelling it. He took off his cap and swept it across his brow. The hottest part of the day was upon them, and it choked out the breathable air.

"Dad, it's going to be OK."

"Is it?" Sam took a hard look at his son, but the resolve wasn't there. He glanced away with a brief shake of his head, letting Samuel know he didn't need, or want, an answer that he knew was yet to play out.

He clasped his hands behind his back and he spread his stance, and he found a spot on the horizon that would help him hold these things in abeyance. He worked the inside of his lip with his teeth, gnawing off small bits of skin from the inside. His eyes blinked, a faltering sentry against his welling grief.

His son moved closer, almost imperceptibly, and then, in an instant, fully there, and Samuel slipped a hand across the older man's shoulders, and Sam leaned into the warmth of his child and waited and hoped for the despair to pass, as all things surely must.

ACKNOWLEDGMENTS

Where to start? The beginning, I suppose.

This is my fifth novel with the folks at Lake Union Publishing, and I never fail to be amazed at their intelligence, their love of the books they take on, and their endless dedication to getting those books into the hands of readers who will also love them. Thanks to my former editor, Terry Goodman, who staved off retirement long enough for one more acquisition from me; my new editor, Jodi Warshaw, and her unerring eye and good cheer; and the entire team that shows such incredible dedication to their authors. My developmental editor, Charlotte Herscher, is simply the best, and this marks three novels with her. I hope there are many more to come.

Mollie Glick, my agent, and the folks at Foundry Literary + Media do great work. I'm fortunate, indeed, to have landed with them.

Jim Thomsen, as ever, is a steadfast friend and a reliable arbiter of quality. His well-considered notes when this book was in manuscript form made it leagues better. Thank you, bud.

Other friends supply encouragement and engage me in conversations that help shape my work in ways profound and subtle. My thanks to Elisa Lorello, Gwen Florio, LynDee Walker, Cass

Sullivan, Ed Kemmick, Lynn Lunsford, Craig Huisenga, Patrick Wilson, Jennifer Rolfsness, Jill Rupert, Jill Munson, and others I'm sure I'm forgetting. These creative alliances buoy me in ways I couldn't begin to quantify.

Finally, I offer thanks to my family. I was fortunate enough to be born into a clan that values intellectual curiosity above all else, and that has served me well at every turn in my life. I had the great fortune of marrying into a family that has lived in the places where this story resides, and if not for those folks taking me in and making me one of their own, I might never have found the thread. There, my gratitude lands most heavily on Angie Buckley, my ex-wife. The marriage is over, but the love and the regard will carry me through the remainder of my days.

ABOUT THE AUTHOR

Photo © 2014 Casey Page

Craig Lancaster is the bestselling author of the novels *600 Hours of Edward*, *The Summer Son*, *Edward Adrift*, and *The Fallow Season of Hugo Hunter*, as well as the short-story collection *Quantum Physics and the Art of Departure*. His work has been recognized by the Montana Book Award, the High Plains Book Awards, the Utah Book Award, and the Independent Publisher Book Awards. He lives in Billings, Montana, and is a freelance editor and graphic designer, as well as a fiction writer.

For more information, visit www.craig-lancaster.com.